Road to Paradise

Road to Paradise

A COLLECTION OF CUMBRIAN SHORT STORIES

By Irvine Hunt
With illustrations by David Boyd

First published in Great Britain in 2003

Road to Paradise is a Cumbria and Lake District Life magazine production, 51 Bank Street, Carlisle, Cumbria CA3 8HJ

Published by CN Group Limited
Newspaper House, Dalston Road, Carlisle, Cumbria CA2 5UA

ISBN: 0952 5742 84

Designed and produced by *Cumbria and Lake District Life* magazine.
Edited by Keith Richardson. Designed by Jonathan Law.
The text is set in 11pt Aldine 721.
Printed by Thomson Litho, Glasgow

With two exceptions all of the characters in this publication are fictitious and any resemblance to real persons, living or dead, is purely coincidental. The exceptions are Charlie Ellwood in Changing Rhythms and Charlie and Tiesy in Wayward Goose. To please them and for their sakes the stories were rewritten to include their real identities though the incidents in the stories are pure fiction.

For Gwyn and Christian and Maisie

My thanks to Tiesy, Ross and Josie Baxter, David Hay,
Captain David Allan, Andrew Austin, Captain Tony Ingram,
and Ronnie and Joyce Tiffin for help with these stories.
My thanks also to Keith Richardson who tolerated
all the changes with astonishing calm.

THE STORIES

Changing Rhythms

AN INTRODUCTION

All at once everyone in the village seemed to know about Charlie Ellwood's pig. It had grown and grown until at last its time had come. And suddenly Charlie was knocking urgently at the cottage door, a bit anxious faced, not wanting the event to be missed.

"Come on, bring your camera. We're going to stick the pig!"

Charlie's modest farm holding lay way up in High Furness. He was a small man, a bit old fashioned looking, yet let him shake hands on a deal and that was more binding than any piece of paper. You would meet him at times unexpectedly, a sack of hay over his shoulder and carrying a pail of mash, trudging up the fell track to his ponies, or he would come walking down into the village past the derelict smithy, leading a cow on a string. And probably that is what he is doing in heaven today for heaven is surely where Charlie landed.

His father was a charcoal burner and woodcutter. And Charlie likewise worked in the woods, and tended his cows and ponies, and his ever-wandering ducks and geese.

Charlie's pig likely sensed what was pending for it began charging around like a runaway. Such a hullabaloo. Such a muddy floundering in the little yard. Then one poleaxe blow did it.

"Here!" yelled Charlie. "Don't stop stirring!" He thrust a long kitchen fork into my hands and a bowl of blood, still warm, brilliantly coloured.

It was the old way of doing things. Perhaps a centuries old way.

"It's for the black puddings!" he explained.

Black puddings lost a bit of their appeal in that vivid moment.

We went to Ulverston to buy him a green painted van and he said it looked all right, didn't it? He said it hadn't all that much rust, not really, and it would do fine, and when he paid, he signed his cheque with his name, but also with an inky cross, which was witnessed, and he shook hands with the seller, saying it was the handshake that meant summat, weren't it? Because a bit of paper had little dignity.

Charlie had dignity. His quiet manner endeared him to many and if to some he seemed years out of his time, his ways were a reminder of how life in the Lakeland dales was changing, how the old ways were no longer the same; how something valuable was being lost, as well as something gained.

Charlie's way of life was at the heart of many of these stories - slow moving Charlie, a little undernourished, living alone after his half-brother died. He chopped his kindling in the outshut alongside a candle lantern long past midnight. Each Saturday he looked forward to the weekly newspaper being read to him, and days later recalled brilliantly the sheep and cattle mart prices just like that. We always knew we would remember Charlie.

In his living room, blackened over the years by the smoulder of paraffin lamps, the ideas for some of these stories began to take shape - the cats who warmed themselves in the nooks of his kitchen range; his black-leaded ovens where he baked bread many a time at midnight; his old potato boxes heaped in a back room; his can of petrol that caused a bit of excitement the day someone mistook it for paraffin.

And so there's a slate worker, and a dressmaker, some roadmen filling in potholes, a few farmers intent on a sharp joke, all living in the Cumbria that once was - Cumberland, Westmorland, Furness and Cartmel, the old places before they were bundled together.

Their world was a quieter world, a less hurried world than ours of this millennium though still, just as now, with its sharp edges and its cruel times. A world of working folk, of feuding brothers, a thieving couple desperate for a crust, an old man, clinging to his farm as eviction threatens.

In the farms and smallholdings of the new county that we now call Cumbria there are still people who have known men a bit like Charlie and his ways; who are conversant with the quirks and merits of each patch of their land; who know the best kinds of wood needed when building a cart; who can stitch up a prolapsed ewe with a bit of string (more often bailer twine now); who knew what it felt like to crawl for miles on hands and knees across turnip fields pulling at the weeds; who remember that there were times when you had to feed a family of six on 16s a week.

The last, of course, is a century gone but the memory of what it meant in terms of hunger and anxiety lingers on, hasn't quite faded. Charlie knew of such things.

The stories that follow range from the recent past and trail back a century or so. Yet even now, in Cumbria there are still the Loving Lizzies, and the Clems and the Mr Ostles, their privacy often protected by the communities in which they live.

There's an old man lodged in a caravan which bulges with beloved books and who lives half hidden in a Lakeland wood, who feeds the red squirrels each morning and strives to drive off the greys.

There's a former pub landlord who loved four-poster beds, who brewed his own mind-searing spirit until he turned to a modest bit of smuggling, and who never received the bottle of whisky I once left for him, though a crafty neighbour apparently did. And there's a faded oldish woman, MA, with her two fell ponies who would be homeless if a compassionate young couple did not allow her to live rent free and tramp-like in the loft of their old Lakeland barn while lodging her ponies gratis below, and who occasionally sits in a beck bathing, and sings glorious passages out of operas, especially *Carmen*.

A few tales failed to arrive, or they exist obliquely - the blacksmith who never made nails at Easter; the 14-year-old lads who earned a shilling a week stripping bark; the driver of a runaway

Charlie Ellwood with his horse and cart in High Furness.

lorry who hurtled down a mountain road, a death-weight of slate breaking loose behind him. Perhaps for them, another time.

Over the years I grew to know Charlie well. Come one New Year we had a treat. We sat at one end of Charlie's long parlour table lit by the paraffin lamp and ate suitably salted pig's trotters. The cats left their oven lairs and sat on the other end of the table, watching, hopeful, their eyes green diamonds.

"A good pig, that," said Charlie appreciatively. "Really good."

At times we went on Charlie expeditions to visit a girl friend, or to rescue a wheel lost in the night off his van, or to chase a missing goose, which landed in a distant sheepwash, enjoying freedom. The last inspired a short story all of its own. It was fiction, of course, though the goose was real enough and the main character, Joseph, was based partly on Charlie, though carefully altered so that no one would know him. That was the intention.

Tiesy the postmistress vetted the tale to see if it captured something of the old ways of Cumbrian life, and immediately she announced that she knew it was Charlie, and really it would be kind to read it to him, and so she did, though I was apprehensive.

Days later Charlie waved me into his house.

"That goose story!" he said straight out. "I know all about it! There's summat wrong with it!"

He pulled his cap down tighter on his head. His face looked pinched and cold. "You've got it wrong. My name's Charlie, not Joseph!"

He was quite emphatic.

"But it's just a story, Charlie, it's not real. It's fiction."

He paused a moment, then said: "It's real enough," and politely he asked if it could have his real name, even if it was just a bit of summat made up.

Over a mug of milkless black tea, Charlie sat by his fire while the cats warmed themselves in the half-open oven, and he listened carefully to the amended version. And later he recited it back again with scarcely a word different.

Wayward Goose

The geese were being fattened for Christmas, and one of them was wanting none of it.

Stubbins the postman rattled impatiently at the cottage door and waited within the shelter of the porch. Half past eight had gone and down-valley from Forge Park the first frost of winter had iced the meadows. Not a morning for hanging around.

A scuff of nailed boots sounded within the house, and after that a working of a bolt in its clasps, and then the door opened.

"Aye, there you are, Mr Ellwood," said Stubbins agreeably to a three-inch gap. A fragment of the thin white face of Charlie Ellwood showed in the slot.

"It's your goose," announced the postman. "She's escaped. Down at the sheep wash playing havoc. I thought you ought to know." Charlie's face disappeared back inside.

Tiesy at the post office called out: "Charlie? Is that you?"

She hurried into the lane, not wanting to miss him.

"Charlie? Are you listening? It's Bosseye . . . up at Newbiggin, at the Sansomes."

Charlie shuffled along the track past the reading room, a bucket on each arm, a sack of straw tied across humped shoulders. The wind blustered bitterly off the fell, pouring through the clustered hamlets of Colby, Forge Park and Rake Howe. It was November at its worst.

Yet another arrived with the news.

"Mr Ellwood!"

The thin voice sounded across the frozen fretwork of last summer's bracken. Charlie bent over a bucket of mash and mixed in more water from the beck. Icicles were hanging from the stones.

"It's your Bosseye, Mr Ellwood."

Young Allonby from Fell Head puffed to a standstill, a breathless twig of a boy.

"She's been at our pigsty, scaring the pigs!" The boy's cheeks glowed crimson with running. "Dad says he'll kill her if she lands at our farm again."

Charlie trudged along his frozen little valley with his laden bucket, his head bowed. The boy followed a step or two.

"He told me to tell you, Mr Ellwood."

Charlie visited each of his poultry huts. They stood on both sides of the beck and hovered uncertainly between usefulness and collapse. In January they bloomed white under snow; in August they were bleached and paintless; and now, in November, they leaned green and brown, embraced in icicles.

"Come on, my pretties," coaxed Charlie. He clucked softly and poured mash into a trough. Squawking feathered bodies struggled round his legs.

Back at the beck he mixed two more buckets of feed and went to the other huts. He was knee deep in hens when he became aware of someone watching.

"Hello," said Stringer. Charlie paused and waited. Stringer was a man he respected.

Stringer said quietly: "Your Bosseye's been ranting again."

One of Charlie's hands tightened on a bucket handle.

"Going daft," said Stringer, "flying off."

Charlie nodded and fingered the twine round his raincoat.

"She broke the hasp," he said at last. As if to confirm this occurrence, he stared back across the beck at the hut where Bosseye nested.

It was a mean, louring day, not one for goose hunting. Stringer said: "If you ratch around in my barn, you'll find a spare hasp lying about."

Charlie trudged off with his buckets.

Heavy sleet swept Forge Park. Despite a rush of welcoming fire up the chimney, the Blacksmiths Arms had only two customers.

"Pint of bitter," said Stringer.

"Just you and me tonight," said Tupshaw. Stringer counted out the correct change.

Tupshaw said: "Anyway, who wants to be out in this lot?"

Dodgson, the landlord, looked up expressionless and slowly pulled a pint of beer.

"Only Charlie, I reckon."

Stringer and Tupshaw drew stools to the fire and steamed. Tupshaw said: "Now there's a man who's a hundred years out of his time."

Stringer supped deeply and let the heat sink in. For a long time no one spoke. It was good just to enjoy the fire.

"He's a proper strange 'un," said Tupshaw. "Charlie, I mean. I've seen him leading his cow on a string like it was a dog, letting it feed on grass at t'roadside."

Tupshaw rolled his eyes towards the bar as if to seek confirmation.

"It's just his way," said Stringer. He caught Dodgson's eye. Tupshaw was not a man he cared for, an offcomer.

Tupshaw snorted: "They say the old devil's lost his goose. Well he would, wouldn't he?"

"Aye?" said Stringer.

"Flying round Furness, attacking folk and God knows what," Tupshaw laughed harshly.

"It happens," said Stringer.

Tupshaw jabbed the fire with a poker and winked heavily: "Have you seen the old devil's van? Dropping to bits. Walks his cow on a bit of string, and drives a bloody van. Now there's a queer mix for you."

"He bought that van," said Stringer, " . . . off me."

Tupshaw's mouth opened, but the glint in Stringer's eyes made him pause.

"Aye, well, no harm meant."

"No," said the farmer. He downed his beer a bit quicker than usual and rose from the stool. "Charlie is a good friend of mine."

Stringer nodded to Dodgson and was gone.

"We are touchy tonight, aren't we!" said Tupshaw, pulling a sour face.

Dodgson pressed No Sale and started to count the copper.

"I'll tell anyone as likes to listen," said Tupshaw. "If that damn goose gets near me I'll shoot the devil."

"You'd never get it in your sights," said Dodgson examining an Irish penny.

"That's what you say," said Tupshaw.

Just before midnight a lantern bobbed and swayed alongside the beck. Charlie came lighting his way from hut to hut, checking doors. Soft stirrings sounded within as he listened. It was cold but the sleet had stopped. He crossed the railway sleepers that did for a beck bridge and peered at the gaping door of the smallest hut. The hasp lay in the mud where it had fallen. It was a bad loss. Charlie stood in the dark below the fell and listened to the beck, still crashing heavily with water. Flying off like that. It was as if some creatures knew why they were being fattened.

Inside the hut something white moved. Charlie, startled, pushed the lantern into the dark of the doorway. A large white goose hissed at him from her box.

"About time, too, you bad 'un," said Charlie, setting down the light. Bosseye had flown full circle. Charlie tied up the door with bailer twine. The goose hissed at being disturbed.

"Hold your peace," ordered Charlie.

The night was bitterly cold, but he did not mind now that his goose had returned. He wedged a rock against the wood. It would take more than a goose to shift that.

Back at the farmhouse he poured a dessertspoonful of whisky

into a mug of tea and sat for a long time staring into the fire. It was a nervous time, the coming of Christmas.

"I reckon it's famous, this goose of yours," said Stringer, holding Bosseye down. Charlie struggled on the grass with a pair of rusty clippers. Stringer had offered to do the job for him, but Charlie needed no one to show him how to clip the wings of a goose. Bosseye hissed nastily, her head clamped in one of Stringer's hefty hands.

"That'll stop her going off," panted Charlie.

Stringer nodded approvingly.

"Shove her in t'oven and stop her better. There's not a man from here to Ulverston hasn't heard what a fine goose you've got this Christmas. Lucky she's come back."

Feathers blew about the turf and settled in the beck. In a flurry, Bosseye was released, furious. She grabbed Stringer's sleeve with her beak. The farmer beat his arms.

"Get off with you!"

But Bosseye held on till Charlie booted her in the backside.

"Peck your eyes out, given a chance."

Little by little Charlie got his breath. His slight body hardly seemed suited to struggling with an irate goose.

He told Stringer: "They've got their ways, same as people."

It would be a shame when it came to killing her. But he would do it himself. The knife was hanging on the kitchen wall waiting. He had sharpened it only the day before.

Her wings clipped, Bosseye's wanderings were curtailed.

Market morning at Ulverston, and Charlie was late. Eighty-one . . . eighty-two . . . eighty-three . . . his fingers stole under each hen bringing warm eggs to light. It was a good haul for a bitter December day; cold hens could be reluctant layers. Mindful of the slippery fell path, he carried the load carefully.

His crumpled van arrived in Ulverston with an orange box laden with eggs. The streets were full of shoppers.

Wayward Goose

"Nay," spluttered Mr Kimberley over his stall. "When are you going to get some proper boxes, Mr Ellwood?"

Charlie pushed it across the trestle.

"Robin, give us a hand," ordered the stall keeper.

"There's none broke," said Charlie.

Mr Kimberley's son smirked: "Allus a first time, Mr Ellwood."

The stall keeper banged the box impatiently.

"Just you shut up! Get these set out. We're losing sales."

Mr Kimberley paid for the eggs from a fat wodge of bank notes.

"You'll be bringing me the goose?"

Charlie counted the notes a second time to make sure there were not two stuck together.

"Turkeys first."

"Of course," said the stall keeper.

"Then the goose," said Charlie.

"Turkeys next week, then. Plucked, same as last Christmas."

Charlie nodded, remembering.

"I've two good customers lined up," Mr Kimberley was saying, but Charlie had already moved away into the crowd.

Five days before Christmas, with fresh snow thick underfoot, and more snow clouds moving in heavily from the North East, Charlie's two turkeys were stolen.

"It's a crying shame," said Tiesy. "Who would rob an old man?"

Dodgson stood at the pub door, broom in hand, looking up at the white fell.

"No one round here I know of."

Tiesy shook her head sadly.

"Things are getting worse and worse."

"Thieves," Charlie told his cows. The two beasts stood in the warm gloom of his shippon. "They'll be after the goose next."

But not if he could help it.

Beyond the head of the valley the wind was building into a fluted howl. A muffled sound of sawing and hammering came from the hut nearest to the beck. An hour later Charlie returned home for more nails.

Tiesy watched from her door and told herself: "He's never repairing his huts after all these years."

Later the slow crunch of boots sounded in snow a second time as Charlie returned for a coil of wire.

"Poor old devil," said Dodgson, knocking snow from his broom. "Tying up the door after it's too late."

As dusk came, Charlie drove Bosseye into the hut. Determined hissing sounded and after a short interval, angry honking. Minutes passed before Charlie emerged panting. He held on to the low roof to get back his breath, then still trembling he locked the door with a shiny new padlock.

Stringer's tractor roared to a halt in a flurry of snow, its lights blazing. The farmer cut the engine.

"Made it harder to get in, have you?"

Furious goose honking sounded.

"Robbing an old man," said Charlie. His face filled with the hurt. Back at his fireside he set the bellows to the grate. Then he oiled his shotgun.

The night streamed with sleet. It blew bitingly out of the North East and Charlie hugged the sacking round him and huddled deeper in among the sodden heather, his cap down on his ears. He waited all night, his teeth chattering. At dawn, soaked, he trudged back to the village.

The second night was dry and crackling with frost. The sleet turned the fell into a vast ice sheet. Charlie saw nothing suspicious and dragged home wearily at daylight.

About ten o'clock Tiesy knocked at his door with a pan of barley soup.

"Whatever's the matter, Charlie? You up on the fell in all this weather."

Charlie mumbled he was all right.

"You take care," she advised. She felt the cold herself a bit these days. "Get this down you while it's hot."

On the third day it began to snow heavily. It started early in the morning and went on and on, cascading as if it were never going to stop.

"We're in for it now," said Dodgson. He loaded the fire with logs. Tupshaw laughed uneasily, peering from the windows. The pub was filling slowly. It was almost Christmas.

"Seen owt of old Charlie?"

Dodgson shook his head.

Tupshaw laughed again for no apparent reason.

"Sharpening his knife for that goose, likely."

With the coming of the snow, the wind eased. By eleven the last of the drinkers had set off to stumble home through the drifts. By midnight the only light in the whiteness was the bulb in the village telephone box.

"It's this un," said a muffled voice.

"How'd you know?"

"I just know, don't I!"

Two figures were close to the beck. The snow had stopped at last leaving the night faintly luminous.

"Wish I knew where the old devil's got to . . ."

"He's back in the village, now get on!"

They stooped at the hut housing Charlie's goose.

"He's got a new padlock."

There was a wrenching noise and torchlight showed through cracks in the planking as they got inside.

"What the devil's he been at?"

The second man whistled softly. "Boxed in his goose, that's what."

"It's nowt we can't shift."

A crash of breaking wood sounded. Twenty feet away a hump of snow stirred. It came apart as Charlie eased his creaking limbs to life. Peering in the dark, he listened as the men argued. The night was rent by a sudden honking.

"Quiet, me beauty!"

"Mind that bloody beak!"

The honking continued, if anything even louder.

"Hell, what's all this wire?"

In the snow Charlie's frosted hands reached for a wooden peg. His fingers struggled to clear it of ice, then gained sudden strength as they closed on wood.

"Rob an old man, would you," he croaked.

He tugged at the wire. Yards away came the sound of creaking timber.

Inside the hut there was a moment's silence, then consternation.

"What's that racket?"

Charlie pulled again and in his anxiety slipped in the snow. As he floundered there was a crash of tumbling wood and rocks.

"Oh, my God!" shouted a voice. "My back! Oh, my God!"

The hut had collapsed, the supports sawn through.

As the men struggled to get out of the wreckage, Charlie, fumbling with cold, pointed his shotgun up into the night and pulled the triggers one after the other. The bangs reverberated round the valley.

Two frightened figures fled down the track through the snow. Later, Charlie dug down among the planks and corrugated sheets to his goose. A sharp eye shone back in the glow of the lantern.

"Safe as houses. I knew you would be."

He undid the padlocked box. Then, his gun crooked under an arm, he led Bosseye back on a string to his kitchen, the goose's anxious honking sounding in the night.

Ulverston market was crowded. It was Christmas Eve.

"Not selling her?" said Mr Kimberley in disbelief.

Charlie shuffled awkwardly on the icy pavement.

"But the goose was promised, Mr Ellwood. Ready plucked."

Charlie shifted from one boot to another, at a loss for words. "She's got to like the kitchen," he mumbled at last.

Mr Kimberley snorted: "I don't mind saying I take badly to being let down."

"We were going to eat your goose ourselves," chimed in Robin. "It was our Christmas dinner."

"You shut up!" snapped the stallkeeper. "Of course, I'll not let it make any difference to us, Mr Ellwood. But I think . . . "

What he thought made no difference for he was talking to himself, Charlie's hunched figure was moving away through the Christmas Eve rush, heading for home.

Stringer sat in the warm gloom of the kitchen holding a steaming mug.

"Given a bit of help," he said, "a goose is as good as a watchdog."

At the other side of the fire Charlie blew his nose heavily into a rag. Their high-backed wooden chairs were drawn close in to the warmth of the range. The fire was burning well.

"I hear tell," said Stringer softly, "that Tupshaw's been in a bit of a car do."

Charlie tensed slightly.

"Brokken a collar bone," said Stringer.

From the corner of the room a bright eye watched them. Charlie stood up, suddenly decided. As the kettle hissed over the fire, he unhooked a long knife off a nail on the wall. Its sharpened edge caught the light as he open a drawer in the dresser and dropped it out of sight. Somehow this Christmas he would not use it.

"I reckon," said Stringer staring into his mug, "Tupshaw must have run head-on into a goose."

Charlie peered at Stringer and their glances met. The old man's face flickered slowly into a smile. Stringer smiled back.

"Aye," said Charlie.

It was a rare moment.

Marry the Spinster

Clem Hodden stared in desperation at his unwelcome caller. "There's no hurry," said the captain crisply. "Martinmas will be soon enough. Then you must get out!"

Clem had never been enthusiastic about repairs, nor was he good with words. Gaunt faced and grey, he followed the captain round the farmhouse looking and listening. "Martinmas . . . Well, I don't know, captain."

Captain Webster paused in the parlour doorway, a hand on the latch, a tweedy-clean presence topped by a sports cap.

"Of course you do. Now dammit, look in here! My property's falling to bits, and you're to blame!" The door had opened noisily, grating on the floorboards. Inside, paper peeled off damp walls.

A cat shot off a mouldy chaise longue. "Disgusting," said the captain. "The place stinks."

"Nay . . . " said Clem.

The captain was already in the back kitchen. Muddy potato boxes were piled ceiling high.

"How you get in here I don't know, let alone work in it."

"Them's good taties, captain," said Clem mustering an argument.

Outside, the captain headed for the long barn. String snapped and a hullabaloo of clucking hens resounded as a bleached door tilted on its remaining hinge.

"Rotten through and through," snorted the captain.

Dust billowed in the softer light of the evening.

"I've got a tin of screws waiting to fix it," said Clem. He stared worriedly as the captain walked about the barn stamping the boards with a foot.

"It's no use, Hodden. I'm determined to have you out this time. Go to court if need be."

Clem struggled to straighten the barn door. The captain joined him and between them they heaved it back up, propping it with a stick.

"Too big for one man," said the captain beating dust off his jacket. "You don't farm it, you don't do anything. Sheer waste."

Clem tried shooing his hens back inside but they wouldn't have it. He put his strongest argument: "There's allus been Hoddens living here."

The captain paused and eyed Clem with some sympathy.

"Three generations."

"Aye," said Clem. "Happen four. My mother . . . "

"Your mother," said the captain, brisk again, "would have agreed with me, had she been alive today. A big place like this is too much for one man. Four bedrooms. What do you do with four bedrooms?"

Clem looked down at his muddy boots and listened to the chatter of starlings down in the rankness of the orchard. It was a warmish evening but he was feeling cold.

"I sleeps in 'em," he mumbled.

The captain snorted, picked up a lump of fallen stone and rammed it back into the yard wall.

"Sleep in them?" he said incredulously. "I'll warrant they've been empty since your sister left eight years ago."

Clem stiffened. His long undernourished face looked greyer than ever at the thought of that day.

"What you want," said the captain, pausing to untie the string at the back gate, "is to get yourself married, that's what! Follow her example. Soon sort out your problems."

"I'm sixty-two," protested Clem.

Marry the Spinster

"Mark my words," called the captain slamming the door of his Land-Rover. He slid back a window. "You've got your own place down the road. Go down there! Marry the spinster: two birds, one stone."

The captain started the engine and the field car bumped away up the rutted lane. Clem listened until the sound died over the hill, then he went inside, a troubled gaze. He stood lost in the gloom of the hall for long empty minutes. Upstairs on the landing he opened a bedroom door. The room was full of furniture, though not of this decade. Wardrobes riddled with woodworm, old chairs, dressers, a commode, bulging boxes. All the rooms were the same, overflowing. Clem paused angrily at the top of the staircase.

"I sleeps in 'em!" he bellowed. His shout filled the house and was soaked up by damp walls. In the kitchen he rebuilt the fire with twigs and sat in his wooden chair, listening to the crickets behind the iron range. At midnight he baked four loaves of bread, and later the cats returned to the oven to sleep.

"I'm sixty-two," he told them.

His mind was made up. Clem set out for Well Cottage. It stood on the broad humpback fell road near Harrow Head. A mile or so away rose the shattered flanks of Wastwater screes, grey and barren. At hand the land was lush with centuries of toil. Whitewashed stone farms gathered the sun into their walls pending the bluster and harshness of the approaching autumn. Cars droned past for it was still the visitor season. Agnes Hastie, spinster, lived at Well Cottage, and Clem was her landlord. His aunt had left him the little house. He came striding down the fell, long legged, a hazel staff in hand and a bunch of marigolds. He was wearing his best cap, an old suit jacket, wide-bottomed flannels and gumboots. Five slate steps let down into the back cottage garden. There was a white painted handrail.

"Nay," said Agnes, coming to the back door. "It's not Tuesday, is it?"

Clem, edgy and embarrassed, ducked into the cosy kitchen.

"Just visiting, just visiting," he said quickly.

Agnes, small and grey-haired, smoothed her print apron and looked at him uneasily.

"You've had the rent," she said, just to make sure.

"Social call," said Clem.

Something about him was different and she soon decided that it was the badly washed white collar. In all the years she had known him he had rarely worn one, except at funerals and the like. Something definitely was up.

"I've got the kettle on," she said and bustled to make a pot of tea.

Clem stared enviously round the familiar room. Clean curtains, a polished slate floor, shiny brass. He sat in the high-back chair just as if he were there to collect the rent, though it felt in no way like a Tuesday.

"I've a bit of business in the valley," he explained. "Just passing."

Agnes took the beaded lace cover off the sugar bowl and set out the cups and saucers.

"Been gathering flowers, I see."

Clem eased the newspaper wodge of marigolds further out of sight under his jacket.

"You'll have bin here thirty-odd years now," he said, by way of an opening. Agnes looked at him wondering what he was at, her hair spilling from her bun.

"And a bit more."

"Aye." Clem stared awkwardly. "Neighbours a long time. Lot of changes."

A lorry groaned slowly up the hill past the cottage. Just at the wrong moment, he began to cough, a deep rasping effort.

"Nay, that's a terrible rattle."

His winter ailments were spilling over into the summers these days. She rummaged in a cupboard.

"You want to look after that chest of yours, living in that great damp farmhouse."

Clem's face grew a shade more hopeful.

"Aye, missis, now that's right, it is."

"None of my business," said Agnes, finding the linctus, "but you ought to be getting yourself a bit of help."

"It's funny you should say that! You might say I'm out doing a bit of courting."

Agnes paused, deeply surprised.

"Courting?"

Clem rushed through his words. "Aye, though the lass doesn't know about it as yet, not exactly."

The flowers. He was taking the woman the marigolds. Clem Hodden of all folk.

"Why, Clem, what a surprise!" said Agnes. Her face lit up.

"It's just an understanding I'm after. Just an understanding, you understand."

"She'll be a local lass, then?" said Agnes, careful not to overdo curiosity.

Clem nodded gravely: "Aye."

"Very sensible. I mean, I don't wish to pry . . ."

"Nay, nay, you've a right to know," said Clem generously. "It's you."

So saying, he produced the marigolds and half presented, half pushed them at her.

The tiny kitchen had grown distinctly uncomfortable. His favourite chair, which he always sat in when he visited, had become hard at the elbows. He stood up awkwardly.

". . . I mean, just think about it," said Agnes. "No woman is going to want a man who doesn't look after himself, now is she? It's a matter of pride."

"Oh, it's pride, is it!"

"Well see yourself in a glass, Clem Hodden . . . I mean, what lass in her right mind would take on a man who never washes?"

Clem, growing more rattled with each second, spluttered and struggled with his thoughts. He knew what he wanted to say but the right bits rarely came out in time.

"I haven't got a glass," he said finally. "And if I had, I wouldn't use it!" He glowered down at her, seeming to fill the kitchen with his dark frame. He clenched his fists. "I'm just not good enough for you, am I?"

"Nay, that's not what I said . . . "

"But likely what you meant," he said bitterly. "Well, thank you kindly, missis, I know when I'm not welcome."

Agnes realised she had said too much.

"You're taking it all wrong . . . " she began. But the kitchen door was ajar and he had gone.

In heavy rain he trudged the bleak moorland. At times he paused to stand for minutes on end, staring seemingly without seeing, then moving on. Once he shouted unintelligibly down the bracken slopes, cursing the blackness around him. Long after midnight he crashed open the farmhouse door and sent the disused butter churn tumbling in a cloud of dust. At dawn he was still staring at the unlit fire.

"Not good enough for her!" he told his cats angrily. "Well, I am!" he yelled.

Gunshots sounded and echoed in the orchard, but the magpies were miles away. The hens squawked in terror at the back of the barn. When he ran out of shot Clem flung the gun into the beck, then hours later he went crawling desperately on hands and knees feeling for it in the rushing water.

A long time passed before his bitterness subsided. On Tuesday he failed to go for the rent. Then an engine sounded.

"Just you let me in!" called the captain at Clem's back door. He rattled it hard. Clem heard the noise but stayed in his fireside chair and coughed harshly.

"I'm getting a court order!" shouted the captain at the keyhole. Knuckles rapped on the window, but Clem did not stir. The sound of the engine faded over the hill. Clem's rasping lungs grew more congested, his coughing spells prolonged. His mind became muddled until he seemed to be climbing along the Miser's orchard wall, wary of the glass in the cement and scragging apples until a long crook lashed his head and the white-haired Miser scattered the spoils all over the ground . . .

The squealing of the pig filled the sty and Clem, his mother shouting suddenly, swung the broom at the animal's head. But too late, his legs were rammed into the corrugated fence as the pig charged and sent him crashing . . .

In the morning each boy lined up in a daring-do. Find the toughest lads. Who could take the strongest blow on the chest? Well, it was easy, a thump of a knotted fist in the ribs one by one, standing in the school yard, eight boys, Edgar Turnshaw winning easily and Clem on his back in the mud, seven blows in his ribcage, gasping and weak-chested ever since . . .

"My god!" exclaimed the captain.

"Is he dead?" said Agnes. They straightened him out on the floor. "It's hospital he needs."

"Pneumonia. He's gone and got pneumonia! We'll need to get an ambulance."

"No," said Agnes. "Quicker if you take him in the Land Rover."

The captain looked set to protest.

"It'll back up to the door," said Agnes firmly.

They struggled to get the patient outside. He huddled in the passenger seat wrapped in blankets.

"Don't you worry," said the captain, clear now about his duty. "I'll get him there."

The vehicle charged up the hill. It was the war all over again.

Agnes looked round the dark kitchen. The walls and ceiling were black, encrusted with years of soot from the oil lamps. A grandfather clock ticked in the gloom of a corner, the minute hand broken off. The table was a clutter of open tins and watchful eyes.

"Shoo!" she said angrily. Two cats crouched, startled, on the table. "Shoo!" She clapped her hands.

"I'll just leave this here," she told no one in particular and placed a brown envelope on the table. She did not like to miss leaving the rent. Then curiosity overcoming her, she explored from cellar to bedrooms. It was a lovely old house, but never in her life had she seen such a mess. Far too much furniture. A hoarder's paradise. Almost no room for people!

At the sprawling hospital in Whitehaven, Clem proved a terrible patient. Weak though he was, he revived sufficiently to protest as they struggled to get his shirt off his back.

"You leave me be!" he shouted.

Pandemonium broke out as the nurses set about washing him. His bellows rattled everyone. A doctor listened to his chest and likened it to a church organ. Come the first night, and Clem failed to sleep. His shouts filled the ward.

"I never sleep lying down! I sleep in a chair!"

"You'll lie down or be knocked down," snapped a sister furiously. The doctor ordered an injection.

"Murderers!" he shouted.

"For God's sake!"

"Shut him up, sister."

"You're an old horse!" yelled Clem. "And a curse to man."

The injection failed. A doctor peered into Clem's eyes and ordered a second jab. Ripe farm language rippled as Clem was wheeled into an annex amid angry threats from exhausted inmates. It was five o'clock before the new patient sank into a troubled sleep. At six the hospital woke to washing faces and morning pills. Clem was left to snore it out.

Agnes locked her back door, put the key in a crack in the garden wall and climbed the five slate steps. Wearing rubber galoshes, she walked over the muddy fell to Clem's farm.

"Bless me, whatever's going on?" she said, drawing near. Two men were carrying a wardrobe out into the farmyard as she crossed the cobbles. "What are you doing? You can't be doing that," she told them.

"Orders, missis," said the bigger man.

The yard was littered with Clem's furniture.

"And whose orders, may I ask?" said Agnes, filled with alarm.

"Captain Webster's, missis."

Agnes, horrified, pushed inside. Upstairs the captain was examining a grandfather clock, stopped at half past eleven eight years earlier, the day Clem's sister had left home to get married.

"And him ill in hospital!" said Agnes angrily. "You are a shameless man!"

"He's ruining my farm," said the captain. "Look at the plaster! Dropping off in platefuls."

"You've no right."

"Every right! I've written to his sister telling her she's to take him in. His furniture can stop in the barn till he's ready to go. I'm taking over."

"This one's next," he told the men. Coffin-like, the grandfather clock began to go down the stairs.

"Stop!" ordered Agnes. "If you take this clock out of the house I'll have the police!"

The men paused. She sounded as if she meant it.

"Now see here," said the captain.

"See here, nothing. Show me the possession papers."

"This is none of your business," blustered the captain, his face puffed.

"Show me the papers."

Captain Webster gave her an odd look. The workmen watched, suddenly touched with doubt.

"Show me them right now, or I'll ask you to leave this house."

The captain glared.

"They're not through yet," he snapped.

"Just as I thought," said Agnes. "And never likely to be, either." She turned to the men: "I'll thank you both to see everything in the yard is brought back inside here within the hour. Taking advantage of a man when he's in hospital at death's door."

"Nay, missis," protested one of the men. "It's not our fault."

"I'll thank you to do as I ask."

Trembling, she went back down to the kitchen and without knowing why hung her coat on a nail. Upstairs there was a rush of talk. She struggled to catch the gist of it . . . the captain was protesting, the men were arguing back.

"Within a week," said the captain.

"Nay," said a voice. "You told Fred you'd already got court papers. We'll have nowt to do with it."

"A technical formality," protested the captain.

Agnes waited, tense and apprehensive. The men clattered downstairs again and went outside empty handed. The captain followed still arguing. An age seemed to pass before the two men reappeared in the kitchen doorway holding a blanket box.

"Will you want this back where it was afore, lady?"

"Everything exactly the same," said Agnes firmly. In the yard the Land Rover's engine roared.

"He said he'd got permission," said the man called Fred. The noise died away up the lane.

As the men carried the furniture back indoors Agnes wrote her address on a page torn out of her rent book.

"You must send your bill to me. It'll save bother."

"If you're sure," said Fred. While the rest of the pieces were brought in, Agnes found kindling for the range and one of the men lent her some matches and she lit the fire. She filled a kettle from a tap outside the back door and hung it on the crook over the cold hearth. Before they went she made a pot of tea.

"I've a lifetime's scrubbing by the look of things."

"Aye, missis, it's a fair old scrow."

When they had gone Agnes began a long search for a scrubbing brush. One by one Clem's cats slipped into the kitchen and sat watching.

Weeks later a hospital car struggled down the lane, jolting about in the ruts. A thinner, strangely clean Clem got out.

"I told yer," he said. "It's allus been rough."

The driver grinned.

"Door to door delivery. Sure you're all right now?"

"Aye," said Clem gratefully. "Champion, thank you."

"District nurse will be along shortly, after that she'll look in each day." The man gave him his small suitcase. "They'll miss you at Whitehaven."

"Nay," said Clem. He looked abashed.

"You're the first 'un to tell that sister where to get off!"

"She was a fearsome woman," acknowledged Clem. They walked to the door and a white edge of paint on the threshold caught Clem's eye. Then he noticed the windows.

"Now what's all this?"

"Everything okay?"

"Aye, fine," said Clem, puzzled.

The driver nodded: "I'll just see you in."

"There's no need. I'm quite all right."

"Yes, but I will, just to be sure."

The key fitted the lock. The driver set the suitcase inside.

"You take care, now."

The car churned in the mud and after a struggle went lurching back over the hill. As the noise died, Clem turned to look about him, burning with curiosity. The inside of the house left him speechless. The lampblack of the walls had gone. Whitewash shone in all directions. The kitchen range gleamed, the slate floor looked as if it had been polished back to new. The farm was the same wherever he looked.

On the kitchen table were several envelopes, each one containing a week's rent.

Clem set a match to the sticks in the hearth and, suddenly tired, sank into his chair trying to take it all in.

"It's a fair miracle," he told his cats.

An hour later the door opened.

"Well," said Agnes, "so it is you. I guessed by the smoke you were home."

"Aye, now missis, come in, come in," said Clem kindly.

"You gave us a bad turn," said Agnes dumping a bag on the table. "I've brought you a few groceries till you can shop for yourself again."

"I just don't know what to say," said Clem, waving at the kitchen. "I reckon this must be all your doing."

Agnes looked at the strangely clean, handsome man in the fireside chair.

"Just say nowt," she advised. "That'll be best."

"Aye, right enough. But you might just stop for a mug of tea," he suggested gently. "I mean, I owe you that much."

Agnes hesitated, ready to go. Then she relaxed suddenly and sat herself down.

"I could do with taking the weight off my feet a bit."

The old range was warm and a comfort. She had always admired it, even in his mother's day. She could do worse. Clem poured boiling water into the teapot.

"It's the best home coming I've ever had." In his eagerness the water spurted.

"Nay, now then," said Agnes. "Just don't be spilling things and getting it messed up again. If I'm thinking of coming here then there's to be a proper understanding before I land."

She settled more comfortably into the chair, enjoying the warmth.

"Aye, well," said Clem nodding. "That's all I was thinking really, nobbut an understanding."

Carefully he poured two generous mugs of tea, taking care not to spill any.

"I'll say this, your old hearth is a lot more comfortable than my little tile one."

Clem nodded. "Maybe I could get us a telly? Make it more cosy."

Agnes smiled: "We'd need electricity for that."

"Aye," said Clem. "So we would."

He nodded agreeably. There was no knowing what might happen from now on.

Robbie's Day Out

The three farmers squatted in a corner of the Drover's Arms intent on a bit of a prank. They were a stolid looking bunch, but they still enjoyed a prank. Atkinson started it. "Tell you what, let's take Robbie to the zoo. Show him the animals. I mean, give the lad a day out!"

He grinned slyly at the others.

Birkett drank down his pint until he could see through the bottom of the glass. Outside the light drained away off the fells.

"Aye, why not?" With farming suffering a bit it would be good to get away from the daily round of vanishing profits. "We might learn him a thing or two. We could manage a Saturday."

Stubbs sniggered. He was thin faced and looked as if he was cold whereas the other two were a bit puffed up in their big green anoraks and not short of a quid or two.

"But will he go?" said Birkett.

"Like a lamb," said Atkinson. "Robbie'll love it."

He could see Robbie's long mournful face trying to take in the news. Stubbs sniggered again.

They had another pint, warming to the idea. Robbie had been around for years, born in the village, a bit of a joke at school, though not with the teacher, Miss Watson, who grew tired of looking up just as Robbie began to scratch himself in embarrassing places. She was never exactly sure, but she sensed that he did it deliberately to upset her, his eyes leering as if he could see right through her print dress. He was a big muscular lad, jammed into a desk at the back of the class, a head above most of the other pupils. There were a lot of sniggers when he first squeezed into his place. Really Miss Watson would have preferred Robbie to have attended another school altogether, Hurton for instance, but the education authority insisted that he stayed.

Miss Watson retired before Robbie left, and now she lived in safety miles away at Coniston. Robbie, of course, left school eventually, but he did not seem bright enough to find a job and he stood about in the village and held his head on one side and stared up at the fells.

"Aye, let's have an outing," said Stubbs. "It'll be a right good wheeze."

Saturday, and soon after dawn Atkinson drove his Land Rover to Ulverston where he parked up and they caught a train to Blackpool. Robbie latched his mouth to the carriage window and tried to fix his bulging eyes on the trees. But the trees wouldn't stay still and he grew peeved. A woman waiting on the platform at Arnside Station turned towards the train just as the carriages slid to a halt with Robbie's limpet mouth stuck to a window at eye level.

In Blackpool a dog sniffed into Robbie's muscular jeans and cocked a leg experimentally, but Robbie hoisted it up by its tail and bit it.

At Blackpool Tower, Atkinson made certain that he was last in the queue and the others bought their own tickets.

"Where's your money, then, Robbie?" said Atkinson. It was a joke and Atkinson paid, putting down the exact sum.

Outside the lions' cage Birkett took the lead: "Look at them, Robbie. Them's elephants."

The elephants prowled up and down, baring yellow fanged teeth, and snarled half-heartedly.

Outside the monkeys' cage Birkett said: "Robbie, how do ya like the crocodiles?"

The crocodiles hung by their tails and picked fleas off one another. Atkinson and Stubbs wet themselves laughing.

In front of the dolphins' tank, Birkett said: "What about these 'ere pigs, then, Robbie?"

Robbie did not think much of the pigs. Robbie knew pigs had got legs and Birkett's nose contracted unexpectedly as a beefy fist arrived out of nowhere.

Then Robbie hit two uniformed attendants and bent the turnstile.

Nobody liked Robbie doing this.

Several oblong attendants helped Robbie out into the street where quickly one sat down on the kerb with a nosebleed.

"For goodness sake," gasped Atkinson. "Let's get out of it!" They hustled the roused Robbie along the pavement and did not stop until they emerged on the promenade.

"This is better," said Atkinson, cheering up. "Let's show him the Golden Mile."

The Golden Mile was ablaze with lights, even in the sunshine. On one side, across the promenade, lay the glorious sands and the lashing of the sea while on the other, down a seemingly endless pavement stretched an amazing conglomeration of booths and stalls. It was dense with people wanting to be happy.

Despite his throbbing nose, Birkett perked up. "Let's have some candyfloss!"

They queued at a cloudy pink stall, engulfed in a roar of music. When they turned to give Robbie his floss Robbie had disappeared.

"Dammit! Where's he gone?" groaned Atkinson.

A shriek sounded and Stubbs caught sight of a sudden heaving mass of people. "He's ower theer!"

A terrified bearded lady cowered inside a crumpled cage, and Robbie was ordered to straighten out the bars while the woman screamed get him off.

"That'll cost you fifty quid!" snarled a dark faced bruiser who emerged with a large hammer in one hand.

"There's no real damage," protested Atkinson. He waved the pink mass of candyfloss.

"Do you want your head smashed in now and then call the police, or the other way round?"

"Here's ten quid," said Atkinson, thrusting the first note that came to hand. At the King Kong show, Robbie stood solidly in the crowd and stared at the booth. No one could move him, not even two clever dicks with sideboards from London who realised that Robbie was a better Kong than the one in the cage. Both experienced a change of opinion as the booth began to sway in their direction.

"Hell's bells!" said Atkinson.

The booth sagged.

"Get him out of it!"

"We should have stayed at the zoo," snapped Stubbs. "There was gorillas in there, too."

"I know what. Food will settle him!"

Protectively they steered Robbie into a cafe and crowded round a table where Robbie's tidal slurpings over a mug of tea initiated widespread interest. A scabby faced boy from Liverpool bared his teeth in a glare but belted back to his ma as a bowl of sugar emptied over his head. Then Robbie vanished into the lavatory and no one saw him come out.

"He's flipping well gone again," said Atkinson.

This time Robbie seemed to have disappeared for good.

"He'll be smashing up summat else," groaned Birkett.

But Robbie was found several minutes later sitting quietly in Gypsy Mable's fortune-telling booth staring at a green glass ball.

Impatiently Madame Mable explained for a third time: "You pays me first, then I tells you. Money first! Get it?"

Robbie's eyes bulged at the lights flashing about the canvas walls. The one pulsating on the table was the worst.

"Watch it, mate! That's valuable."

Like magic, Madame Mable's spooky voice collapsed. She was, decided Robbie, a he with handsome genitals and in the ensuing

conversation a string of light bulbs ceased to work.

The crash of splintering woodwork brought the farmers rushing. They hauled Robbie clear.

"You idiot!" bellowed Atkinson. "You blithering gormless fruitcake! A peanut would behave better than you!"

Atkinson was the only one who could talk to Robbie like this. Robbie became immensely sad, his lips pressed together in a quiver.

"Oh, don't start blubbing," sputtered Atkinson. "We bring you on a nice trip to the seaside, and what do you do? Smash everything up, that's what!"

"What we should do," suggested Birkett, "is keep him away from people."

"Well that'll be easy here, won't it!" snapped Atkinson. The promenade was heaving.

An enormous tear began to run down Robbie's long face.

"See, Robbie, we'll get you some chips," volunteered Stubbs. "You'd like some Blackpool chips now wouldn't you? There's nothing like Blackpool chips."

But no, Robbie didn't want chips. Not even Blackpool chips. Robbie didn't want anything. He stood hulk-like in the middle of the prom and began to blubber in earnest.

"For goodness sake Robbie, quit it!" snapped Atkinson."Or we'll go back home right now!"

Robbie's tears increased.

Then Birkett had a brainwave. "Let's go paddling."

"You'll not catch me paddling," protested Stubbs. "I'm seventy!"

"Salt water! Do your corns good."

They paddled, three Cumbrian farmers and Robbie, their pants rolled up and shoes in their hands. The sun was hot and magically even a few feet into the water seemed a world away from the sticky crowds of the Golden Mile.

"Aye, now,"said Stubbs, surprised to find that he was enjoying himself. "I haven't done this since I was a lad."

Robbie splashed ahead, kicking up waves, the tears forgotten.

His face shone rapturously. In all his life he had never paddled at the seaside before.

"Good job the missis can't see me," said Stubbs grinning cheerfully.

It was now that they met Miss Watson.

Miss Watson had always come to Blackpool for her annual holiday. She waded blissfully, holding her dress clear of the waves with one hand, while the other held a small camera.

Robbie's arrival was not welcome. Robbie's eyes fastened on Miss Watson's knees. Robbie had always wanted to see Miss Watson's knees. Now, after all these years, there were Miss Watson's knees. Waving a beefy hand excitedly, he splashed nearer.

"Keep him away!" shrieked Miss Watson.

But Robbie only wanted to point.

"Don't let him near me!"

He meant no harm.

"A photograph!" cried Atkinson desperately. "Robbie, let's take your picture. You and Miss Watson together. Robbie!"

They got a stranger to take it. Atkinson and Stubbs stood on one side, Miss Watson and Birkett on the other. Robbie towered in the middle wearing a ferocious smile of satisfaction.

They arrived home at midnight.

"We'll have to visit Blackpool again," Atkinson told Robbie. "It's been a real nice outing."

Next morning Robbie went to look in the pigsty. Four each. He had known all the time. Pigs always had legs.

The Bones In The Land

The kettle boiled unheeded on the kitchen range. It was Sunday morning and Cloggy's wife was in a sniping mood.

"You're not going down to that shed again," Millicent snapped. She was following him about the kitchen as he worked towards the back door.

"Aye, well," said Cloggy slowly buttoning up. "There'll not be much sense me spending Sunday idle here in the house will there?"

Millicent locked her hands in a tight clasp. She had her austere look.

"You'll be able to get your own dinner."

Cloggy wrapped on a muffler and said nothing. Whatever happened, he was not going to get into a row.

"It isn't often," said Millicent, "I get a chance to stay at our Betty's, not two or three days together, anyway."

She waited for Cloggy to react, but the stocky little man had started to wheeze and for a moment he propped himself with a hand on the side of the slopstone. He puffed at his inhaler.

His wife seized the sputtering kettle and wafted at the steam: "You'll wheeze yourself to death in that damp shed of yours."

"It's not damp," gasped Cloggy. "It's as dry as snuff."

"So you say. God knows why we ever got married - you're always hiding down there."

"God had nowt to do with it. God was on his holidays the day we got married."

He opened the back door and gulped at the cold air gratefully. His clogs clattered on the path.

Millicent called: "I wouldn't wonder if I didn't stay in Ambleside with our Betty till Wednesday."

He vanished into his shed and locked the door. She had not been inside for years, and he did not intend to let her enter now.

Millicent smiled with crabbed satisfaction. She glanced at herself in the kitchen mirror and patted a few whisps of grey hair into place. She would set off now and if the whim took her she would definitely stay with Betty till Wednesday. Counting tonight, they would probably get in three good sessions that way.

Elterwater was embraced in drizzle as Cloggy trudged to work on Monday morning. Clouds wreathed in heavy layers on Lingmoor. During the summer the old work of quarrying was glossed over by the rush of tourism and streams of polished cars, but now in dull winter the village had quietened and locals reclaimed their seats at the pub. For many winter came as a blessed relief.

He clattered along the quarry lane soon after seven-twenty and out of habit stopped off the main track to check the door of the gunpowder magazine, then in a grey gloom he splashed on to the office amid a desolation of corrugated sheds and slate piles.

"Morning," said Mr Johnson standing behind his desk. "Raining brighter again."

"Aye." Cloggy picked up the day's schedule. "Mebbe it is."

The foreman reached for a pipe: "Another happy weekend with the wife, then?"

Cloggy scowled: "Gone to her sister's. Off among the spirits."

Mr Johnson turned to the iron stove: "We'll have a brew and start the day proper."

He saw that Cloggy was less than cheerful, and the one man no one liked to see depressed was the one in charge of the gunpowder magazine. Gloomy men had been known to do gloomy things.

The magazine lay in a deep cleft away from the cutting sheds, and for good measure had been capped in concrete. Cloggy unlocked the steel door, paused to slip on rubber overshoes, then opened an inner wooden door. Surprisingly, the room was clean and light and almost empty. The roughness of the fell track contrasted sharply with the magazine's white plank floors and walls. A dozen cardboard boxes made up the entire contents. Methodically he drew out four pills of dynamite, six pounds of gunpowder, a coil of fuse and three silver detonators. The last he treated with extreme respect. He took it all to the main shed. Wednesday, Millicent had said, but it would be more like Thursday before she was back. Peace for a few days.

An hour later he returned the explosives to the magazine. The drizzle had turned to heavy rain. It blinded in across the fells, cold and drenching. Deep in the quarry crater the four men struggled in the mud to free a compressor. It lay tilted awkwardly, a bulky yellow machine trapped in the gloom. Enthusiasm was at low ebb.

"A sod of a day!" shouted Tailor.

"Let's leave it," urged Blackett. He was a shambolic, balding man, drenched to the skin and feeling a lot older than his forty-one years. Mr Johnson was the only one showing any determination. Knee-deep in sludge, he flung a cable round a wheel and pushed the end at Tailor.

"Lash it to the dumper!"

"We'll never get it out now."

"Just do it!"

The quarry walls rose in sharp cliffs around them. As the cable tightened, the dumper slithered sideways. Nothing more seemed to happen, then the compressor began to tilt upright.

Mr Johnson waved urgently: "Slower! Take it slower!"

Mud and water poured off the machine, poised dangerously now on the edge of a boulder.

"Steady!" shouted Mr Johnson. He moved in.

The compressor was almost out when a gunshot crack sounded. Blackett screamed: "Look out!"

The whip end of the cable sang across the quarry floor. Mr Johnson and Blackett met the mud in parallel dives; Cloggy sank less quickly. Almost in slow motion, the wire coiled into the air, turned leisurely and lashed him in the side.

Millicent sat upright on a bedside chair.

"How much longer am I expected to manage on half-pay?"

She dumped a bag of scones on the table.

"It's all right for you, everything provided for in hospital, but I'm having to manage on a pittance."

"In another week," said Cloggy, "I'll be out." He looked down the ward. "After that it'll only be a matter of time before I'm back at work."

She emptied the scones into a dish.

"Grapes is too dear these days."

"They'll do champion," said Cloggy wearily from his bed.

Millicent sniffed her annoyance. All these weeks visiting; she was worn out with the effort and at the end of her patience.

"There'll be no money spare for drink once you're out. And little enough for Christmas."

Cloggy, his side no longer the agonising mess it had been, looked at her pityingly: "Have you come here to lecture me, or see if I'm any better?"

"Don't talk nonsense. I'm pointing out you'll not be visiting the pub as often."

"It was little enough before."

"If slate don't kill you, drink will."

"Is that so? And a drop of warfarin too, I suppose?"

"Don't start that again!"

He had never got over the unease he experienced the day he had found a new tin of rat poison on a shelf in a cupboard.

"What do we want with this?" he demanded.

Millicent blustered about seeing a rat down by his shed, but she had been strangely unconvincing and he dumped the tin in the bin and for a time remained wary.

She sat up straighter and fiddled with her hair as a braid slipped askew from under her hat. Her face looked yellow and parched.

"I'll tell you summat for nowt. I'm sick of slate; sick of that ugly quarry; sick of Elterwater. Slate is all I've known ever since we married."

"There's nowt wrong with slate," said Cloggy defensively. Heads turned their way. Cloggy caught a wink from the Larson lad in the next bed; he was another who was in slate, a lorry driver.

"Slate and me," said Millicent, "don't mix. Never has."

"You never listen," said Cloggy. "Slate is the bones in the land. Runs through it. If you take it apart like we do . . ."

She gave him a scornful glance.

"You're a bigger fool than I thought. I'm going."

"Slate," persisted Cloggy softly, "is summat you know nowt about."

He wanted to say more, but Millicent stopped him with that curious little jerk of her hand that she often used.

"I'll not be in again till Sunday."

She walked down the ward past the huddled groups of talking people. Her shoulders were bony and square, set high in her coat. She hated hospitals. She left as Blackett came in.

"You know," said his mate, flopping onto a chair, "there are times I feel right sorry for your missis." He grinned, brown-toothed. "Her and her miseries."

"Off to chat up the spirits," said Cloggy. He was glad to see his mate.

"Wife's sent some biscuits." Blackett dumped a bag on the table. "Grapes is a fortune these days."

Cloggy nodded gloomily.

"Got at you again, I see."

Cloggy sighed: "No more than usual. But there's times I think she hates me."

Blackett took a cautious look up and down the ward then below the level of the bed conspiratorially unscrewed the top off a half-bottle of whisky.

"Have a sup of this, now."

"No thanks, you know I'm not a great one for whisky."

"Aye, but this is special, hospital treatment! Go on. Do you a power of good."

Cloggy did as bidden, though reluctantly. Beer was one thing, but spirit seemed to affect him differently.

"Trouble is," said Blackett, "women get stuck at home and have too much time for worrying."

"Aye. Perhaps if they were working the rock face they'd understand better."

Nothing was so beautiful as green slate. Cloggy had brought down more tonnes than he could remember. Mostly it ran in swaithes, from east to west, giant bones, hidden from sight, but lying there waiting to be found. He wasn't the only one who thought so.

"You know, I've been thinking, when I die I want to be buried east-to-west, like the rock."

"Oh, aye?" Blackett's shaggy eyebrows rose. "And just when do you think you'll be dying, then?"

"No, you know what I mean. We need never be lost, us, knowing the rock. Like a compass. We allus knows our way, even when there's mist."

Blackett nodded. It was true. Quarrymen saw the grain in rock like other folk could see it in wood.

Cloggy said: "When I'm out of here you must come to my old shed. I've summat special I want to show you."

"You'll be another week, yet."

"It'll surprise you," said Cloggy.

But it was a fortnight before he was out, and when he arrived home he was too weak to think about his shed.

A cold peace existed. Christmas came and went with the minimum of frills. There was a mood of brooding, which persisted as January blustered in.

Millicent stood in the kitchen in front of her favourite mirror. She had several hanging about the house but she preferred this one. It was oval and set in a frame of green and red metal flowers. This and the dresser were the only two things Betty had not grabbed when their mother had died. Millicent had carried them off with considerable satisfaction. The mirror framed her face perfectly. When she stared into it it was as if she were looking into her own private world. At times she wondered who else had looked into the glass and had watched their lives slowly passing by; mirrors saw it all, wrinkles, tears, the lot. If only they could speak! Looking more carefully, she leaned in closer to the glass and nipped out a blackhead.

Cloggy opened the shed door.

"Grand little den you've got here," said Blackett. An old wooden chair, shabby shelves, cobwebs and all the clutter of years of comfortable hoarding.

"Just a minute, I'll light the lamp," said Cloggy. Occasionally his side still ached; otherwise it had healed a treat. He pumped up the Tilley to a bright green glow. It filled the hut with hissing light. For years it had been Cloggy's den; and before that it had been his father's and full of hens.

"Have a look at this."

In a corner stood an upright lump covered in sacking. Cloggy revealed a long slab of green slate. Blackett peered at it open mouthed.

"There's still the date to go in yet."

"Nay," said Blackett at a loss.

"Took a bit of doing, that did. Out of the Back Quarry. I cut every bit myself."

Blackett looked sideways at Cloggy: "It's a lovely piece of work," he said cautiously. He read the text carved into the stone.

"Aye," said Cloggy modestly. He reached for the sacking and covered it again. "I reckon it's one of the best bits of old Lakeland that ever was."

"I didn't know you were a poet."

"Aye, well. Me cousin Bob's a teacher and he helped with the words."

The last inch of fuse burned into the rock face. In the rippling explosion that followed, a wall of slate crumpled down the cliff into the quarry.

"Down like a lamb!" said Mr Johnson as the dust settled.

Tailor gunned the bulldozer: "Let's get at it!"

The sun was shining and though it was now into March, there had been little snow. The twin peaks of the Langdales stood out, etched sharply and beautiful. The detonation and crash of falling rock had sounded like a hammer crack and told the whole valley what was going on. Cloggy was back on form.

Sunday night, Cloggy went out to the pub. It was Millicent's chance. She rummaged in a drawer and found the big screwdriver, the one with the black handle. Angrily she went outside and attacked the hasp on the shed door. Hardly back at work, then down at the pub. Hatred welled within her. She should have left him years ago! There was a time half jokingly, half seriously, when she had considered trying to invoke the spirit world to lay a curse on him. That would teach the devil! And who knows, it might have worked, but she encountered unexpected opposition from Betty and a row had blown up. In the end Betty had threatened to exclude her from their seances. The spirits, Betty had declared robustly, were for the good of the soul, not for evil. Millicent had bottled up her anger. She could wait!

Another time, inexplicably, without knowing how the idea arose, the word poison had filtered into Millicent's thoughts. This had both startled and frightened her, though almost at once it had even occurred to her how it could be done . . . little by little, in the food, accumulatively, so that only she would know what was happening. On an errand she had gone into an ironmongers in Ambleside and stared at the shelves. When the assistant asked could she help,

Millicent on the spur of the moment had said she wanted to kill some rats and she left the shop clutching a tin of warfarin. But she had never used it, regarding it more as a psychological weapon than a real one. She had hidden it in a cupboard where it remained forgotten until frighteningly Cloggy had rummaged there. She had mixed feelings as he threw the tin away.

The quarryman had said nothing to her, but later, without thinking why, he had mentioned it to Mr Johnson.

The chief had just laughed: "Wants to poison you does she!"

"Probably," said Cloggy.

Eventually the matter was forgotten. Driven by curiosity and a wish to hurt, Millicent found the coalhouse hammer and banged the screwdriver down behind the hasp. If that lump of a man Blackett could get in then so could she. An owl hooted from the tree beyond the back yard. That was one more thing Millicent hated about living in the village. She loathed owls. She renewed her blows until the metal snapped and the door moved ajar. Alarmed at her daring, she stood uncertainly in the dark, then holding the hammer tightly she pushed inside.

Blackett was in a pleasant alcoholic muddle.

"I'm runnin' out of b-brass," he stammered. He felt happily uncoordinated. The night was bright, with all the noise of the village concentrated at the pub.

Tailor said affably yet again: "I'd swear there's beer in this 'ere alcohol." But the joke had died long ago, about fifty times ago.

Cloggy sat hunched at a table. The evening had not been a success.

"There's not much pleasure in life these days, when you think on it," he said morbidly. He was unnaturally hot. Minute specks of sweat stood out on his forehead.

"Beer's allus a pleasure," said Tailor.

"Not when you've s-spent up," said Blackett.

"Don't know what you do with all your money."

"Aye, well, and where's the witch tonight, then?"
Cloggy scowled: "Chatting with the spirits, like as not."
"Hah. I seen that on telly - shoving a glass about on a table."
"It don't get shoved," said Cloggy. "It moves itself. She told us."
"I'll believe that when I see it!"
Cloggy didn't know whether he believed in spiritualism or not. Just once when Betty came to their house with the awful Annie Marchmont and her cousin Partridge, he landed home a bit early to find the three of them along with Millicent sitting at a table in the middle of one of their sessions, as they called them, mumbling together as a glass slid about on the board. Of course they all had a finger on it and were sitting with their eyes staring. And it was then it happened, before anyone could say anything about him standing in the doorway the glass seemed to crumple in the middle of the table, not even a cracking noise or sound of any kind, but just a sudden sagging away and the whole thing lay in a heap in the middle like so much coarse salt.
White faced and scared, the women had quit the house, Millicent apologising and trying to say it was a faulty glass with a crack and they shouldn't have used it in the first place, and the spirits would understand, and the others were not to go and leave her.

For the second time the landlord's voice announced "Time!" He came through, picking up empty glasses with a flourish.
"Come on," said Cloggy. "Let's be out of it."
The cold air hit them.
"Got a funny taste that bitter tonight somehow." Cloggy had not felt right all evening, even on the way to the pub.
No one lingered. Too bloody cold. They went their ways.
Tailor said: "He were a bit odd, weren't he, old Cloggy? Bit of a misery, like?"
"It's them hospitals," said Blackett. "Once you've tasted luxury, home's bound to seem a dump."
Cloggy let himself in quietly. He did not believe in direct

confrontation, especially when unwell. It was not the best time to stand up to a bitching wife.

He moved through the parlour without putting on the light, but spoiled everything by stumbling into the coal bucket. He swore softly. What was that doing in the middle of the room? After this he did not bother to stay quiet any longer. On the kitchen table was a note from Millicent. She had gone to her sister's "for good."

"And good riddance," declared Cloggy who had gone through this several times before. His eye took in the coalhouse hammer lying on the table. He brewed a pint mug of sweet tea and sat by the empty hearth and felt that somehow the grate was a bit like his own life. Cold ashes. Cold heart. Cold world. All his own fault, he guessed. He wished he was already in bed. Stiff and aching, he locked the front door, wound the chiming clock on the dresser and emptied the tea leaves down the sink. If she were away then it did not matter. He glared at her favourite mirror as if Millicent's own face were staring out of it. He had never liked it. Betty's by rights, and really she ought to get it one day. He'd never felt right about the way Millicent had sneaked it out of her mother's house, her mother's cold body lying upstairs on the bed. He looked closer at the glass. Serve her right if he chucked it out altogether. Mould was spreading from the bevelled edge. It was an ugly affair but he let it be. It would be the first thing she would miss.

The hammer on the table was different. He picked it up, puzzled. Now why was that lying around? Late though it was, he took it outside and found the shed door open. With a soft moan, Cloggy pushed at the handle. He fumbled for matches fearful of what he would find.

Inside his loving piece of carving lay scattered on the floorboards in bitter fragments.

Lights came on down the cottages. Muffled voices sounded. It was hardly midnight and all Elterwater seemed to be wakening.

The shopkeeper rushed up in a thick duffle coat.

"The man's murdering her!"

"No, she left in a taxi."

A double crash of breaking glass filled Cloggy's cottage.

"What's the fool doing!" Splintering wood and more glass breaking.

The crashing went on for several minutes. Cloggy was wreaking a terrible revenge with the coal hammer. He came to the kitchen cabinet.

"A drunk, am I!" he shouted. "Smoke like a chimney, do I? You bloody witch. Take that!"

The cabinet disintegrated. Bottles tumbled in a noisy cascade. One heavier than the rest rolled sharply against the brickwork of the sink.

"Hah! So that's it, is it!" He lunged forward. "Whisky! A bloody bottle of whisky, you old hypocrite!"

Incensed, Cloggy turned, caught a movement on the wall and a moment later a blow from the hammer sent a shower of metal flowers and glass streaming to the floor.

"Hypocrite!" he shouted. "Damned hypocrite!"

Midnight had gone as the front door of the cottage burst open and Cloggy stumbled out.

"Bugger off!" he shouted.

"Now see here," began a shopkeeper, but one look at Cloggy stopped him short. The last the frightened villagers saw was a dark figure vanishing into the night, a lamp in one hand, a bottle in the other.

The shopkeeper said: "He'll do murder in that mood. Someone must stop him."

But there were no takers. The villagers shook their heads and one by one disappeared back indoors. There was a cruel wind.

The chipping of metal on rock came to them, a low clear sound.

"Whoever's that?" said Tailor.

"It's someone at work already!" said Blackett.

It was Monday morning, start of another week. They had trudged along the track, the twin peaks of the Langdales still untouched by the sun, the valley cold and uninspiring. The sound of rock being chiselled this early came as a surprise.

"Hell, it's at the magazine!"

"You're damn right!"

They ran now, nailed boots grating on loose slate.

Tailor cried: "It's open!"

A Tilley lamp blazed in the morning blackness. Outside the explosives store a figure in an old raincoat was hammering at a rock.

"What's the fool doing!" cried Tailor.

"He'll have sparks all over bloody Langdale."

"Cloggy!" shouted Blackett, then something made him come to a wary halt. "Cloggy!"

The figure straightened, the bright flash of a chisel head in his hand.

"Get back!" rasped a strange voice. "Get back!"

"Jesus," exclaimed Blackett. Cloggy swayed and waved an arm.

Tailor said: "He's drunk!"

Blackett yelled: "Come out of it, Cloggy."

But Cloggy's face burned with suspicion.

"Don't you come near! Don't come one step!"

The quarryman broke off to swig from a bottle, carefully keeping the two men in view. Tailor and Blackett gaped uncertainly, their eyes on the open door. A single spark was all it needed.

"Stop here. I'll fetch the boss."

Mr Johnson walked along the track towards the hut.

"Be sensible, Cloggy," he called. Blackett and Tailor stumbled nervously a step or two behind. It was lighter now. They were scarcely twenty feet away, close enough to see his strained expression. They were still dithering with uncertainty as Cloggy snatched a twisted bundle off the ground and held it sharply above his head.

"I warned you," he called. A fist full of fuse wire, and the bright gleam of silver. The three men took one frightened look and ran for their lives.

"Damn fool!" croaked Mr Johnson, back in the safety of the trees. He was trembling. "What's he doing with bloody detonators!"

Blackett squinted along the track. "He's as flip as a bat." Cloggy of all folk.

"One spark," said Tailor. "One spark - he'll send the hut sky high."

"Us with him," said Blackett. Thinking this they retreated hastily still further.

Word spread. By eleven o'clock a score of villagers watched in the woods. Above the fell the sun bathed the valley in deceptive light, bright but without warmth. The Pikes stood back aloof.

Twice Mr Johnson tried to reason with Cloggy, but the quarryman would have none of it. There was no doubt he had gone soft in the head. The second time Mr Johnson approached, Cloggy turned abruptly and hurled a piece of slate into the heart of the magazine. Appalled, they heard it strike the wall and clatter to the floor. By a miracle nothing happened. Cloggy watched a full quarter of an hour before he moved back to the hunk of rock and resumed chiselling.

"It's the whisky," said Blackett. "He just never touches whisky."

"It'll be his wife's likely."

"Good lord," said Mr Johnson. "I'd forgotten all about her. We'd best have her here."

"I'll go," said Tailor. "She's in Ambleside."

"If you hear a blast," said Mr Johnson. "You can slow up."

Cloggy had stopped hammering and began to watch the men. He felt strangely elated. All night he had toiled and the bitterness had faded slowly. Now he had finished and taking up the bottle again he enjoyed the relief of a job done. Well he'd just have himself a pipe of baccy and, to his surprise, he even felt like singing.

"You come right out of that, Cloggy Dixon!" shouted Millicent. She stood white faced and rigid among the trees, her voice a thin frightened screech.

Cloggy peered out. He felt warm and safe. He drank again from the bottle, now almost empty, trickles escaping down into his coat.

Where were his matches? He struck one with a sharp rasp on the floorboards and soon his pipe was drawing well.

"You stupid old man," shouted Millicent. "Come on out at once!"

Funny stuff, gunpowder, he thought. He'd seen a lighted candle drop straight into an open half barrel of the black and not a thing happen. The candle had lain in the middle of the powder and burned right on. He had lifted it out himself, still lit, and no harm done. Yet let there be one spark . . . dynamite, likewise, had its quirks.

Another raw gullet full went down.

Millicent said: "He'll not come out. He's stupid."

"Try again," urged Mr Johnson.

"It'll do no good."

"*There's an o-o-o-o-ld mill by the stream* . . ." The wavering sound came through the trees.

"God preserve us," said Mr Johnson. "Whatever's that?"

"He's singing," said Blackett.

"Sounds more like he's dying."

"*Nel-l-lieee Dee-e-e-n* . . ."

Cloggy finished the bottle with a flourish and swayed in the doorway. He felt lightheaded, almost floating. He beamed into the light and waved his pipe. Now it was over he could leave. Not for years had he felt so cheerful.

"*And the wa-a-a-ters as they fer-low* . . ."

"At last," said Mr Johnson. "He's coming out."

"Anything to stop that bloody racket," said Tailor.

All Langdale heard the explosion. Rooks screamed up out of the trees; in the village the postman paused outside the pub; a winter hiker, startled, turned to look back along a lane. Slowly a puff of smoke lifted above the tree line then expanded and drifted away.

Millicent never flinched. She stood on the path, a stiff, rigid figure as slate and concrete whirled and crashed about her. She stayed immobile until the last flake of stone had clattered to rest among the trees, leaving behind an intense silence. Only then did her shoulders sag and a faint tremor run through her austere frame.

"You stubborn fool," she cried bitterly.

Trees lay twisted and broken. Lumps of concrete had ripped through the branches and as the smoke cleared the lines of the blast stood out like knife cuts. Cautiously the quarrymen approached the ruins. Where Cloggy had toiled through the night lay a mound of rubble. Half buried in it was the blackened rock on which he had been working. Of Cloggy's body nothing was to be seen.

"Blown to smithereens," whistled Tailor in awe.

Mr Johnson hesitated. "He must be here somewhere." But there was no trace.

"He was mad," said Millicent. Her voice was taut with scorn.

Blackett wiped his mouth with the back of his hand.

"No," he said slowly. "I reckon you're wrong there, missis."

He stared into her face and felt a pang of pity. She looked old, her neck scrawny and wrinkled. But worse than any of that, imprinted in fine lines around her tight mouth were the signs of all the years of hatred that she had felt.

"I reckon that for once in his life," said Blackett. "Cloggy was a happy man."

Millicent turned away stiffly and began to walk back along the track. After thirty years she was free at last. Now she had only herself to think about. Well, she'd return to Betty's for a start and collect a few rightful belongings, then she would sell up and move to somewhere nice. She had always fancied Silverdale.

Mr Johnson watched until she was out of hearing then he coughed quietly. The fright of the blast was still with him.

"Right now I feel sorry for her."

"What a way to go," said Blackett. He kicked at the rubble. "Anyway, they don't have to put up with one another any more, and I suppose that's summat."

"Aye. A while since he thought she was going to poison him."

"What? She wouldn't have!"

"She had rat poison, but he found it. Makes no difference now."

For a while they searched in the woods, half expecting to make an awful mangled discovery, yet that was the miracle of it, except for a few shreds of blackened clothing they found nothing. If his body was there, then it must be under the mass of rock. It would be up to the police to do a proper search.

Blackett was the last to leave. Curiosity took him back to the heap of rubble and he stared for long enough before he bent to drag at the stone that half-buried the long rock. It took a while before he could examine the pitted surface. He read a few words, some roughly chiselled, a few simply scratched:

Cloggy Dixon
Bury us down int' slate,
Down int' green sea.
And once I'm gone
Speak soft like,
Lest dust on your coat
Be Me . . .

"Nay," said Blackett softly. It was the second time he had read them, but they still surprised him.

Loving Lizzie

At first the day was no different from any other. A dull thump sounded within the caravan as a hot water bottle landed on the floor, then a heap of blankets heaved itself about and to a low waking groan an old woman struggled up from her bunk.

"It's no use us lying in," announced Lizzie, her feet finding her plimsolls.

In a corner a battered looking ewe bleated a welcome.

"Now then, my pet," acknowledged Lizzie.

She peered from the windows. Scarcely six o'clock, the sun rising above the coastal fells, and still the barley was not ripe. A no-good wind had lashed the field all night long.

"We'll just have a pot of tea, Rags, my pet," said Lizzie.

Ragged Wool made a futile attempt to struggle to its feet but the effort failed and it subsided in a heap and watched Lizzie get herself a brew.

Where Lizzie's caravan stood near the top of Roman Hill she could see across the salt marshes and the little port of Ravenglass. Behind the caravan, the woods climbed away towards the high fells of Lakeland. It was a lonely spot, but Lizzie enjoyed it that way. The tea was hot and sweet and soon she felt stronger. She tied on a raincoat and lifted a paraffin heater from a cupboard, but frustratingly several matches failed to light the wick.

"Empty already!"

It seemed only a couple of days since she had last filled it.

"Now you wait here," she ordered. "I'll not be long."

Outside, the wind was rushing about the hillside as she pulled a tin from under the caravan and went for paraffin.

"It's the old witch," said Jim Nicholson staring up the road from his garage.

"That's no way to speak of my aunty," protested Henry.

"She needs a right good defumigating," said Nicholson. "Her and her flipping ewes."

"She's doing no one any harm," said Henry. All the same he watched the approaching figure warily.

"Coming for paraffin, she is," said Nicholson. He turned to the garage. "Billy!"

A lanky youth in overalls looked out of the workshop.

"Billy, you get Lizzie her paraffin."

"Oh, not me, Mr Nicholson!" protested Billy.

"You get it or else," threatened Nicholson.

Billy muttered over the scattered pieces of a dismembered motorbike and banged down a spanner.

"He's getting big for his pants is that one," said Henry.

"They all do," scowled Nicholson. "But I don't want him flying off now he's getting the hang of things."

Lizzie homed in.

"Billy!" yelled Nicholson, and disappeared through a pile of junk into the back. Another spanner crashed in the workshop.

"She just smells so," Billy protested to Henry.

"Hello, Billy lad, it's me, Loving Lizzie wanting some paraffin." She grinned, brown, wrinkled and unwashed. Billy had his own ideas about Lizzie, but he was never rude to her face.

"Give us your tin, ma," he said. He grabbed it off her and moved to a drum to get it filled.

"And what are you doing here this time of morning, Henry?" demanded Lizzie. "Wasting the day."

Henry edged up-wind.

"Not me, Aunt Liz. I'm wanting a spare bit for the tractor."

Lizzie snorted: "If you thought anything of your old aunt you'd be ratching in your pocket for a coin or two; you being a rich man."

Henry winced, though he was not exactly surprised.

"I've next to nowt on me, Aunt Liz . . ."

Billy appeared round the garage door and hastily dumped a tin on the ground.

"I've put you ten shilling's worth in."

"Oh, have you? It wasn't that much last time," said Lizzie, with half an eye on Henry.

"It's gone up, ma," said Billy awkwardly.

"It was only eight and six pence last time."

"Well it's gone to ten bob now."

She took a while rummaging in her purse, long enough for Henry to ratch through his pockets.

"Here, I just happen to have ten bob."

Billy grabbed the note and disappeared inside.

Lizzie smiled gratefully: "You must come up to my caravan and let me make you a nice cup of tea. I enjoys a bit of company."

But Henry wasn't getting caught that way.

"Not now, thank you, Aunt Liz. There's work to be done. Top field gate's nearly off with this wind . . . perraps another time."

Lizzie peered at the pile of junk.

"Suit yourself," she said picking up a tin. "I've work to do misself."

"There's lots who haven't work these days," said Henry.

But Lizzie had work. Wrapped in a thick woollen skirt and several cardigans, she stood in the barley field waving a yard-brush at the sky. Shadows swooped about her and cries filled the air.

"Get off, you devils!" she called. "Get off!"

The brush churned the wind and the crows flew anew.

"If it's not crows, it's wind tearing the heart out of the land, or rooks poking their beaks."

Black trailing bodies sailed across the field uttering defiant cries.

"Get away you ugly things!"

Back and forth she moved, swinging the brush, a ragged old woman brooming the sky.

Later Sewell paid Lizzie.

"You're doing a grand job looking' after my barley," he said gravely.

"It's nowt."

She stared round his farmyard.

"That ewe of yours is improving, is it?"

"They don't call me Loving Lizzie for nothing," said Lizzie simply.

Sewell dug into the midden and turned over a fresh dollop. He never could understand folk going on about Lizzie, but Sewell had little sense of smell, and for that matter neither had Lizzie.

Lizzie climbed back up the hill. The wind blew straight in from the sea, blustering through tiny Ravenglass and its one main street. Long ago the place had been busy with Roman galleys and long after them had come the Norsemen and in turn, down the centuries, fishermen and smugglers. Nowadays it was mostly tourists.

"Here I am, my pet," she announced, panting as she reached her caravan. A welcoming bleat greeted her.

"Well now! Out you come while I get you summat ta eat."

Armed with a sickle, the old woman cut at the banks down the barley side, working till her back ached. The pile of fresh green grew till Lizzie saw there was enough, and to her satisfaction the ewe ate the lot.

A cup of tea later she filled the paraffin heater. The weather was turning cool. Well, she'd light up early. Meeting Henry had been lucky. Feeling pleased, she struck a match and bent towards the stove.

There were two garages at Ravenglass. One was a tangle of past enterprises, dismembered machines; heaps of empty tins and rusting exhaust pipes. This was Nicholson's.

He bent down and picked up an oilcan.

"Did Lizzie not take her paraffin, then?" he asked Billy.

"Aye, of course."

Billy was struggling to give birth to a world-beating motorbike out of the parts of three others. He did not hold with over-talking.

"Then whose is this lot?" said Nicholson, sniffing at the tin. A tractor rumbled past, but Nicholson found himself listening to a second muffled distant sound. It reverberated back down the hill from beyond Bail Rigg.

"Now then, that was odd."

Billy had heard it too. They stood on the forecourt staring. Nicholson fingered a wart on the side of his neck.

"I'd swear that bang were up Lizzie's way."

"Aye," said Billy. He stared uneasily at the tin in his boss's hand.

"Funny she never took her paraffin."

Billy began to pale.

"And what's the matter with you?"

Billy looked as if he were about to be sick.

"She . . . nay, I reckon she's gone and taken my petrol."

He gulped awkwardly.

Nicholson ran as a man his age ought not to run. Fearing the worst, he scrambled towards Lizzie's neck of the wood, Billy on his tail. He almost collided with the blackened figure as it emerged from the top of the coppice.

"Rags," wailed Lizzie, her face filled with anguish. "My poor old Rags is dead!"

"Rags?"

"Me old ewe."

Nicholson wept with relief.

"Damn the ewe, it's you I'm bothered about . . . "

"I lit the stove," said Lizzie. "An' it went off!"

Lizzie, in a state of shock, stood in a shamble of scorched clothes.

Along the road came the urgent sound of fire bells. The firemen grumbled their way up the hill.

"You keep out of my barley!" shouted Sewell.

The caravan was a write-off. A blackened heap. An hour passed before they were satisfied there was no danger of fresh smouldering in the wood behind.

"Crazy old woman," said the fire officer. "Whatever was she doing? Never known one go off like this before."

Nicholson caught Henry's eye and dropped his gaze.

"She's lucky to be alive, I'll tell you that," said the fire officer prodding at the steaming ashes.

"Roast mutton," said Sewell.

"Aye," said Henry.

"She must have been blown straight out in the blast," said Nicholson.

The fire officer sighed.

"Lucky to be alive," he said again.

The family met in Henry and Peggy's lace-curtained bungalow at Holmrook. Nicholson had been invited. Down at the bridge the River Irt was running sweetly in its bed to the estuary and tourists were eating ice cream, their chatter sounding in the road. The chill wind of the past few days had died away. It was suddenly hot summer and doors and windows were open wide.

Peggy said: "I'm not keeping her! She'd smell us out."

"Well I'm not," said Alice angrily. "Her caravan stank like a pisspot."

Alice drained the dregs of her cup of tea.

"Anyone's house would stink with sheep dottles lying all over the floor. Anyway, Peggy, you've more room than the rest of us. If she stops with anyone I reckon it needs to be with you."

"Thank you very much!" Peggy glared at her sister. "You manage your home, and I'll manage mine, thank you."

"Now then," said Henry.

Nicholson, uncomfortably quiet until now, began to feel obliged to play a part.

"Perhaps . . ." he suggested. "Perhaps she could stay on at the nursing home?"

Alice snorted scornfully: "She'd not agree to that till pigs yodel."

"Well she'd have to," said Peggy, "if we say so."

"She'll cost us a fortune if she stops on in that home," said Henry.

That was the crux of the matter.

Nicholson sank deeper into his chair and wished he was back at home. Knitting needles clicked in the corner.

"Someone . . ." said Aunty Tate. "Someone has to take her. It's only decent."

Alice clasped her hands firmly: "It's no use, our Peggy, you'll have to have her first. After that we'll take turns."

"It's all right for you," snapped Peggy.

Sewell dug the grave. Lizzie, still patched with bandages, seemed to have lost little of her agility.

"Now set her in," she ordered. The trees swished in the wind as Sewell shovelled the remains of the body to the edge of the pit.

"Lower her gently, my poor lamb."

"It'll drop to bits if I pick it up," said Sewell "It'll get a shove and that's all."

"Right enough, then," said Lizzie.

Sewell pushed at the remains of Ragged Wool, then shovelled earth in till the grave was full.

"Never in all my days," said Lizzie, "has my stove blowed up before."

"You'll want a wooden cross," said Sewell.

"Aye, that would be a kind act."

"I'll see there is one."

"It's bad enough losing me home," said Lizzie as they moved past the remains of the caravan, "but being told what to do by all them hospital nurses, that's what I call lacking dignity."

Sewell got out his pipe as they looked at the barley.

"A bit longer yet, but I reckon the tops will start turning soon."

Peggy got to the point: "So you see, Lizzie, it'll be us you'll be staying with first . . . "

Lizzie sighed and tried to settle into the leather and chrome chair.

"Aye, well, it's very kind of you Peggy."

"You'll have a nice room all to yourself. Electricity and a wireless, all modern like."

Lizzie frowned: "I'll not be wanting electricity. Having it come out in the night, getting hold of you."

"Now don't start that again, Lizzie. Nothing gets hold of you. When you turn off the light it isn't there any more."

"Aye, so you say. But I know better."

"But it's true," said Peggy with a touch of exasperation. "It didn't harm you in hospital, did it? And it won't harm you here."

Lizzie shook her old head: "Coming out in the black night and a body dead 'afore it wakes up in the morning!"

Peggy went on hurriedly: "You'll be very comfortable, but there's summat Henry wants me to mention. We hope you'll make sure your blouse stays fastened. I mean, you keep showing that old man's vest again."

The clock on the mantelpiece ticked several leaden seconds.

"Nay," said Lizzie slowly. "That'll not matter, will it Peggy? Folk will only say it's Loving Lizzie."

Peggy's voice grew smoother: "That's just it, Lizzie dear, it does matter. If you're staying with us then you've got to be dressed proper. You never know who calls."

A flicker of defiance appeared in Lizzie's faded eyes.

"Aye, well," she said slowly, "you'll just have to take me as I am, won't you . . ."

But Peggy had not heard: "Another thing, you'll have to have all your clothes washed in proper disinfectant. Henry can't abide the smell of sheep in t'house. We allus tries to keep a nice clean place."

A difficult pause followed during which the net curtains stirred half-heartedly in the heat. Then Lizzie said in a small voice: "No smell of sheep?"

"We'll wash all your clothes with summat nice and strong."

"Oh!" Lizzie had just worked it out. "What about Bowlap? Where I go, Bowlap goes."

Peggy's mouth closed slightly then opened as a nasty suspicion crossed the whiteness of her face.

"Bowlap? Who's Bowlap? Not another ewe, I hope?"

"Of course she is!" said Lizzie indignantly. "Bowlap was up on the fell when yon fire got me. You don't think I'd leave Bowlap behind now old Rags has gone, do you?"

A disgruntled family gathered in the parlour.

"She upped and said she was going back to the nursing home," said Peggy angrily. "But it was a lie 'cos all the time she's been sleeping in the wood in nowt but her old clothes."

"Showing us up," said Alice.

The family chorused its disgust. Lizzie was the talk of the neighbourhood. Two days missing, and now turning up living rough in the coppice above her old caravan spot.

Henry pushed his greasy cap back on his head, then jammed it on again in exasperation: "If she stays in our 'ouse then she comes without that perishing ewe. I'm not having that stink!"

He was emphatic.

"Aye, well," said Alice worriedly. "What are we going to do? I'm sick of her!"

"There's only one thing we can do . . ." The wizened face of Aunty Tate lifted up from her knitting. "We'll have to buy her another caravan between us. Second-hand. And Jim Nicholson can pay his share, 'cos he's caused this mess."

Peggy was alarmed: "That could cost us three or four hundred quid!"

"Aye, but what'll it cost in that home? She could last ten years in there! They dies hard does their side of the family."

"Then it's about time she did die," said Peggy.

Faces turned sharply her way.

"Well you know what I mean . . ." Peggy had gone red. "She's had a good innings, and none of us is getting any younger."

Alice refilled the teapot and set it down with a bang: "A second-hand caravan will cost a lot less than keeping her in luxury."

"She's done it again, hasn't she!" said Henry. "Beaten us!"

"She allus does," said Peggy. "She's allus caused us bother."

A few minutes before six Lizzie woke up at the start of another fine day. She got out of bed and found her plimsolls, then she put a new tin kettle on the stove and looked out of the window. Her caravan shone with bright surfaces. The windows were clean, the chromium shiny, the walls freshly painted in marble cream. Everything was really nice. Even the carpet.

"We'll just have a nice pot of tea," said Lizzie cheerfully. Bowlap bleated, sagging against the door, its coat tangled with briar. "And then I'll pick all that stuff out, pet."

The tea was hot and sweet and soon she began to feel ready for the morning. Outside, at last, the barley was a swaying ripened sea. A warm wind blew up from the creek and ran through the stalks in waves. Lizzie pulled on her new khaki army coat. She was feeling better. Even her aches seemed to have faded.

"Out you go, now," she told Bowlap. With a heave she shoved the ewe into the open.

Down the field the crows were raiding the far edges, though it would not be for much longer. Today the barley would be harvested.

"Aay, you black devils!" she shouted.

Bending over, she pulled an empty tin from under the caravan and with Bowlap at her heels she set off for Nicholson's, telling herself that it would be about time for Henry.

The House On The Ridge

No one had lived in the farmhouse for eight years, but now someone was going to.

The pony and cart came into view, trundling along the potholed road, swaying in the Saturday morning haze, top-heavy with furniture and creaking at the joints; and as it came up to the final turn, encouraging cries of "Whoa!" and "Steady theer!" sounded from the driver high up on his seat. Walking alongside, picking through the ruts, a young couple pushed at chair legs and boxes where they seemed set to break free. Arthur and Emma Stamper, not a week wed, were carting their belongings into their first home together.

Where the ground dipped the driver turned off down a track. "Oh, now then," exclaimed Emma, as the stone farmhouse came into sight. "It's not so bad."

She was plain faced, a mop of brown hair cropped short on her neck, but young enough to carry it, and it did not look severe. She stared down the meadows towards the building and the fells beyond. It was Cumberland at its loneliest, a corner of the old county with rough walled farms and pot-holed roads.

Arthur, taller than Emma by a couple of inches, hooked his thumbs into the broad braces that held his cords.

"This is it, then, Mr Mossop?"

"Aye," said the driver, "this is it."

The cart turned across the front of the house and swayed to a halt by a drystone walled garden. Mr Mossop's thin face had developed a look of urgency. He clambered down, giving Arthur an apologetic smile before vanishing round the building. His disappearance was so rapid that Emma found herself staring but Arthur gave her a knowing wink and her question was never asked.

"See, there's a water hole," he said.

A glimmer of reed-choked water lay alongside the track that fronted the house. Emma, however, was staring at a mass of nettles waving above the garden wall.

"What a scrow!"

There was no hint of the farm's past. No sign of the watcher. The building was small with a barn on one end. A blue slate roof covered the sandstone walls, bleached and weathered by a couple of centuries of gales. Paint was flaking off the window frames, but this they had expected.

Arthur said: "What do you think, then?"

Her face lit with a quick smile: "It'll do fine."

He nodded, satisfied: "I thowt it might."

Mr Mossop reappeared.

"I get taken a bit short now I'm getting on, you understand . . . but you'll be wanting the key."

"Aye," said Arthur politely. "It would help."

The carter produced a large key and inserted it into the lock. It turned with a harsh click.

"Oh Arthur, don't!" laughed Emma, but he had picked her up and was crossing the threshold into the welcome coolness within. She slid to the floor and looked about her. The living room was flagged in sandstone. At one end was a black cast-iron fire range and alongside it a stone staircase led up in a spiral. She opened a door and peered into a larder. It was the simplest kind, just one thick sandstone shelf and a space underneath for buckets.

Mr Mossop said: "The old house is not much to look at, but it's cheap."

His face was creased into a walnut of a smile.

Emma said: "Nowt a broom and whitewash won't see right."

"It'll do us," said Arthur. He paused, awkward and shy, then added: "Two shillings was right?" It did not sound much.

"Aye. In advance."

"Aye." Arthur produced a purse from a pocket deep in his britches and took out two separate shillings. "We'll not be the kind that gets behind with paying."

Mr Mossop wrapped the rent in a large green handkerchief and put it away.

"Mebbe it'll need a slate or two puttin' right, but it's a solid old place. I'm only sorry there's no land left with it."

Emma climbed up the stone stairs, treading in deep hollows. Eight broad steps and at the top two bedrooms, one with a hole in the ceiling plaster. She untied a piece of wire from a nail and pushed open a window. From up here the garden looked worse than ever. Arthur's voice sounded through the floor: "We'd best be unloading."

"Not before I've swept out." She hurried down, counting the steps again as she went.

"Here's thee brush." He gave it to her with a knowing smile. "Now both of us is sweeping for a living!"

An hour later the room was piled with furniture and more stood out on the cobble path.

"I've nivver brokken a thing yet!" said Mr Mossop, panting. The piano came off last.

"Be careful," said Emma. "Ohh . . . "

Arthur and the carter did their best but it landed on the cobbles with a crash.

"Sounds real musical," wheezed the carter.

"It was my mother's . . ."

They struggled indoors and set it against a wall.

"You've a good lot of things," said Mr Mossop. He climbed stiffly up into the driver's seat where his thin brown face hung over them for a moment longer.

"Mebbe I'll look in on you again in a day or two . . . "

They watched him go, the pony picking its way up the track. Once he had gone they began to sense their isolation.

Bit by bit as they sorted out the furniture they made discoveries: a date on the spice cupboard, 1747; a tin full of rusty nails; a deep smooth hollow on a door jamb.

"They've sharpened a knife or two on that," said Arthur.

"We'll do the same," said Emma. She reached up and gave him a kiss. Not until the furniture was in some sort of rough order did they realise that the farmhouse had no tap. They searched from end to end. There was nothing by the iron range except the water boiler, wanting filling. At the back of the house Emma pushed open a door into the barn. One wall bulged badly inside, a drift of fallen stones lying at its foot.

"That'll need putting right," said Arthur, but there was no tap there, either.

"There must be watter somewhere," said Emma desperately. "Folk couldn't have lived here and not had watter."

"Mebbe there was a spring."

No tap, no pump, no well. It was a mystery.

"Why ever didn't I ask? I'll have to go and see him."

Emma went to the front to stare at the pond. So far they had hardly given it a glance. It was an old water hole, miry and trodden by cattle, green with algae.

"We'll not be drinking that," she said emphatically. As she spoke a rat ran down a waterlogged trunk on the far side. "Did yer see that?"

"Aye, and where there's one, there'll be others."

He took himself round the house and stared down the fields. They stretched emptily to the edge of the ridge and sank into the dale. Beyond that the fells rose steeply. Armed with a white enamel pail, he searched the hedgerows, swallows swooping as he went. He found nothing down the fields and turned up towards the track. Half a mile back along the road where they had first come he heard a gurgle in a bank. In the grass was a single stone step and a spring.

A fire burned in the hearth by the time he had walked back with the brimming pail.

"It's best watter I've ivver tasted," he told her.

Emma smiled, relieved: "I'll brew a pot of tea . . . but it's going to be hard work on wash days."

She hooked a kettle over the fire. The range was rusty and wanted cleaning; for now though it would do. The chimney drew well and that was something.

"Now we know why the rent's only two shillings."

At dusk Arthur lit an oil lamp and placed it on the table in the middle of the room. Both were tired.

"We've been lucky," said Emma, setting out supper.

"Aye, but the old devil said nowt about there being no watter!"

They lay awake in a massive double bed. The windows were missing a pane or two and cool air filled the room.

Arthur said: "Are you still sure you wanted to marry a road man?"

"Why ever do you ask?" said Emma, surprised. "Of course I'm sure."

"I mean, we haven't even got a tap . . ."

"I'm not grumbling, love."

Even so he felt that she needed some sort of compensation.

"I'll have a go at that garden for you."

"And the range . . . the chimney back's all brokken."

"Aye. We've a bit ta do before we'll be properly set."

They drifted into sleep. Hours later Emma sat up quickly.

"Arthur?"

It was dark and the noise had been close by. She listened, her senses fully alert.

"Arthur, did you hear?" He surfaced slowly from a great depth. "Listen!"

As she spoke something skittered across the joists.

"It's nobbut a rat," he told her.

She waited for a long time in case it was repeated. A pang of unease touched her at the upheaval that had taken place in her life - in both their lives, for it was the same for Arthur. She listened for the rat, but the noise was not repeated. There was nothing to bother about till morning.

Arthur carried in a bucket filled with lime cement and set it down by the hearth. It stank as ripe as a mouldy midden.

"That's fair horrible!" said Emma laughing.

"Bit of cow muck mixed in," Arthur explained. "To help it set."

He pulled the loose blackened stones out of the back of the fire range and using a small shovel plastered the cavity with the mix.

"Now give us that stone . . . that's it."

He soon made good the worn chimney.

"Well, that's a new one on me," said Emma. "Cow muck, I mean."

"There's nowt better." Arthur smiled in the slow way that she liked. "Give it an hour ta go off a bit, then bake it slow with a small fire. It'll set as grand as owt."

Emma remembered: "My granddad said the old folk used ta burn dung instead of wood."

"Aye. Had to then, folk was that poor. Worse than now. What we want is ta find a good cut of peat if we can. One all our own."

Doors and windows open wide to the breeze, she scrubbed out the living room, shifting chairs as she went, and bit by bit the flagstones began to recover something of their original pink sandstone warmth. They would not stay that way but they might as well start out looking right.

On Monday morning, Arthur set off for work, a giant broom across a shoulder, a sickle at his waist. Emma walked up the track with him, carrying the pail.

"There's farms selling up all ower," he said. "Things is real bad for folk."

"Well at least we can count our blessings."

"Aye, the house is cheap enough. But we've got ta save somehow if we want ta get started on our own. What we need is a bit of our own grazing, and some sheep."

Their place showed in among the scattered trees as they followed the road. Beyond it lay the fells, hazy in the heat. Emma switched the pail to the other hand and pushed an arm through his.

"I don't mind if you're a lengthman all your life."

But Arthur shook his head. Sweeping roads was an old man's job and he wanted better.

At the spring Emma filled the pail while Arthur walked on to Three Lane Ends where his length of road began. He would be sweeping up over Craggside and down to the schoolhouse, and home early by five if he were lucky. He whistled cheerfully: *She was only a girl in a Gilded Cage* as his boots stirred the dust. It needed more than a broom to put Cumberland's old roads in good fettle, that was a fact. The potholes were summat chronic.

Emma cleaned and black-leaded the range. It took all morning. The oven was thick with rust and she became coated in grime; the hot water boiler and tap were little better. But it pleased her to discover that the latter was brass, and not until it shone brightly was she satisfied. The range looked as fine as a picture. Furthermore, the chimney back had baked rock hard.

In the days that followed before the stranger appeared Arthur and Emma brought the farmhouse to better order. The garden got a first clearing of nettles; Arthur repaired the gate and replaced the broken glass in the windows. A loose slate caused him a long struggle, for he had to improvise a ladder from scrap wood, and during this he made the curious discovery that a number of the slates had been latched to the roof spars with sheep bones for nails. That was the old way, for sure.

Beyond the house farm hands occasionally passed with horses and carts but in the main few folk came near from early morning till the sun went below the fells at dusk.

When she was least expecting it, Emma saw another rat. It was in the barn where a pile of old hay had been dumped. She grabbed a rake to take a swing but it disappeared into a hole.

"I just don't like 'em," she told Arthur later.

"They'll not harm you, Em, if you leave well alone."

"They spread disease."

He was not one to argue. Instead he got the ladder and some cement, filled the hole with stones and plastered it over.

"There's that bit of barn wall that's tumbled, as well," she reminded him, but Arthur was tired. For now the wall would have to wait.

Not until the middle of the seventh week did Emma sense that she was being watched. A first uneasy suspicion came as she gathered firewood in the fields below the back of the house. The weather had changed; the spring haze had turned to misty mornings and then to fine rain. A piece of sack across her head, she worked along the hedges dragging out dead branches, for there was no sense in waiting till winter before laying in fuel.

At a stile she paused in the drizzle to get her breath. Without knowing how, she was suddenly sure that someone was nearby. There was no great movement, only a light stirring of trees. Even so, something had sharpened her awareness. She walked back up through the wet fields, a bundle of twigs in her arms, watching without appearing to watch, and as she climbed over the last stile a patch of black shifted by a distant hedge. It happened fleetingly so that she might almost have been mistaken. She hurried indoors, her heart palpitating.

That evening Arthur said: "Emma, is everything all right?"

The fire was blazing. The wind was getting up. Without meaning to, she answered severely. "There was another rat in the barn . . . I wish you'd do summat about 'em." Her tone was sharp. He did not reply. They had been married barely a couple of months.

That night as they lay in bed they heard squeaking and this time it came from inside the walls.

"I'll see to 'em," promised Arthur.

At breakfast Emma said: "I'm sorry about last night . . ."

He looked up from his porridge: "Nay, there's nowt ta be sorry for."

"I'm a bit on edge."

"Aye . . . don't you bother. I'll settle them beggars soon as I've worked out best road ta do it."

Emma found him his cap.

"I'll make thee summat good for supper."

She waited until he had gone from sight along the road, catching a last glimpse of the broom where it bobbed above the hedge, then she set a sack across her head and shoulders and went out into the drizzle. Her dress soaked up the water from the long grass as she worked towards the corner where she had seen the movement. No one liked being spied upon and she knew now that someone had been watching her. Well she would find out who.

A low groan came from a ditch. Startled, she paused near a split ash, then walked slowly along the hedge and looked through. An old man lay asleep, his mouth open as he snoozed through a bushy grey beard. He wore a blue Melton coat, tied round his belly with string. Everything about him was faded and worn. She stared, wanting to get away without waking him, and succeeded only by a determined effort. A twig snapped underfoot but the old man did not stir.

Slowly the afternoon passed. Emma stayed indoors, darning and thinking, and because she was quiet the rats seemed to grow noisier, skittering inside the living room walls where they emitted sharp squeaks. She put up with it for a time, then unable to ignore the noise any longer, she sat at the piano and began to play loudly. Anything to drown them out.

It was a strange performance, her out-of-practice fingers finding the notes with difficulty. *Watchman, What of the Night? Annie Laurie* and, the irony not lost on her, *Home Sweet Home*. She thumped the keys, making the notes echo through the old house and she guessed that it was the first time there had been music of any kind in that living room for many a year.

When at last she stopped the rats were silent.

". . . so you see, he's in the ditch," she told Arthur. "And he's old."

She paused uncertainly, wondering what he would think.

Arthur, dry now after a day-long soaking down by the

schoolhouse, reached forward and banged out his pipe on the hot range. Rain was one of the pains of his life which he understood all too well. Decided, he said: "We'd best go and see." She smiled, grateful.

They could not find him. The ditches were filling with water and beginning to flow again. The drought days of early spring already seemed of the long past, though it wasn't cold.

"Perhaps he's moved on," said Arthur, "gone from t'district."

Of course, she had not thought of that.

Arthur trudged ahead, following a ditch down one field, then across a hedge and along another. Water filled his boots. Somewhere there was a warm, quiet corner of the world where it never rained, but he was damned if he knew where.

Wheezing sounded in the gloom.

"He's here," announced Arthur. "I've found him." He helped the slumped figure to his feet.

"There's jus' Sandy and me," said the old man. He broke off as he began to cough. Arthur waited until the spasm had subsided and then asked: "What do they call thee?"

"John - Old John and Sandy."

"Both names, are you?" said Arthur. He picked up a soaked bundle.

"No, no," said the other. "Sandy's gone on."

Arthur spoke gently: "You'd best come with us. We'll find you a warm spot for the night."

"I'm not wantin' to cause anybody any trouble."

Emma eyed the old man's bedraggled clothes. He was soaked. His wheezing worsened as they came to the steep bit.

"Will Sandy know where we've gone?"

"He's a good nose," said the old man.

"Nose?"

"Sandy's me dog," said the stranger.

Sandy had not appeared by the time they had reached the farmhouse.

"But it'll be warmer in the house," said Arthur.

He refused politely.

"No, the barn'll be best for the likes of me, thank you."

"There's no need," said Arthur. Emma, however, was signalling.

"He'll be all right in the barn," she said quickly. She had remembered the hole in the ceiling of the other bedroom. Arthur gave her a strange look. Emma flushed.

"We haven't a spare bed ready, that is . . . ."

"Aye," said the old man gravely. "Just dig us a hole in the hay mow and set us in. It'll be right again by morning."

Emma carried a lantern into the barn. The old man sat on an upturned bucket getting his breath while they scooped a shallow trench in the pile of loose hay, then he settled himself into it.

"Now if you'll kindly cover me ower, I'll be right enough."

Emma and Arthur did as he asked, burying all but the stranger's face and his beard, which was left out on top of the hay. And that was all that showed, his brown weathered face and his beard.

"Best bed there is," wheezed the old man with a grin.

"If you're sure that'll be all right?"

"I'll be champion, thank you both."

Out in the yard Arthur said: "Champion! Come morning he'll be frozzen to death!"

But in the morning the stranger was awake and fresh and cheerful when a little after six Arthur set a pint mug of tea on the bucket and grinned at the old man's beaming face.

"And I thowt you'd not be with us this bright side . . ."

Old John lay in the hay dry and warm. His aches and pains had subsided for now.

"Sandy and me keeps each other warm."

"Ah, he's back then?"

The old man eased himself up, picking hay out of his beard and winked: "A devil for the bitches."

He slurped down gullets of hot tea.

"That's uncommonly good," he exclaimed gratefully.

"Emma and me's been talkin' - if it suits you, you don't have to move on, not if you want to rest up a while."

The old man looked candidly into Arthur's face: "That's very civil."

"We've an old bed we can fix up in the house."

But the other's face puckered.

"Nay, I'll be best out here, if that doesn't disturb you and your missis."

Arthur laughed: "Mebbe it's you who'll disturb a few rats. But we'll find you summat better ta sleep on."

So it was agreed.

Emma was scrubbing the hearthstone when Old John appeared. She was still feeling guilty about the previous night.

"You won't come and stay here in t'house, then?"

"The barn'll be right fine, missis, thank you."

"Emma," she told him, suddenly decided. "You can call me Emma." Missis made her feel about forty.

"Then I'm real honoured," said the old man gently. He paused, then added: "Mebbe Sandy and me could rummage out a bit of kindling for you."

So Old John was set up in the barn loft in an iron bedstead with a line of empty tins hanging from the rails ready to scare away any rats. A whack at the bedrail would set the tins jangling.

There was not long to wait. Late that night a distant crash made Emma sit up in the dark.

"Whativver was that?" she said, alarmed.

Arthur, deep in the covers, emerged from sleep, listened briefly, then flopped back mumbling: "It'll be the old devil scaring off the rats!"

Emma pulled the covers over her head.

The fire was burning in the grate when the old man appeared next morning.

"That crash!" said Emma. "I thought you'd fallen out of bed."

His eyes lit with a smile of satisfaction: "Aye, it frightened the rats all right!"

"Not just the rats."

He grinned: "One of them beggars was that surprised it fell right off t'beam and landed on me chest. They don't like them noises!"

Across the dome of the fells the wind curled in a mournful song. Gaps at windows and doors added in their own low wails. It was a night to be at the fireside. Carefully the old man undid his pack.

"Here's health ta you both." A golden ripple sank down his gullet.

"Here's health," said Arthur. Emma took the bottle, unsure.

"Go on, Em, sup it down."

"I've nivver had whisky afore."

"Then now," said Old John, "is the start of a lifelong friendship."

Emma drank and sneezed and the bottle went round.

And Old John said: "I tell you, you can make warts vanish just like magic. All you do is crouch down in the coal hole and wait a bit . . . where the lines of energy meet, you understand."

Arthur and Emma looked baffled.

"It's like divining rods," explained the old man. "You tap into the energy and it whisks the warts away just like that."

He looked into their faces to see if they had got his meaning. Later he got onto another subject: "Must be Woodbines. Nowt else will do."

"Whativver for?" asked Emma seriously.

"I know that one," said Arthur. "For sheep ticks."

He supped again, and then more slowly. Old John coughed and wheezed but stopped when he got the bottle.

"Ticks as big as bladders. Woodbines burns 'em off a sheep's arse just like that."

"Well I nivver," said Emma, impressed. "With Woodbines."

"No better cure," said the old man. "As soon as you burns 'em, the little buggers turn round ta see what the funny smell is - and off they drop!"

She laughed: "You're worse than my Arthur. Oh . . . "

For a moment the world reversed a little.

"Well," said Old John, "I remember one year there was frog spawn everywhere. The water hole outside this spot looked like a sago pudding. And once the little beggars hatched out, there was merry hell!"

"Frogs jumping all ower?" said Emma, fascinated.

"No, a damn great heron spiking and gobbling them up!" The old man's eyes wrinkled in a devilish smile. "It's the honest truth . . . there were no babbies that year, well none as I remember. The herons were that fat they couldn't lift their bellies off the ground ta fly!"

The wind howled in the chimney.

"Herons?" said Arthur quietly to Emma. "Herons don't bring babies."

"I know, but it don't matter," said Emma.

"Another thing," said the old man, "one day Sandy and me, we look under the henhouse and two eyes shine out bright as raindrops. 'It's a badger,' says I, 'get me gun' and I shoots it. But it was no badger - not at all, it was me best old fat ewe, and I'd gone and shot it. Fair made me weep, it did."

"H-how awful . . ."

The wind whistled at the windows as the rain beat harder out of the dark. A trickle of water began to flow down the stone staircase.

"I'm g-going to bed," said Emma.

"Me too."

Old John nodded: "Ah, well." He tipped the bottle up against the firelight and saw it was done. "We'll all be better if we're nearer the Good Lord."

And in the morning the old man woke up fresh and cheerful; and Arthur and Emma woke with heads ringing like chapel bells on Coronation Day.

Emma was sitting alone by the fire darning a sock in the lamplight when she heard a gentle scuffing. Dismayed, she watched a rat squeeze through a gap at the foot of the front door. Then came a second, and another until four had found a way through. They ran in short stops and starts across the living room to another hollow in the floor and squeezed under a second door into the larder.

She sat petrified, then as a fifth head began to work its way in,

she picked up a poker and threw it. The crash stopped any more heads appearing. For a while she did not dare to see where the others had gone, but her curiosity grew too strong and clutching her dress, she took a cow rake from the hearth and looked into the larder. The rats were up on the sandstone slab eating a piece of cheese, and they were still there as she fled upstairs.

Folk were hurrying down the track.

"Keep one for us!" shouted a ginger-haired youth. At the water hole a dozen men clustered excitedly as the Wilson brothers from Sawmill Edge dug with their sharp spades. This time four rats broke at once. Shouts rang out, sticks rose and fell in rapid blows, dogs darted and barked. More rats emerged, more excited cries, more smashed grey bodies were slung into a bin.

Old John directed the diggers to another dark bank and Emma noticed that he seemed to know exactly where to look.

"Quick try here, lads! Keep the beggars moving!"

The Wilsons were powerful diggers. Their spades bit through the bolt holes. Sweat poured off their necks and faces and soon their shirts were ringing wet. The excitement grew.

"Look!" shouted Emma.

Rats bolted from three holes. Sticks struck swift sharp death. With a yell, Mr Mossop did a wild dance as a grey body went straight at one of his gaitered legs and clawed up to his thigh before he knocked it off.

More folk arrived. News of the rat hunt had spread round the parish. A labourer out of Gamonby appeared with two Lakeland terriers, bright, quick little devils, perky and deadly. But if the hunters could bite, so could the rats and the men knew it and protected their necks with mufflers, and put bicycle clips round trouser ankles, and tied string round the wrists of their jackets.

"By the back of the barn," cried Arthur. The excited hoard poured round the building.

"Try this bit!"

"You'll be into summat hard theer," advised Old John, but no one was listening. The excitement of the hunt was on them. Again the diggers attacked the ground.

"Hell! It's all rubbish!" Bits of corrugated iron appeared and an enamel bowl.

"The crowbar, fetch the crowbar!"

Within minutes rats were bolting again, large grey lumps, shrill thin devils; pink blind young exposed in nests, steamed and drowned. Terriers, sticks and stones dealt out swift death. Emma could stand the sight no longer and stumbled away, colliding with Mr Mossop. Arthur came and put an arm round her shoulders.

"It's got ta be done, Em."

"It's just that you all enjoy it so much!" she said bitterly, her cheeks tear stained.

More excited shouts, and then a sudden howl of agony. Arthur, alarmed, hurried back.

"Whativver's happened?"

A cluster of chastened men examined young Willis.

"It's the lad's own fault," said his father severely, but he was also concerned.

"You 'it me yed," howled the lad. "You 'it me yed!"

"It'll be your backside next time," glowered his father. Angry wields were beginning to show on the boy's face and neck.

Mr Mossop told Arthur: "We walloped the lad instead of a rat! Too quick he was. Jumped in under the sticks, he did!"

Later they counted the bodies.

"A hundred and thirty-seven," said Arthur, marvelling.

"And young Willis," said the ginger youth. But this remark was thought to be out of place.

"There'll be more rats around yet," said Old John. "But we've knocked 'em back."

Arthur nodded his thanks to the old man.

"We'll have another hunt in the autumn," he said enthusiastically.

Emma and a Wilson girl emerged with trays.

"Tea," they announced. The rat hunters sank to the ground supping and exchanging yarns. Time had gone rapidly. The smell of burning rats rose into the sky for a while and then dispersed. In the days that followed, Arthur dug up the hollow doorstep and set in a new one, and that cured the rats for a while.

Emma tugged at a patch of ground elder and tried to pull out all the bits of root. It was pernicious stuff. The meadow sweet she left.

"Get the lot out," said Arthur. "Have it clear."

"But I like meadow sweet, though it's blocking the light a bit." It waved in a creamy wall across the front of a window.

"Weeds, all on 'em," said Arthur.

Emma changed the subject: "Whativver do you think happened to Sandy?"

Arthur, sitting on a big smooth cobble by the door, relit his pipe and did not answer immediately. He had puzzled about the absence of the dog, but had put it down to an old man's ways. In Arthur's view everyone was entitled to be a bit peculiar if they wanted to be.

"He's talking as if Sandy's still here," said Emma. "I mean, at times I could swear he is."

She gathered up another load for the waste heap. She had removed a lot of weeds already.

"Mebbe it ran off on his travels," said Arthur, "and he doesn't like to think it's gone."

Emma sighed. She didn't ask Arthur to help with the weeds; he saw enough every day of his life.

"He put a dish of watter down t'other day . . . by the door and for a moment I could have sworn I heard summat lapping it up."

She laughed and glanced at him. "Proper daft, aren't I?"

Later, Arthur set the pile smouldering with a cage of twigs. He liked making fires. It was the surest way to stop weeds growing again, especially ground elder.

A week or two after, in the welcome cool of the kitchen, Emma said to Old John: "You used to live here, didn't you? I mean, you knew the best spots to hunt rats . . . and about the frog spawn."

The old man looked at her, suddenly cautious. He didn't reply at first and Emma did not press him.

"Now then, missis," he said eventually. "A long time ago so I did."

His shoulders gave slightly as he sat alongside the big table. Outside the sun was back in a blaze, drying the land after a storm, pouring heat into stone and earth. The water hole flickered, shrank fractionally, flickered again.

". . . so me missis said 'Just be sure you eat a proper meal every day, or else,' and then she passed away without another word, and there was just Sandy and me left. And all me land seemed ta be worth nothing. Every day I walked round me fields recognising the hollows and the bad stone patches, and the dyke where my old horse Pilot broke a leg . . . it got so I couldn't keep nettles out of places, and I knew then that it was no good. Not once the nettles are in. Well, I sold off the land and one morning I closed the door and just walked away."

He fell silent.

"You and Sandy?" said Emma.

But Old John did not seem to hear. He sat staring at the iron range as he edged towards another night.

Emma said: "There's a drop more tea."

She left the mug by him, steaming in coils and went outside to look at the garden.

The lane shimmered with heat. An hour earlier a horse and cart had trundled past with a load of coal for Risedale. The soft clopping of hooves had faded step by step, muffled in dust. There had been no other traffic all day. Arthur sat on a bank at the roadside, a pan of water coming to the boil. Hours of work with a shovel lay behind him and he was hot and tired. He wanted no more of patching roads till another day.

". . . so you gets 'em filled in, and then they gets unfilled," he said. "The only time a pothole is any good is when it's filled in again."

Old John had come across the meadows and they sat out,

two hazy figures, and marvelled at the heat. It had been a funny year for weather. September had never been hotter.

Arthur said: "Dad was on the roads before me, but before that - and him gettin' wounded in France - he'd been a blacksmith up at Ellenrigg. Used to work every day there was, even Christmas once when t'doctor wanted out to an emergency. But he never worked on Good Friday. 'You'll not catch me nailing Christ to the cross' he used to say. You see, it was blacksmiths what made the nails. Then the Army sent him home and the council put him on the roads. And after that he used to sweep with his broom right up past the smithy where he once shod many a hundred horses . . ."

The water began to boil over.

"It fair broke his heart."

"Aye," said Old John. "Things is cruel at times."

Arthur leaned forward and set out two mugs of tea on the ground. Unusually for him, he felt the need to talk. It was too hot to work.

"It's gettin' now with tarring everywhere that horses finds the roads too slippery to travel on . . . I'd not want an automobile myself, not with the noise and smell. Of course, a horse smells when it farts, but that's natural. Anyway, there was this carter, Rikky Dickson drunk hissel silly every market day. Got into Penrith right enough, but he never would have landed back home had it not been for his pony Nell. Used ta deliver pig carcasses to the butcher at Robin Row. But sometimes he landed back with some not delivered. His cart allus arrived at a terrible clatter, Nell pulling away, no sign of Rikky till we looks inside t'cart. Aye, and there he'd be, drunk as owt, lying in among the dead pigs, smiling. Dad used ta point at Rikky and say 'We'll have that one fust. They tastes better when they dies happy!'

"He was a one was my dad."

A crow croaked close by overhead, causing Arthur to look up. Across the fields the fells shimmered slate blue, loaded with thunder. More hot weather, though it could not last forever.

"Emma?" said Arthur. "Aye, you've gathered, then, she's going ta have a babby . . . the old stead will do us for now but there's no knowing where we'll find ourselves. I know I've had enough of potholes."

They walked back to the farmhouse, each silent with his own thoughts. There had been only one cart all day. The first cool air of autumn flowed over the land.

Arthur picked up the old man's pack and showed him the strap he had fashioned.

"It'll loop over thee shoulder." Emma said: "There's no need to leave, John, not if you want to stay on . . ." His sudden announcement had dismayed her.

"Aye," said Old John, trying the strap. "That'll do grand."

Then he said: "You've brought an old man a bit of peace and happiness, and I bless you both for it. But I need to go now before the snow comes. It's Sandy," he explained. He seemed anxious not to be delayed. "He's a terrible one for wandering."

They stood in the garden and for the first time since they had met there was an air of awkwardness.

"A devil for the bitches," said Arthur, though he knew it sounded lame. Emma shivered and wished she had put on something warmer.

"There 's just one thing," said Old John. "If it'll be all right with you?" He looked at them hesitantly.

"Aye," said Arthur. "Of course."

The old man led the way into the barn, Arthur and Emma exchanging puzzled glances. In the corner where the wall had rushed the old man stooped over and laboriously began to pull aside the fallen stones, letting them tumble about his boots. Arthur, not sure what was happening, moved to speak but was silenced by Emma. Chaff dust billowed as the old man felt about in the hollows then, grunting, he grasped at an object and eased out into the light a ragged hessian bundle tied up with a maze of twine.

In a strange soft voice he said: "Come on now, you little devil. It's time we were going . . ."

Outside he hooked the strap of his pack over a shoulder.

"You must stop by whenivver you've a mind to," said Arthur, eyeing the bundle.

"We'll have t'kettle on," Emma said.

"Aye, I might just do that," said Old John with a grateful nod. "It's a kindly spot you have here."

He smiled warmly, the wrinkles deep about his eyes.

"I've felt really at home."

Walking slowly, he turned up the track, the hessian bundle under his arm.

"Well," said Arthur at last. "What do you reckon to that?"

He was unsure, but Emma knew.

"It must be Sandy. He went and left Sandy in the rubble that first time he left . . ." The conviction grew within her. "Sandy's been buried in the wall all the time."

The sky was turning wild with fast-moving clouds. It was going to be a cold autumn by the feel of things. At the top of the track the old man turned onto the road and moved away half seen through gaps in the hedgerow.

Just a few old bones, mused Arthur, but he kept the thought to himself.

"You coming inside, Em?"

She watched for a moment longer, hoping for one more glimpse, then she turned indoors knowing that despite the old man's assurance he had probably gone for good.

"I'll miss him," she said.

Fireside Chat

Two odd things happened during the same week at Sharpbeck, Back o' Skiddaw.

Billy Dixon the roadman disappeared after Sunday chapel, and Aggie Boyle, without any explanation to anyone, refused to open the door of her cottage, not even to the postman. Several days passed before anyone in the village thought to put the two bits of gossip together.

"Now just you drink up your tea, Billy, or it'll go cold,"said Aggie comfortably.

"Aye, lass. I will."

She raked up the fire till it was a bright red and the glow filled the tiny parlour. She settled at one side of the hearth and Billy sat at the other in the big armchair, the one he'd bought her in a saleroom at Cockermouth.

"Three sugars, just the way you like it."

Billy didn't interrupt. As Aggie said, it was enough just to sit by the fire and feel the warmth. The roadman was still in his Sunday best and Aggie liked him for that, one of Burton's.

"If my old mother was still alive she'd be right upset if she could see us now. That she would! Never let us marry, would she! Though I don't know why I tell you that again. A girl wouldn't put up with it nowadays!"

"No, lass, girls don't these days."

"Aye, well, I've never had a man of me own, not down all the years. Not till now!"

Aggie smiled warmly at her visitor, and leaning across she fondly straightened his tie.

"'Men is devils. You keep away from 'em Aggie Boyle,' she used to say. 'Don't let me catch you playing their funny tricks or you'll be sorry you will!' Allus ranting how she'd lock me up. And then one night she did! The night me and Bob Robertson played bloomers in his dad's barn."

"No, how did she find that out?"

"Billy, to this day I don't know how she found that out! Raging mad she was. Shoved me screaming into the cellar. Left me in the dark all night! I proper hated her for that! Now see . . . your tea's going cold. I'll make us a fresh lot. You like it better in a mug, don't you?"

"Aye, you get more in a mug."

"Course, it was not so gladsome me not liking her, but there must have been summat wrong with her in the first place. After all, she had me dad. So why couldn't I have a man? Some days I'd see me old school pals getting wed, and with babbies, and I'd think that would be lovely. But that's what she was afraid of, the children. Having 'em turn out like her. Well, that always seemed a bit daft cos she couldn't help having them looks could she?"

"No, Aggie, no one could."

"Course you never saw her at her worst, when she was nasty, but if you had you'd have understood better what she was like.

"Here . . . let me help with your tea, love. Come on, don't be shy, open your mouth a bit; we mustn't go spilling down your best suit. Well, that first day you winked at me, eh, I'll never forget that. You're a real devil, mother was right on that!"

"If you say so . . . "

"Well I does. She'd have killed us both if she'd known we was courting. Oh deary me, yes. You should have seen her with a chicken axe. Chop right through their necks with one blow she could."

"Aye, so folk have said. A fearful woman!"

"See, love, let me get a towel, save spilling down your shirt. I've allus liked your shirt. Blue stripes suit you, Billy. Goes with your blue eyes."

"Now then, Aggie. Don't go on . . ."

"Eh, just to think, all the years you bin sweeping roads! I reckon you must have worn away a dozen brooms down our Chapel Hill. And that time you fell in a snowdrift and nowt showing but a brush head where you'd gone in! I've had many a good laugh at that! Course I wish you were feeling better. Bit late now for us to wed. Too much bother. Anyway, you got your own place, and me I got here. But it's daft really, two folk being lonely 'cos of someone like her. All we wanted was a bit of company.

"Shall I undo your boots? Let your feet feel the air? No? Perhaps not . . . never know who might drop by, though the door's locked so you'd have plenty of time to get 'em back on if you wanted. I know what I wanted. Just one wee lass of me own. Not much to want in life is it, a la'all body to drink at its mother's breasts? Little Agnes.

"You know, while we're sitting here chatting I could just be cutting your hair."

"Aye? Will you, Aggie?"

"Course I will! I've always wanted to cut it for you and now's a good time. I'll set a towel on your shoulders and keep your suit clean. My hair's gone thin now, of course. Used to be really thick when I was young. Blonde it was. Mother was jealous of my hair. Used to chop it off when I was young, far as she dared with dad around, but it grew back as good as ever, thick and beautiful. I think she used to hate my hair more than anything. You'd have loved my hair if you'd known me then, Billy.

"Funny about me dad. He stuck with her for years and then did a bunk. Gone to Keswick. That's what mother telt me first time I asked where he was. He was there one day, and next day he'd gone. More work for mother. Meant she had to dig the garden veg bit all by herself. Strong she was. 'I'll do it' she'd say. Wouldn't let anyone touch the garden from then on. Lost her temper when I tried to help. We never heard of dad again. Some men are like that, just push off. Aye, he'll be pushing up daisies somewhere now, he will.

"There, that's your hair done! That's nice. You've a lovely head of hair you have Billy. I've always liked you for it. Dad was the same. It ran in his side of the family . . .

"Yes, all right. We'll have our supper soon. Two nice pork chops, and after that a drop of port."

"Aye, Aggie, chops and port! That sounds good."

"Aye, lad. Hello, there's someone else coming up the path . . . I wish folk would stop keep coming and bothering. Now don't you say owt. Save your strength and leave the talkin' to me."

"Just you open up, Aggie," insisted PC Watson. "Can't chat through a closed door now can I!"

He knocked again, a shade louder. The old woman stood quite still behind the door, a hand to her mouth.

"Aggie if you don't let me in I'll have to knock it down, won't I! Now you don't want me to have to do that do you!"

She turned the key.

The waft of air from within the cottage made PC Watson step back a bit.

"Are you all right, love?" His eyes stared into the gloom within. "Phew, you've got a nasty smell in here, lass!"

Aggie stroked Billy's hair just one more time.

"He's asleep, poor old man. He'll wake up soon." She smiled and nodded in approval. "You'll be waking up soon, won't you Billy lad?"

"Yes, Aggie, course I will, pretty soon."

"Then we'll have that drop of port, you and me."

"Aye, all right, love. Just a small glass."

PC Watson stared open mouthed at Billy, and then at Aggie. For a moment he did not know what to say.

Both voices had come from Aggie.

Later she sat and finished a mug of comforting tea.

"Be sure you look after him," she told the stretcher bearers. "Like I said, he's not as good on his feet as he was."

"No, I'm not, that's right love."

The district nurse reached for Aggie's coat and the old woman told her in confidence: "Billy and me's had a real nice chat we have."

"Have you, Aggie?"

"Aay . . . he were a lovely man."

Later the police took away the axe and decided to dig up the vegetable patch.

Mr Ostle's Great Loss

It was spring in name only, March at its coldest, a dismal day to be out on the lake in a leaking rowboat. A day awaiting calamity.

"Don't just sit there looking stupid!" yelled Ostle. "Bail!"

The wretchedness that was little Ronnie Hadwin trembled as his cocoa tin splashed in erratic scoops in an unfair attempt to empty Windermere out of the boat faster than it was leaking in.

"It's squirtin' terrible quick, Mr Ostle sir," he wailed. "Terrible quick, it is."

The carpenter snorted disdainfully, flailing with an oar at the tangle of submerged branches across the bows.

"It'll hardly squirt itself out, will it, you gormless sprat! Now get on with it!"

Hadwin bailed as fast as he could. Scarcely a month in the job, and already he hated the lake. He had decided he was more a mole of wood shavings and cluttered workshop corners rather than the water rat his master imagined.

"Damned branches!" yelled Ostle.

The carpenter, precariously balanced, struck downwards, rocking the boat.

"Mr Ostle, sir!" protested the boy. He held on to the sides as his master cursed - the one, thin-necked and fourteen years old, the other hunched, bald under his cap and fast losing his temper.

The boat began to swing in the wind.

"Mr Ostle, sir . . . we'll go ower!"

"Are you givin' me advice?" snapped the carpenter. "There, that's got it!" Suddenly he was triumphant as the oar hooked a branch. "Now we're gettin' somewhere!"

The little man was strong. He hoisted the gory tangle till it came waist high. Success at last, and he was poised to swing it clear as a fresh squall came sweeping down out of the north and caught them broadside.

Ostle yelled as he tumbled inboard and it was at this confused moment that his bottom set of teeth seemed to jump right out of his mouth and in a pink blur sailed over the side of the boat into the lake.

In view of the greater crisis, the leak was forgotten.

"The bugs will have got 'em," said Hadwin.

"Bugs?" demanded Ostle. What bugs?"

"Mud bugs," said Hadwin. "The lake's fair crawlin' with 'em, Mr Ostle, sir. Everybody knows that."

Carpenter and apprentice peered into the bay, but made little of the choppy water.

"The bugs will have got 'em for sure," said Hadwin.

"Workhouse rubbish!" snorted Ostle. "Can you see me teeth or can't you?"

"I saw 'em go down, all pink and white . . ."

Ostle blew in exasperation: "I know what they looks like. It's where they are now, you dimwit!"

The rowboat rocked in a series of troughs. To the north another grey belt of rain was blotting out the mountains.

"It's gettin' proper rough, Mr Ostle."

"I've got to have 'em," said the man worriedly. He struggled with a difficult thought. "There's a wedding."

"Yeah," said Hadwin.

Ostle glowered. Another miracle of botched carpentry, and half his teeth gone! He'd give John Edgar hell when he got back to the workshop. The old carpenter had fouled up the repair good and proper.

But hope came.

"Mr Ostle, sir," cried Hadwin excitedly peering over the stern. "Does that look like 'em down there!"

A lighter patch seemed to eddy vaguely on the bed of the lake, at this point scarcely twelve feet below.

"By God, you're right!" Ostle exclaimed. "It's them!"

"Down among t'bugs like I says," said the lad. "But they're too deep. We'll never get a hook on 'em."

"Hook?" said Ostle staring into the water. He turned and glared at the apprentice. "What do you think I employ you for?"

Had Hadwin's wits been sharper he would have remained silent.

"Mr Ostle, sir?"

"Can you swim?"

"Aye, master, sort of . . ."

The confession was sufficient for the carpenter.

"Then you'll soon get 'em!"

The enormity of his employer's intention was still registering as Hadwin found himself hoisted by the back of his britches and propelled over the side into England's largest lake.

The apprentice yelled as he went under, and was still yelling as he surfaced.

"Me clogs! Me clogs has come off!"

"Don't just splash around!" yelled Ostle. "Get down after me teeth!"

The clogs bobbed to the surface and Hadwin grabbed the side of the boat long enough to throw them inboard.

Ostle protested: "Me teeth will have gone for good if you don't shift!"

"It's freezin', Mr Ostle, sir!"

"Get down now!" barked his employer. Already the boat was drifting.

Ninety minutes later a blackened kettle steamed in the carpenter's workshop. It stood on an iron stove which roared noisily with blazing off-cuts. Embraced gratefully within the heat was the chilled figure of Hadwin, wrapped in a blanket, not, however, a triumphant Hadwin.

"I've just got to get some more dentures," said Ostle desperately.

His old carpenter, John Edgar, plucked curls of shavings out of a plane and looked sombre.

"It's a bad do," he acknowledged. "But nobody'll notice owt's wrong. They'll be looking at the wedding folk, likely."

"I feel naked without me teeth," said Ostle. "We could see 'em plain as anything!"

He glared at Hadwin.

"Thing ta do," suggested John Edgar, "is ta get another pair, temporary like."

Ostle spluttered. There were times when the workman was as gormless as the apprentice.

"And where might I do that, with the wedding termorrer?"

"Aye," said the old man. "That's an uncommon difficulty."

Ostle yelled at Hadwin: "Don't just let the kettle boil away. See to it!"

"Of course," said John Edgar, "for a small sum you could borrow mine."

Ostle paused as the old man took out his bottom deck and held them for his employer to see.

"Mebbe they're a bit like your old uns?"

"They need a good scrubbing," said Ostle critically.

All the same, the carpenter gave them a quick rinse under the tap and tried them for size. Chomping experimentally, he went down the workshop to examine the result in a piece of glass. Not at all bad considering they were an odd set.

"By, that's a right good fit, that is."

He bared them. Not at all bad.

"It's lucky us having the same sized mouths," he marvelled.

"Nobbut thre'pence," said John Edgar. "For the loan, that is."

"Tuppence," said Ostle. "And I'll give 'em a good scrub for you."

"All right - tuppence. Just for termorrer."

The wedding was in Ambleside and everything went smoothly. Afterwards the bride and the bridegroom posed on the church steps in a gusty wind; then the bridesmaids, relatives and friends were waved in for a group picture amid flying veils. The bride and the bridegroom smiled, the guests smiled, but none seemed to smile brighter than Mr Ostle. Years later whenever the wedding albums were examined people picked him out.

Mrs Ostle, a generously made woman with a lifetime of cooking behind her, produced a hot dish out of the blackness of her oven range.

"You near drowned that lad," she accused her husband.

"Oh, and who says?"

"Everyone. The whole village is talking."

"Hah! Well I don't pay lads to hang about when there's work to be done."

Hadwin's soaking was the only satisfaction in the whole business.

"You've a nasty mean streak when you want," said Mrs Ostle setting a plate of pig's trotters in front of him.

Ostle glared: "What's this? Trotters? How can I eat trotters?"

"Always complaining, you are! They'll practically mash with a fork. What's more, first thing tomorrow you can go and buy yourself a new set of teeth."

"I'm not wasting good money on anything of the sort."

For a while the carpenter's gummy mouth wrestled with a trotter, then exasperatedly he dumped it on the plate uneaten.

"I'm going to be a shadow at this rate."

"You'll do as I say," advised his wife. "I've never been so ashamed in all me life . . . going to a weddin' in borrowed teeth. I can't think of anything worse."

As if by accident a gentle clicking of dentures greeted Ostle on his arrival at the workshop next morning.

"And what are you grinning at, you old bat?" he demanded of John Edgar.

"Aye now," said the old man broadly. "I'm thinking you'll be buying some new teeth."

"At a pound a bottom set? Ower my dead body - now get on with summat."

There was plenty to do with six rowboats to repair.

"It beats me how folk managed before there was false teeth," confessed Ostle. He grabbed a work list down off a shelf and revealed his remaining dentures sitting in a glass of water.

"They look proper lovely like that," observed John Edgar.

"Well they're no good by themselves!"

Young Hadwin whistled noisily as he cleaned out the stove. Sight of him made Ostle pause, and at this instant a brilliant idea struck him.

"Now then, that's it! Just you come here, me lad."

Triumphantly he told the apprentice exactly what to do, giving him a sixpence out of the kitty in the Oxo tin.

"And no dawdling, 'cos I'll know."

Hadwin's thin face flickered with uncertainty. "But how'll I tell which ones Mr Ostle?"

"Always scrawkin', aren't you?"

At the same time he saw that Hadwin had a point and reaching for the jar he fished out the dentures.

"Match 'em with these. Now get along before I finds you summat nasty to do."

The boy took the glistening plate of teeth with little enthusiasm and pushed them deep out of sight in his apron pocket.

"Not in with the nails!" bawled Ostle.

Eventually Hadwin disappeared with the dentures wrapped in a sheet of *The Lakes Chronicle.*

"We'll soon be right now," the carpenter confided to John Edgar.

Cookson's funeral parlour was a combination of silver embellishments and heavy black drapes which sank down the walls into soothing grief-absorbing carpets. Cookson himself was no longer the owner having invested deeply in his own trade, and the business had been taken over by Arnold Southward, an offcomer from Workington whose cumbersome coffin-building hands contrasted strangely with the narrow sleeves of his black professional suit.

"Teeth?" said Mr Southward. "Of course! We've lots of teeth."

The undertaker produced a cardboard box from a cupboard and tipped an impressive collection of used dentures onto the counter.

"I'll risk my reputation you'll find something here even Mr Ostle will find suitable."

Hadwin eyed the yellowed heap in dismay.

"Does f-folk give 'em to you, Mr Southward, sir?"

"Gives 'em, leaves 'em, what's the difference, eh? It's the widders what decides. Now this is a fine outfit. Just Mr Ostle's style, I fancy. Good hard biters."

Hadwin left sixpence on the counter, stuffed the teeth into his apron and fled. It was five minutes down to the workshop.

"Well?" said Ostle.

Hadwin handed them over.

But the dentures were not a success.

"Nowhere near," groaned the carpenter. He took the set out of his mouth and examined them. "Got too many teeth, that's what"

"No," said John Edgar, putting on his specs. "They can't 'ave."

"Well they have," said Ostle. "Sixpence? Well you can take 'em back and find summat better."

Hadwin trudged back up the hill to the undertaker's. Another search, another stab in the dark, but no better luck. The second set was equally ill fitting.

"It's no good," grumbled Ostle. "I'll have to go meself!"

"You should send the lad to Woollies in Kendal," wheezed John Edgar. "They sell new spectacles a tanner a time. Maybe they sells dentures with 'em."

"And waste more money on the train? Get on with summat, or we'll all land in the workhouse!"

By the time Ostle was free to visit the undertaker's it was late afternoon and the chilliness of the lake had seeped into the village. It hardly seemed any warmer at the undertaker's parlour where Ostle banged on the counter bell.

Mr Southward emerged from behind a curtain wiping his hands. The interruption was not altogether welcome. He was anxious to put the finishing touches to a freshly delivered arrival.

"It's not often we have the pleasure, Mr Ostle."

"It's not often me teeth lands in the lake."

"Just so . . . you've come to try for yourself."

Ostle's eyes glinted at the box of dentures.

"Now this is more like!"

"You carry on," said the undertaker. "I have, as it were, another client waiting."

The first set felt sharp and uncomfortable. Ostle tried another, and after that, another. Some were too big, or too narrow, or simply just awkward. One set tasted disagreeably of camphorated tooth powder. He marvelled that people's mouths could be so different.

The box exhausted, Southward produced a second collection.

"London made, most of them. Nothing finer on the market."

"I don't care if they're from 'Merica as long as I get some that fit."

The new batch was no better. He tried them all without success. Ostle banged the bell a shade harder. Southward was keen to be rid of the carpenter, with or without teeth, but he wavered as a further thought struck him.

"There's one more chance, Mr Ostle . . ."

The corpse lay fully dressed on a slab of black slate.

"The Captain . . . rather sudden."

"His should be good 'uns," said Ostle.

"It's only a remote chance."

Ostle took the teeth half-heartedly, wiped them on a sleeve and tried them. The effect was considerably better than he had expected.

"Now then. They're not bad!" he acknowledged. He bared the teeth at a mirror. They looked rather well.

"A good strong set," said Southward reassuringly. "The Captain was one for the best of things."

"Is that so?" Ostle nodded in approval. The teeth felt comfortable, not as good as his old ones, but an improvement on everything he had tried so far. "Aye, these'll do!"

Southward smiled wanly.

"Slightly better quality than the rest. A ninepenny pair, I think."

Ostle's face grew several more lines: "They were only a tanner this morning."

"A captain's dentures," said Southward. "We all have to live, Mr Ostle."

Eventually Ostle compromised. Straining generosity, he left eight pence, counting it out twice. Yet all was not well. If the carpenter was pleased, Mrs Flora Ostle was not.

"A dead man's teeth," she said in disgust. "Don't bring them near me!"

"I tell you no one will know," said Ostle. "They were made in London."

He opened his mouth and clicked experimentally. There was a tendency for them to slip a little but Southward had assured him he would get over that once he had worn them a day or two.

"You might at least clean 'em before you use 'em!"

"All right, all right. I'll boil 'em if that will satisfy you! Then let that be an end to it."

For twenty minutes the pan of water bubbled on the kitchen fire. Women, Ostle reflected darkly, were always fussing about nothing. The teeth were a bargain and he was going to wear them, dead man's or not. He listened as they jiggled up and down against the metal then at last he removed the pan from the flames and examined the contents. The result was not what he expected. A bellow of rage filled the kitchen.

"You damn fool, woman!" he bawled indignantly. "See what you've done!"

The quality dentures had disintegrated.

The next morning, the three-horse Belsfield bus was struggling up Cragg Brow heading for Windermere station as Ostle stomped down through the village to his workshop. He felt despondent and cold. Several people owed him money and until the season got going there was little likelihood he would be paid. Ostle likewise owed money. Ten bob to the grocer, seven pounds to the timber yard, and smaller sums to others. In winter everybody owed money to everybody else. There was just no way he could see himself buying new teeth for weeks.

To add to his misery, John Edgar did not turn up for work.

"That's all I need," said Ostle banging around in annoyance. It was the third time in a month.

"Get that stove lit!" he bawled as a thin figure edged across the line of his vision. "If the old devil's tight again I'll brain him - and that goes for you too!"

The apprentice fled for kindling.

The only touch of brightness down the whole of the long workshop was a forlorn top set of dentures sitting pink and white in a jar of water. By ten o'clock Ostle was thinking about sending Hadwin along to the old man's cottage when the workshop door opened and Flora Ostle flustered in laden with shopping baskets. It was apparent that she had important tidings.

"Dead?" said Ostle, letting the news register.

"Sitting in his chair at his fireside."

The carpenter sank down onto a bench.

"He might have picked a better time," said Mrs Ostle, "what with the season just starting."

"Now then," chided her husband. "The man's hardly gone . . ."

He stopped, ever so slowly, his mouth still open, as a simple but brilliant realisation began to overtake him.

Mrs Ostle was horrified, of course, at the very thought, but she always was. And, as Ostle said, it was a perfect keepsake in memory of his old and trusted workman, and they were a good fit.

What was more, in the end he had got them for nothing.

Silence is Golden

Tyson's road gang arrived to fill in the potholes.Their pony and cart climbed steadily up the forest road through the mist of early morning, the four men walking alongside, clogs clattering on stones, everything slightly ghostly. No one was expecting anything out of the ordinary.

Where a beck crossed the track they set up a canvas bivouac, lit a coke brazier and unloaded a few shovels and then, as if that was all that was expected of them, they slumped with familiar ease to their Ten o'Clock break. No one was tearing to make a start. After a while the biggest among them, Tyson, looked up and in a low voice remarked: "Well, I'm beggared, he's here again."

Three heads turned to follow the foreman's stare. Stubbs, his mug of tea steaming, Allonby, pipe half lit, and young Dixon of Scaleby who at first stared without seeing anything different and then realised that he was already looking at the ragged figure standing in among the trees.

"It's Michael," said Tyson.

"Oh, is it!" said Stubbs, his face hardening as he got to his feet. "Well I'll fettle him . . . "

The little roadman gestured at the watching figure: "Get off with you, you bastard! Get out of it!"

"Hey, now then," said Tyson. But Stubbs was not to be deterred.

"I'm not putting up with him for another two weeks. Not again! He can bugger off!"

The outburst took Dixon by surprise.

"Whativver's the matter?" He had never heard of Michael until now.

"You'll see a sight too much of him if he doesn't get along, that's what! Never says owt. Stands around if you let him like he was dead."

Dixon glimpsed a wizen-faced figure moving away among the larches.

"So what's he about, then . . ."

They settled to the brazier, intent on enjoying its increasing heat, but the harmony of their arrival along the quiet woodland road had been spoiled.

"He never says anything," Tyson explained to Dixon. "He's got no tongue, see. He's a mute."

"Well it doesn't stop him sneaking around," snapped Stubbs. "He'd creep up inside your jumper if he got the chance."

Allonby knocked out his pipe: "He does no harm."

But Stubbs' scowl grew darker.

"Always watching and hanging around."

"He hangs around," said Tyson. "'Cos he's a loony."

It was gone half-ten before they turned to the road. They got up slowly, finding their own shovels and rakes, Stubbs still in a foul mood.

At a distance Michael Flosh appeared to be a young lad, though closer to it was easy to see he was in his forties. His face was wrinkled and parchment coloured. He seemed to be standing lopsidedly, an odd figure in a stained raincoat and boots.

All morning he watched the four men as they raked and filled in holes. A year had passed since they had last been in the valley and he saw that one of them was new. The big one with the wide leather belt round his breeks was the gaffer; he'd been gaffer last time and said what he pleased; Michael liked the big one. Next was the wiry one, who drank from a bottle when he thought no one was looking. The man had a thin angry face and never laughed. The third was the old man who was always stopping to pee. He was quiet like the gaffer, but Michael had never seen anyone pee as much as the old man. And now there was a new one, with the big shovel and bulging muscles, called Dixon. Michael watched the newcomer gather up stones out of the beck and barrow them to the road. He would wait to see if he liked the new one.

"That's the place, on the side of the ridge," said Allonby resting on his rake. Dixon stared at the spot, a grey slate roof high up among the trees, hard to see unless you knew where to look.

Stubbs said: "Know what his old mam does? Every day she feeds him on a wall. Puts a bowl of food out on top of the stones like she was feeding the birds!"

"Aye? And who told you that?"

"I've seen him waiting there, haven't I? Out she comes with tatie pot in a dish and sets it on the wall."

"Tell us another! The birds would have it."

"No they don't! She leaves a plate on top, see, so the birds can't get it."

They were a quarter of a mile up the road from the bivouac filling in a long draw where a swollen rill had gushed across the track in the last storm. It had carved a wide channel through the clay and shale. Stubbs spat at a stone.

"Free grub if you want it." He laughed uneasily. "I went and ate it myself, once."

"You?"

"Cold mutton and mash, but I left the mash. He ate that."

"Is that so? I'm surprised you didn't manage the mash as well."

"He nivver said owt."

"He says nowt," said Tyson, " 'cos he's dumb."

He eyed the little man disapprovingly.

Later they huddled in the bivouac, the heat of the brazier scorching their faces. Four eggs bowled around inside the black heart of the kettle.

"He's like a lot round here," said Stubbs. "Radge as a maggot. His mam and dad were cousins, married too close. Bairns starts coming out queer then."

Streaky sunlight daubed the valley. It picked out the first of the turning trees. Autumn was beginning to flare but the road gang scarcely noticed. Autumn simply meant winter was next.

At five to twelve an old woman with grey hair appeared at the back door of the farmhouse. Ella Flosh carried an enamel bowl and set it on top of the wall.

She didn't look to see if anyone was there, but following long custom she took hold of a metal bar and rattled it on the stones, then she went inside, leaving the bowl steaming gently under a tin plate. It was a daily ritual. He squatted on the ground and scooped up the stew with a spoon. It tasted good and salty and he licked the bowl clean. When he had done he left it tipped over in the grass and went down to the beck and drank noisily.

On Friday morning Tyson failed to appear. The others huddled in the bivouac and stoked the brazier as if it contained the last hot coals on earth. From time to time Allonby peered down the track where it snaked through the trees. The morning had a hint of sunshine, though little warmth.

"Oughtn't we to make a start?" said Dixon. He did not enjoy hanging around. "It's gone nine."

"He'll be along soon enough," said Stubbs. "Time to start when he gets here."

"But he'll want to know what we've done."

"Let him. Anyway it'll be time for Ten o' Clocks soon enough."

Dixon carried the kettle down to the beck and filled it at a pool. The crash of water was louder after the night's rain and he listened, enjoying the sound. As he climbed back up through the trees a movement caught his eye.

Michael was standing between a tumbled wall and a larch. Perhaps two or three seconds passed, sufficient for Dixon to see the mute's drawn face. Unexpectedly Michael gave a shy smile. Dixon went back with the kettle.

"You were long enough," said Stubbs accusingly.

"He's out there . . ." said Dixon, for want of something to say. But he regretted the words as soon as he had spoken. Stubbs glared.

"Michael, I mean."

"I know who you mean, that spying bugger! Well, I'll fettle him!"

"Don't," said Dixon looking bothered. "He's harming no one."

Stubbs had grabbed a broom.

He shouted: "Come here, you varmint!"

In the trees Michael watched as Stubbs approached. He felt no sense of alarm, rather a limpid curiosity which turned to mild surprise as the roadman began to tow him by his sleeve towards the track.

"Here! Take this!" ordered Stubbs. "Go on, you lazy devil! Do summat useful."

Michael was unsure what was expected of him. He clutched clumsily at the broom.

"That's it!' said Stubbs. "Sweep! Sweep!"

He made with his hands. Still uncertain, Michael pushed at the brush, sending a stone skittering.

"Go on," ordered Stubbs. Allonby was beside him, laughing. "That's it!"

Another stone flew into the leaves. And then Michael understood. Clasping the broom in both hands, he pushed at the ground; and then he pushed again, and as the leaves flew up before him he went on pushing.

"Now bugger off!" snapped Stubbs. "Sweep the bloody lot!"

They watched the ragged figure moving away up the track and by the time Tyson had arrived, Michael was out of sight.

The roadmen made good progress repairing the potholes. By the end of the second week they were half way up the valley and had moved their canvas den twice to new places among the trees. The days of mist had cleared and sunlit skies prevailed. The slopes

were bright with orange and yellow splashes running in vivid swaithes up the hillsides where they vanished along the skyline. For himself, Tyson was well pleased. They would have the job finished before the snow and be comfortably back at the distant depot for winter maintenance. Dibs and dabs of news about Michael came as others passed: some charcoal burners over from Wallthwaite had chanced on him sweeping far up in the woods; a string of carters leading timber had met him; so too had two tramps, wanting a brew. None of the roadmen saw anything of him. Stubbs' broom had done the job.

And then one afternoon he appeared to young Dixon. The roadman was retying the strings round his britches and knew nothing of the mute's arrival until a light hand touched him.

"Ohh, you had me by the ears then!" said the startled roadman. He looked and then he glanced again. Michael's hungered expression shocked him. It took Dixon only moments to reach into the bivouac and grab one of his beef sandwiches from his bait box.

"Here," he said. "Get this inside you."

The mute wolfed it down and Dixon quickly found two more. Plainly the man was famished. Dixon was thinking to rummage for another butty but a streak of caution got the better of him. Instead he opened his palms to show that they were empty.

"That's your lot," he said, suddenly brusque. "There's nowt more."

He would have two shadows for the rest of the week if he kept on feeding him. He felt guilty, but slowly the roadman walked off up the track, not looking round. The others would be along soon.

Trees had grown close in round the farm, concealing all but a couple of green slate roofs from the rest of the valley. Michael took up his tin bowl again and rattled it on a stone, but though long moments passed no one came out of the house to fill it. The blue and white chipped enamel still felt greasy, just as he had left it the last time. There was no smoke from the chimney. For a long time he waited, his head angled at the bowl where it lay on the grass.

At the door Michael paused. A couple of centuries lay sagging in the hollow step. Inside, the dark stone passage seemed to be holding its breath. Nothing stirred. In the downhouse Ella Flosh sat huddled beside an unlit iron range, her plaid tight around her shoulders. Michael poked gently at his open mouth but she paid no attention, and she was still there staring when he went outside again to look at the empty bowl. Nor did she move for two more days, and then she tilted forward stiffly and lay heaped on the slate floor as cold as the stone.

The roadmen paused and stared.

"Ye gods!" exclaimed Stubbs. "Look what's coming!"

Michael shambled towards them, his face haggard, his coat torn. He was spattered in mud.

"What's up with him?" said Allonby. Tyson watched as the mute neared. Something seemed to be different, he seemed to be excited.

"What is it, Michael?" Tyson asked.

The mute opened and closed his mouth as if he were trying to speak. One hand was wrapped round the handle of his brush, the other was deeply clenched.

"He wants a new broom, that's what," sneered Stubbs. The bristles were worn down almost to the wood.

Michael's eyes rolled at the trees, then shifted back towards the road gang as if he could not keep his gaze fixed permanently on any one of them. He lifted his clenched fist and after a long moment his weathered fingers opened slowly like some gnarled brown flower.

"Bloody hell," said the foreman softly.

Two gold coins shone in Michael's palm as bright as the sun.

Sitting on an upended barrow, Michael ate ravenously.

"They're Roman, no doubt about it!" said Stubbs. He laughed again, over-loud.

"And how do you know that, then?" Stubbs bit at one of the coins.

"Well it's not the king's head, is it? The king doesn't go wearing a helmet and things like that, does he? It's one of them legion ones . . .

I tell you, it's Roman gold. And he's found it!"

Their gaze shifted eagerly back to the mute. He was eating everything they had been able to muster.

"Getting his strength up," said Stubbs approvingly. "It's Roman gold, all right."

"It scarcely seems possible," said Tyson.

All afternoon Michael led the excited men from one path to another.

"Sweep, sweep," encouraged Stubbs for the hundredth time. "Show us, Michael. Go on, show us!"

And Michael, shambling ahead, was anxious to help. It was a new experience. Never before had anyone been so intent on his company. He hurried through a coppice and on up a hillside, shouldering his worn broom, his boots scuffing at the tree roots; then on along a twisting path, his eager companions close on his heels. Yes, this was the way, he'd been here already alongside the marshy stretch where a spring gurgled summer and winter, past the white patch boulder to the joining of two more paths. Deer paths both of them.

He stopped in a glade alongside a mound of autumn colours, glistening wet leaves heaped as high as his chest. The excited men barged past, searching the ground.

"Is this the place?"

Stubbs kicked the pile apart as if his life depended on it. Michael stared, his head suddenly on one side. Their search proved useless.

"They won't be buried under a pile of leaves," said Allonby.

"They could be anywhere," said Dixon. "Here's another path. Michael, is it this 'un?"

Michael, still remembering the way the leaves had been kicked, nodded.

"This must be the way!"

The mute ahead, the roadmen moved on quickly, tearing apart each heap of leaves wherever they met them. And whenever they grew tired and began to argue or have doubts, the sight of the two coins set them back searching.

They looked again the next day, and the next. The thought of more coins waiting to be found burned as bright as autumn itself. Somewhere a hoard of gold existed and Michael the mute had found it.

It was like returning to the start of a maze.

Allonby said wearily: “We’ve been along this one already.”

Michael was shambling ahead, clutching the broom. But the exhausted gangers had had enough. For three days they had trailed along paths on both sides of the dale, following the mute wherever he led them, and always it had turned out to be the same, Michael’s piles of leaves and no sign of more coins.

It took Tyson a while before he could say what he had been thinking.

“Fact is,” he said slowly, “he doesn’t know himself, does he? Not where he found ’em? Not any more, he don’t . . .”

Michael was showing them any old path. The mute had forgotten what they were looking for. Even fresh sight of the coins created no response. For the first time he paused to beckon them on and found that they did not follow. The roadmen were trudging back down the valley side to the bivouac.

“There’s more gold here somewhere,” said the foreman. “I feel it in me bones.”

“Might as well search all Cumberland,” said Stubbs bitterly. “Anywhere would be easier than these ruddy woods.”

“We’ll come back and have another look,” said Tyson. It was time to return to Keswick.

Thinking on, he left Michael a new broom, ramming the handle into the ground so that it stuck up like a signpost. He’d book it to Wear and Tear.

After they had packed up and gone, Michael ate the last of the bread and cheese. He decided that he liked young Dixon, and he liked the big gaffer; and the old one who peed. But the other one he did not like, not the thin one. Behind the skin of the man's face lay a yellow skull.

The wind grew stronger. The great tide of autumn stretched to the skyline. Time to begin. Armed with his new broom, Michael started in among the leaves. There was plenty to do. He'd sweep all the way down to the beck again, and later for a change he'd go up to the shale bank and sweep out some more of the pretty golden things.

Road to Paradise

They were two specks crossing a bleak upland, a couple of tramps heading north hoping for a bit of good luck, wanting to reach the city.

"It's no good," wheezed Eskin fretfully, "you're going too fast all ower again . . ."

The wind whipped the words away out into the broad sweep of Cumberland. It was the melancholy back-end of the year, the few travellers on the road finding little shelter. Through this desolation they trudged, winter on their heels.

"Are you lis'ning?" The big man in the lead checked his pace reluctantly.

"We gotta keep going," said Bottle, his mind on the horizon.

"It'll be no good once it's gone dark."

Eskin caught up.

"It's me chest," he said apologetically.

"Nay," said Bottle, "it was yer corns once back."

"Aye, but it's me chest now . . . me corns is fairly improving."

They were the long and the short of it, Bottle, a bulky once-strong man trapped by worsening sight and a tiny pair of steel-rimmed spectacles. And Eskin, small and bald pated, fighting an unequal struggle with life on a misery of a day and wheezing as if he were leaking.

"We haven't rested all morning," he groaned. "I haven't the strength I used to have."

"Well we ain't stopping now," said Bottle, setting off again, though more slowly. "We're nearly there."

And so they were.

Carlisle - there was a musical chime to its name - the cathedral, a castle, a city, small of course but still a city. It promised much and it lay just ahead. Bottle knew what to do once they reached it.

"It'll be no better than the rest," predicted Eskin.

"Just you wait," said Bottle. "We'll have a good laugh in Carlisle. It's a good place for a laugh is Carlisle."

The journey north was not so humorous. Under dismal skies they tramped up through Lancashire into Westmorland, sleeping under hedges when dry, and in doss houses when wet. They passed through Kendal and over the grind of Shap Fell and its bleak wastes; and then down to the wealthy market town of Penrith, encased in sandstone warmth. Now they trudged north along a stony road, their next destination nearing, Cumberland's only city, and a smoky huddle at that.

Unexpectedly Bottle sneezed, scattering a flurry of dewdrops. The sharpness of the burst took him by surprise.

"Damned if I ain't got your cold."

"Flu-henza," said Eskin. "Everybody gets flu-henza these days."

"It ain't 'fluenza," said Bottle.

Kendal and Penrith were disastrous. Bundled by the police out of the first, and not a charitable penny at the second. Any hope the tramps had was pinned now on finding a generous vein in Carlisle. The promised land, they could see it ahead, rooftops, chimneys and factories coming into view.

"We'll do a bit of gentle knocking," said Bottle planning aloud. His ugly old boxer's mug tightened its creases.

"I'm feeling lucky again. A bit of cold puts folk in a better givin' mood . . . more spiritual."

"Food," said Eskin, "is all I want."

It was amazing how hungry he felt. He paused in the road, momentarily, and then had to stop properly, caught in a fit of coughing. Bouts had come and gone for several days.

"You want a long red flannel vest for that cough of yours," advised Bottle. He waited patiently. "Tight down over yer arse."

He looked into the little man's troubled eyes.

"Keeps the cold out, see, and the farts tight in."

Eskin's face lit up at remembrance of red flannel.

"You don't see it much these days. Not so you pick it up cheap like."

"Nowt's cheap any more," acknowledged Bottle as they set off again. Twopence an ounce for bacca; beer a penny, there seemed no end to it.

Eskin sighed: "We're in bad times."

"We'll be all right in Carlisle," promised Bottle.

The city was close now, firmly ingrained in the Border plain. Some two thousand years earlier the Romans had been garrisoned there, a bulwark against the north, but now the city stood feet higher, a new civilisation grown up on the rubble of the old. Little by little the tramps began to meet more people. Horses and carts, hurrying cyclists.

"Go on," said Eskin. "Tell us about Carlisle . . ."

It was a sure way of slowing the big man.

"Aye, well," said Bottle, and as if in response to some hidden chord his pace slackened. "Merchant's 'ouses, railway workers. Lots of money."

"Grub - what about grub?"

Bottle turned, a big man going round-shouldered. He peered down through his glasses: "Hot grub. A good doss'ouse, see. Soup - a ha'penny a bowl, with bread. Keep the winter out."

"Ha! I've never kept the winter out yet," said Eskin bitterly. "Winter's bin in me bones all me life."

"You will. I promise you."

And suddenly they had arrived. Solid workers' streets

encompassed them. Bottle reached a corner and instantly recognised the place from years before, a good begging pitch - two lines of gardenless houses, and the cobbles less regular. It was the same street.

They peered about them, suddenly nervous.

"Well, it's clear enough," reported Eskin. For the present at least his cough had subsided. Begging required concentration.

"Come on, then," said Bottle. "Let's try our luck."

The old art. Eskin started eagerly on the nearest shabby house, knocking firmly, showing confidence. Eighteen pence between them, that was all they needed.

The door opened to reveal an unpromising woman in a starched pinafore, her long face stamped with irritation.

"Good day, missis," began Eskin in a suitably humble voice. And all at once the eyes of the little tramp had developed kindly wrinkles, his taut weathered expression had become faded and gentle.

"A morsel, missis . . . could you be sparing a poor old man of the road a morsel?"

"My name's Stubbs," announced the woman. "What's yours?"

"Why . . ." said the tramp, surprised. "It's Eskin."

Her eyes gleamed nastily.

"You're the fourth that's comes begging in two days - well you can clear off Mr Buggerlugs Eskin, or I'll call the police."

"Nay, missis," said Eskin, suitably shocked. "That's not necessary."

"Clear off," she said menacingly. "And next door is me mother's, so you can miss her as well!"

The door slammed.

Eskin shivered and moved on. "And next door," he mimicked, "is me mother's."

Across the street Bottle fared better. At the first house he was given a penny.

"God bless you missis," he mumbled, a grimy finger to his forehead.

At the second house no one answered. At the third a door opened to reveal a cluster of ragged children who stared the tramp in the face as their mother searched her bag for a coin.

"I know I've got one here somewhere," she said anxiously, and then she found one, and after that a second. "It's as much as I can spare," she apologised.

"Say nothing, I quite understand," said Bottle, pocketing the coins. He moved away, avoiding the next few doors, conscious of the silent children watching him go.

A couple of cheerless streets later they totted up in a doorway.

"Fivepence ha'penny, and a ha'penny . . . that's sixpence. And two farthings - it ain't enough."

"It'll do us for now," said Eskin, trying to shelter from the wind. "Let's p-pack in."

He coughed until his eyes watered. There seemed to be a devilish patch of phlegm in his chest that refused to shift.

"Just one more street," said Bottle. "Our luck's running good."

Eskin deep inside was beginning to feel deadly ill but he didn't protest. He took the even numbers, and Bottle the odd.

"Bugger off!" bawled a thick-set man, emerging from a house. Bottle hastily obeyed. "And do some bloody work, you idle bastard!" the man bellowed.

Further down the street Bottle slowed up, glowered through his scratched lenses and then, composed again, knocked at a battered door. Some days there was nothing but abuse.

A tiny woman with a face as ugly as his own stared sharply up at him: "I haven't even got a penny for the gas."

Bottle looked sympathetic and counted the three rings on her fingers.

"Perraps a brew of tea, missis? Me and me mate has walked a terrible way."

"Nay, I don't know," she said distrustfully. She peered harder, staring at his tiny spectacles. At once a mental limp formed in Bottle's old face - all the miles he had struggled to get to this dank

Carlisle street, the journey across cold wet fells, past empty autumn fields; the need more than anything for a brew of tea to warm the chilled inner parts that only a man who had tramped through Lancashire, Westmorland and Cumberland could possibly have. It all showed in his red patchy cheeks. The woman hesitated, then relented.

"I'll go and look, but I won't promise."

"God bless you, missis," said Bottle reassuringly. He waited on the pavement, benign as a bishop and was still in an ecclesiastic frame of mind when she reappeared with a twist of newspaper.

"There, it's all I can spare."

"The merciful lord be with you," began Bottle, but the door closed swiftly on religion.

Eskin was almost out of sight down the other side. There was no knowing how he was doing. Bottle tried again. Bright green paint and a black knocker. It seemed a good omen.

A comely woman in a vivid pink dressing gown looked out, her fair hair a battery of curlers. Bottle's face warmed.

"Might a good lady like yourself be sparing the price of a brew for a gentleman of the road?" he asked. At the same time he conveyed a considerable air of appreciation, as well he might, the lady's charms being well observed and a delight.

"A brew, petal?" she said cheerfully. "What's a big 'andsome feller like you wanting with the price of a brew? You 'ang on pet while I looks in me purse for summat better."

Bottle felt greatly cheered. Sometimes in moments of greater clarity the old bruiser saw deep into the heart of other people's lives and wished himself back in a warm place of his own. The misery of his long ago dismal attempt at family life vanished at sight of a generous bosom and a shining parlour.

All this in a moment as he stood at a scrubbed doorstep on a cold day in Carlisle, and then the smiling woman reappeared, cosy and confiding.

"Here you are, my petal, a thre'penny bit to see you on your way!"

"Most generous," mumbled an impressed Bottle.

The woman beamed and winked.

"Had a bit of good luck last night you might say . . ."

She seemed bent on explanation but the nature of her luck was never to be revealed for she glanced up the street and at once her manner changed.

"Lawdy, it's the police!"

Bottle had hardly time to observe the uniformed man at the corner before he found himself towed into the woman's parlour, the door closing behind him.

"Out at the back!" urged his benefactress. Her eyes were big and round with concern. "Quick, petal, get on out at the back!"

"I'm very grateful . . ." began the tramp, but she hustled him and pushed him on through a gleaming scullery.

"The door!" she said.

Bottle, galvanised now, opened it quickly enough and was surprised to meet a man in a check overcoat and cap coming the other way.

"Here! Who the hell are you?" demanded the newcomer.

"Bugger! It's me 'usband," said the woman. "Straight on," she urged the tramp. "Eric, I can explain everything . . ."

Bottle was already unlatching the back gate as a torrent of questions washed the yard. He did not linger. In a lumbering trot he hurried to safety along a cobbled back lane.

Fine drizzle sifted into the streets as they totted up their earnings.

"One an' fivepence; one 'an six, one 'an sevenpence ha'penny," said Bottle with satisfaction. "That's nine pence ha'penny each, and a hextra two farthings for meself."

Eskin's teeth were chattering. He felt chilled to the core and wanted to finish. Almost dark, already a lamplighter was turning on a gas lamp, though it was hardly half-past three.

"A proper c-cracker," said Eskin.

"Plump as a peach," affirmed Bottle. "I thought for a moment I was on to a good thing."

Eskin's face shone dismally: "Aye, but we never is. Not us."

"I really fancied her," said Bottle.

The two moved on through the wet. Thought of further knocking had gone; knocking in bad light only brought suspicion to doorways, certainly not charity. Yet their good luck was not quite over. From way behind came the plod of hooves, and little by little a horse and cart overtook them. It was heavily laden, the driver huddled in his coat.

A pile of tarpaulin-covered boxes edged past.

"Well now," said Eskin softly.

"I'm lookin'," said Bottle.

The tail of the cart was beginning to draw away before they closed in. For two or three paces they kept up with the load, then Bottle nodded.

"Lift," he ordered.

Eskin swiftly obliged, holding up the wet cover as Bottle seized a cardboard box.

The cart rumbled away and in an alley they examined their prize.

"Soap," said Eskin in disgust. "I thought it was Woodbines."

Bottle carefully repacked the tablets.

"Three dozen. It's all right. We'll easily sell this lot termorrer in the market."

Eskin's thin shoulders seemed to shrink even more. He felt too miserable to care.

"Let's get some grub, I'm fair perished." He had never been bothered about soap.

They moved deeper into the city, heading for a doss house. More and more living rooms were laid bare as gas mantles were lit - families preparing for tea, a man taking off a coat, a woman holding a pan. Patches of greenish light splashed out onto the streets and then as suddenly curtains were drawn and the plainness of illuminated blinds added to the loneliness of those passing by.

A bout of coughing behind him halted Bottle. In the gloom the indistinct figure of Eskin stood humped over, leaning

CARLISLE
30
MILES

his forehead against wet brickwork.

Bottle went back.

"It's me chest," said Eskin apologetically to the wall. "I'm proper knackered."

The big tramp put down the carton of soap.

"Nay, old pal, don't talk so." He grappled about inside his coat. "Get yourself a swig of this."

Another horse and cart rumbled past while Eskin gulped greedily, and then coughed as coarse gin stung his gullet and escaped down his chin.

"Don't be wastin' it," cautioned Bottle. The treatment took time to work. Eskin turned and lent back against the bricks and slowly his wheezing subsided.

Eventually he said: "No bloody gristle any more. Gettin' bloody old."

"Don't waste your strength talking."

"One time I could go on knocking doors all day long."

Bottle took a swig for himself, then handed it back.

"Terrible stuff this. I mean, it rots your eyes . . ."

"Aye. Hot piss would taste better."

Even so, Eskin accommodated another gullet full and felt easier.

Bottle said: "We'll pack it in for today."

"It's all right, I can manage another door or two yet."

But Eskin couldn't manage even one. A few uncertain steps and his chest seemed to be gripped in a clamp. The two men sank down against a sheltering wall while the little man recovered.

"S'all right for some folk," said Eskin, a phlegmy dewdrop refusing to quit his nose and no strength in him to waft it. "They ends up all right."

"Well, we've done all right," said Bottle consolingly.

"I mean when we're done for good, where do we end up?"

Eskin's thin face looked into Bottle's: "Like as not we'll be found in a ditch, frozen to death and no one knowing owt about us."

Bottle didn't like the sound of that: "That's no kind of talk."

"Aye, well," Eskin drew in a deeper suck of air. "There's many a man buried in a roadside grave if folk only knew it. Once I slept on top of a dead old sod . . . in a doss 'ouse at Preston! He'd bin dead a while, see, but no one wanted to know."

Eskin's face filled with a soft smile.

"He'd been shoved under a bed stiff as a plank and left for someone else to find. And guess what, it was Joe Soap wot found him! Middle of the night, feelin' for the piss pot, I was. Got hold of the old bugger's nose. Scared me daft, it did."

The little man laughed.

Bottle waited for a suitable interval then said: "Can you manage to walk on now, old pal? We'll find a proper doss 'ouse . . . get warm."

"Real scared I was," said Eskin proudly.

The streets flickered with people. A tram clanged past, its lights a little cosmic city all on its own. The two men followed the sandstone pavements till they rounded a corner.

"Now then," said Bottle, suddenly looking ahead. "How about a boozer?"

The green tiled walls of the Bourne Arms stood weeping in the drizzle. Bottle leading, they pushed into a bar and found it occupied by two or three drinkers. It was instantly smoky and warm, a den for men.

"Aye there now?" said the barman. He was another big man, but fatter bellied than Bottle.

The tramp gave an affable nod, shifted the carton to the bar top and carefully put down some coins.

"Two beers, mate, with plenty of hops in 'em."

The barman filled two glasses from a barrel.

"Selling soap, are you?"

Bottle supped deeply and wiped his face on the back of his hand.

"Lavender," he said, handing out two or three for examination. "Couldn't want better."

"Pinched, was it?" The remark slid in from the other end of the bar and sniggers followed.

"Bought" said Eskin firmly. "Bought for termorrer's market. Twopence a time."

A heavy-faced navvy leaned forward: "It says a penny on the box."

"For three," said Bottle. "Penny heach . . . twopence for three."

The man sniffed at a tablet.

"It's got a fair whiff."

"Nobody," said Bottle making to gather in the goods, "need buy owt if they isn't interested in quality offerings."

"I'll try three for luck," said the navvy.

With this lead, others bought several more.

Trading was transacted to a background of fresh coughing. It brought the barman's face round.

"That sounds badly."

"It's the smoke," said Eskin.

"We must go," said Bottle. Clutching the carton, he helped the smaller man out into the cold air of the city street. It was some time before Eskin felt able to gasp an apology.

"Don't fret a fart about it," said Bottle generously. He wiped at his glasses. "Me own lanterns was running with that fug."

They did not linger. Bottle had set his mind on reaching a doss house, somewhere out of the cold. The pub had been a bad idea. High walls of warehouses rose above them, then they turned under a bridge, the cobbled road alive with cyclists. Overhead a train went across noisily, blasting the air with sudden gusts of smoke and steam so that Eskin seemed to feel the clutch of it at his windpipe.

To Bottle it was all very familiar.

"First time I was here I was a big name." His face filled with the memory. "Whitsun hirings, years gone. Big Bottle the Bruiser! Boxed against all-comers, I did."

Eskin, despite his aches, was interested: "You, a bruiser!"

Bottle went on: "We had a proper boxing ring in a tent, down at the Sands, where they sell the cattle. Big farm lads with faces like back end of a cow used to take me on thinking to win a quick shilling . . . well, that was what they thought!"

"What happened?"

"Bam!" said Bottle. "Bam! I knocked 'em straight out of the ring, into the crowd! Booed me, they did!" His face lit up at the memory. "I once knocked a bloke so hard I broke one of me own fingers." He cracked his knuckles a couple of times to remind himself.

Darkness was on them and it was now, just when the old bruiser was least expecting anything special, that he chanced to see one more familiar gas lamp bracketed to a wall of a solid brick building.

"Now why didn't I think of this before! Hey, Esky, listen! We can get warm in here!"

Bottle clutched the little man by an arm and headed for the door. Slowly, as if they were entering a grand theatre, they climbed a flight of steps and were swallowed by the benevolence of the municipal baths. Such luxury! Paradise indeed! Clouds of steam poured into the corridor where ripples of untuneful singing were accompanied by the fierce gush of running taps. Bottle and Eskin occupied adjacent cubicles. A weary faced attendant had issued towels, eyeing their clothes - and then, doors bolted, wonderful oblivion! - cascading boiling water surging into the baths. Whatever else, municipal hot water came in vast quantities.

Unwrapping them one by one, Bottle peeled the papers off a dozen tablets of soap and dropped them into the steaming cauldron. He stirred the water with a handy mop so that soon suds began to billow up in a sparkling wall till they spilled over the edge and ran to the floor. It was a kind of heaven. The cold of the street was forgotten. Here within the baths the world was suddenly warm and generous and gloriously perfumed.

Naked and hairy, Bottle dropped six tablets of soap over the top of the partition.

"Use the lot," he called.

A tremendous splash sounded as Eskin, fully clad, still in an alcoholic haze, collapsed into the steaming water clutching at the bottle of gin. Never in all his life had there been so much warmth.

Bottle, scabby, flabs of old man's muscles from his boxing days, set his dentures on the edge of the bath. He placed his spectacles beside them, tested the water with a dirty foot, added a gush or two of cold and sank happily into a steamy paradise.

Later, fierce bangs crashed on the doors. Bottle was singing lustily; from Eskin's side rose clouds of steam. Closing time was nearing and Bottle was not wanting out.

"You've been in there two whole damn hours!" bellowed the attendant. "You've five minutes to get out. After that it'll be a kick up the arse, d'ya hear?"

"Go boil your rudder!"

Baby pink, and astonishingly clean, Bottle sat blissfully in the bath washing his boots.

"Time's hup!" he shouted to Eskin.

More angry bangs sounded as he towelled himself.

"If you don't come out," called the attendant, "I'll fetch the constable!"

"Aw right, aw right! Give us a minute, will ya!"

Bottle heard the man grumble away down a corridor.

"Come on, Esky! Let's get off before we're thrown out."

The warmth had seeped to the heart of Bottle's being. Nothing could spoil it now. He rinsed his dentures and put them in.

"Come on, you old screw."

But Eskin evidently had his own ideas about time and did not budge.

"Stir it old pal," said Bottle good humouredly.

Dressed now except for socks and boots, he struggled up onto the edge of the bath and peered down from the top of the partition.

"Ain't yer coming then?"

Eskin was still in the hot bath, water up to his chin, suds all over the floor, but no, Eskin was not coming.

"For Chrissake!" said Bottle impatiently.

But not even for Christ would Eskin stir. Eskin's eyes were rolled back till the whites were bulging like blobs of cold porcelain. Eskin wasn't paying much attention any more.

As Bottle realised the truth he stared agonised into the little man's face. There was no movement, just the awful unseeing mask. He held on till his arms began to ache, then he lowered himself to the floor, and stared dully at the wall before him. His mind seemed blank as his gaze sank down the tiles to his hairy feet.

In a rush he gathered up boots and socks, pocketed an unused tablet of soap and cautiously slid back the bolt on the door. His big rough face an aeon older, he padded along the corridor intent on escape. Shouts sounded as he got out into the dark. The old tramp hurried along the street, his steel-rimmed spectacles blank with rain. Not until he had passed a second lamppost and had turned a corner did he stop against a wall to drag on his socks and boots, then without a backward glance he hoofed it away into the night as fast as he could go.

At times it was hard to know which way lay the road to paradise.

Black Lead Beauty

POLICE GAZETTE; APPREHENSIONS SOUGHT
Cumberland, Keswick, October, 1908. For stealing a Horse.
A MAN - Age about Sixty, thin shoulders, light build,
sallow complexion, greying hair, squeaky voice when excited,
believed to be a Carter; dark jacket, brown cord trousers, blue tattered
melton overcoat, grey muffler, grey cap, clogs (believed new).
Also A WOMAN (supposed wife of above) - Age about Sixty,
slight build, long face, grey hair, dark eyes, bad teeth,
long pointed chin; shabby frock, several shawls, clogs.

In the gloom of an archway two nervous figures stood undecided. "He's inside, he is," hissed Fletcher again. "Will you be told!"

"Aye," said the old woman. "But if he's not?"

"You worry too much," said her husband. "Look on in and take note."

"And be seen meself!" she protested.

Fletcher snorted his annoyance.

"Get and look, will you! He'll see nowt except two poor devils short of a crust. Now stop dithering."

"It's this 'ere lamp." She clutched her shawls about her nervously. The lamp overlooking the cobbled yard was too bright. Fletcher snorted again.

"Nowt's ever right for you is it!"

Darkness had seeped in over the mountains and the green glow of gas-lamps had bloomed into life in Keswick's winding streets. Through an alley off Market Square John Dykes, farmer, was in the Pack Horse moderately drunk, unaware of a pending crime. In the yard fronting the inn his pony and cart were tethered to a ring awaiting departure. It was late, the bustle of the market over and only the inns and taverns were still lively, and especially the Pack Horse where a few farmers were holding court, their laughter spilling into the night.

Maud muttered to herself as she edged up to the window. She did not know why she put up with Fletcher and his ways, but any effective protest was no longer possible. They had been stuck with each other too long to change. She did as her husband ordered, keeping her head low, she peered in. At first she did not pick out her quarry, then she drew back as the bulky figure of Dykes moved on the far side of the room.

"I see 'im."

"What's he about?"

"He's drinking like the rest."

"Then now's our chance," said Fletcher hitching at his coat in excitement.

The pony was standing in the dark, its head bowed from a long day of waiting. Fletcher and Maud had observed it for close on an hour and it had hardly stirred. An easy picking. Maud came up on one side, Fletcher the other, feeling along the shafts.

"Quiet there, me beauty," whispered the old man. "Whisht, there."

It was a sturdy grey, about fourteen hands high, well fleshed. In all Keswick they had chosen carefully and it would be a fine prize.

Their arrival was not exactly welcome. The nag stirred uneasily, moving a step or two on the cobbles.

"Now, now, me beauty," said Fletcher soothingly. "Gently, there, gently!"

Two wary eyes latched on to the man and woman as they unhitched the traces. The pony distended its nostrils, testing the air suspiciously.

"Grab that shaft," ordered Fletcher as he freed the tugs. "And let it down quiet!"

"Orders, orders! Allus giving orders, you is," hissed Maud angrily. She struggled with the shaft as quickly as she could. The nag whinnied nervously.

"Hush, me beauty!" Fletcher tugged at the bridle wanting sharply away, but contrarily the pony failed to budge.

From the inn fresh laughter sounded, increasing Maud's fears.

"Leave it, Fletch," she implored. "Let's be gone."

But he towed on the bridle and this time the treatment produced the wrong effect. From stubbornly holding back, the nag now clattered forward, a little too sharply so that the old man found himself unwillingly in tow.

"Damn you!" exclaimed Fletcher struggling to hold on, but his clumsiness encouraged the creature to keep going. Too surprised to let go, he found himself being towed along the alley and out into the street.

"Me clogs," shouted Fletcher, suddenly thrown off balance. "I'm losing me clogs!"

The pony did not stop. Whinnying loudly, it set off across Market Place, leaving Fletcher in a heap.

"You misbegotten ribcage!" He scrambled up angrily. "Come back!"

His voice rose, screechy with excitement, but he was shouting in vain. The pony was moving through the town as if it had realised it had gained its freedom. Briskly now it headed towards the muddy ruts of the Cockermouth road.

"Blast its hide!"

In grubby feet the old man gave chase, cursing in its wake; and long after he was beyond the gloom of the houses a ragged woman followed clutching at a clog, grumbling in the dark.

Back at the inn a befuddled John Dykes swayed in the light of the gas lamp, his face stretched and blank. Others were leaving with him.

"What is it, John?" cried one.

"Nay," exclaimed Dykes thickly. "If I'm not John Dykes, then I've won meself a cart. And if I is John Dykes, then I've lost a bloody nag!"

Fletcher and Maud found the pony foraging out beyond the town. It had gone lame in one foot.

"Hah! A first bit of good luck!"

They got the pony in tow without difficulty and then the trio hobbled along through the night past the long cold sheet of Bassenthwaite Lake and on towards Cockermouth with many muttered curses.

"Me only clogs," moaned Fletcher.

"Nivver mind," said Maud consolingly. "The nag'll fetch us a good price.

"Not two months old they was."

"One's still good."

He snorted. "And what good's the one, you stupid fillet! Will I be hopping along on the one!"

And then to the pony: "Wait till I get you home, you devil!"

In a dismal quarter of Cockermouth, close to a pungent smelling tannery, the couple's hovel was a picture of shabbiness, trodden rubbish and a weary turnip patch. At one end a lean-to sagged heavily against the masonry, a structure not enhanced by the half light of a chilly dawn. A long struggle was under way.

"Get in, you devil!" yelled the old man. Red in the face, he waved his stick, but the nag was having none of the blackness of the open doorway and set back its ears defiantly.

"Blast it!" said Fletcher, dodging a vicious lash of hooves. "A mad bull would be easier!"

Man and beast confronted each other.

"You come up on its right," Fletcher ordered his wife.

But Maud was scared.

"Let it go, Fletch. We'll nivver get it inside, this rate."

"And have all Cockermouth see it on the loose!"

Waving his stick he tried again and the struggle went on, but always the pony shied each time he tried to force it inside.

"Wait," said the exhausted Fletcher at last. "We need ta think this out proper. What would me granddad 'ave done? Kicked it up the arse I bet! I know what, we need a rope, that's what! Cross its back end."

Maud tutted and went off to find a one, then husband and wife tried again, hitching the line across the creature's hind quarters.

"Now pull, you old witch!"

"Don't you witch me!" protested Maud, but nonetheless she pulled. The line did the trick, the pony felt its back legs giving. For a moment it teetered between daylight and darkness, then it went in through the opening with a clatter.

"God bless me granddad!" exclaimed a triumphant Fletcher ramming the door shut. Instantly a tremendous blow struck the planking.

"The bar . . . get the bar!"

A second crashing blow landed. In a panic Maud and Fletcher forced a crossbar into place.

"Got you!" said the old man. "Our fortune's made!"

"Hah! You and your easy pickings!" complained Maud. "We've gone and got us a bad 'un, that's what."

"We gotta eat, woman."

"It'll kill us before we get a gob full down."

Fletcher felt cold and ill.

"I'll sort it, just give us a chance."

They tumbled into bed exhausted.

"It'll be different after a few hours in the dark."

Distantly another crash sounded.

"Them whites of its eyes is a bad sign," said Maud.

For a long time they listened as the town began to wake to a new day. Close by a cock crowed. Then another crash echoed in the lean-to and defiant whinnies broke on the lane.

"It'll have the place to bits," said Maud tearfully.

Fletcher despaired. Deep within him he felt a pit of misery. It all seemed to be going wrong, but he was too tired to care. He pulled the covers over his ears and sank into a troubled sleep.

Little by little the shed door began to splinter. Fletcher hammered a second barricade together from scrap wood and pushed it up against the old one. The whole lane was gossiping, and the old man was afraid the wrong kind of folk would come snooping.

Suddenly decided, he opened the tea caddy, took out a thre'penny bit and set off for the other end of town. Desperate measures were needed. The beast must be watered and fed to keep it looking good.

An hour later he was back with a green glass-stoppered bottle. Carefully he mixed a turnip mash and poured in a pale brown liquid.

"Gypsy magic," he announced.

"Not in me copper bedpan!" protested Maud as he prepared to feed the nag.

"You'd not have me stepping in there meself?"

"Me mother gave me that pan," wailed Maud.

"Then it must have bin with this devil in mind."

"What are you giving it?"

"I telled ya, gypsy magic."

She sniffed heavily.

"Magic nowt - that's laudanum!"

"Same thing."

The old man pushed the long-handled pan under the door into the dark beyond, then he settled to wait, squatting on the chopping block. Maud came and went from time to time. Neighbours stopped to listen, and eventually there was the first faint sound of the pan being nudged. Cold and weary , Fletcher leaned forward.

"Now, me devil, get that down and we'll see who's master."

An anxious time passed before he dared to peer through a chink into the gloom beyond.

"We've done it!" he cackled.

Cautiously they opened the door to reveal a desolation of shattered wood. In the middle stood the drowsy figure of the pony, Maud's bedpan crushed asunder.

Heavily dosed, the nag lost its fire.

Black Lead Beauty

Frosty nights had overtaken the land and an early winter seemed likely. Husband and wife were hard pushed for food. Fletcher chopped fiercely with a hook at the ground and dug out three more frozen turnips. They were like lumps of rock and skilfully he split them with wedges before putting the pieces into an iron pot and setting them over the fire. It was oatcake and 'nips for supper again. The sooner they sold the pony the better.

Fletcher, on the other hand, was in better spirits. He dosed the nag again and together he and Maud trimmed away the mane and shortened the tail. They clipped its coat until the creature began to look altogether younger.

"Get the black lead," ordered Fletcher.

They stood in the gloom and brushed liberal patches of black onto its flanks, rubbing it well in so that few might recognise the nag.

"It's hooves, eh?"

"Yes," said Maud dutifully. She got on her knees, nervous at the creature's nearness, but knowing that the laudanum had transformed it, and so she rubbed each hoof with oil until they shone.

"Gypsy luck in them now."

Fletcher cheerfully patted the pony's head, frowned at a sudden black patch on his hand and polished a bit more off the shiny hair. No need to overdo it.

"Termorrer, me beauty, you'll be the best nag Wigton fair's ever seen."

Stupid with laudanum, the pony never moved an inch.

"We could file its teeth . . ."

But Maud was having none of that.

"You'll not get me near its mouth!"

Fletcher nipped a dewdrop of snot off his nose. He sent it spattering generously to the ground, leaving behind a pinch of polish.

"There's five golden sovereigns coming from you, me beauty. Then it'll be giblet pie and the fat of the land for us, it will."

The pony shone with apparent good health.

It was hardly midnight as the old couple set off along the road to Wigton, the nag in tow.

PACKHORSE

Maud said: "Mebbe the police will be at Wigton watching?"

"Let 'em. No one'll recognise this 'un now."

That seemed true enough.

"Are we going' to put it into the ring?"

"What! Pay auctioneers for doing nowt? We'll stand in the street and sell it there, same as others."

They made good progress, walking steadily through the night, speaking rarely, and by the time the sky began to pale with the first hint of dawn the worst of the journey was over.

"*Our fortune's in the ma-aking*," warbled Fletcher as weak winter light filtered across the land.

"You've still got a black nose," advised the old woman. Nor were they the only people trekking in to the little market town, for soon they came up with a string of gypsy caravans; and after that carts and horses, a heavy Shire or two and still more ponies heading for the sale. A band of tinkers was camped at the roadside.

"A pound of spuds for your old nag," bellowed a rough faced bloke.

"Get along!" retorted Fletcher scornfully. "Five sovereigns it'll be fetching at Wigton before the day's out."

"And 'ow much black lead into the making, eh?"

Fletcher's eyes narrowed, but he did not stop walking.

"Ugly mugs," he muttered.

Once over the rise he stopped.

"Get some dust," he ordered. "He's right, the nag looks too clean."

"We've just gone and got it in right good fettle," protested Maud.

But Fletcher ordered her to help rub away some of the shine.

"Police'll be looking for nags that're too sparkling. They're not stupid."

On again past weather-worn signposts, their wooden arms pointing the way across Cumberland.

"Way-hay! Way-hay!" Along the rutted road came the thunder of hooves. Fletcher stared as a bunch of ponies appeared. "Stand clear! Stand clear!"

A lean-faced man charged up on a black hunter. Close on his tail galloping loose-headed came a dozen of the wildest fell ponies Fletcher had ever seen. He struggled with the tether and dragged his nag aside. In fine style, the posse swept by, a second rider at the tail, driving the creatures at a furious pace.

"Pigs!" shouted the old man, but he might have bawled out a midden for all the good it did for the ponies had already disappeared.

Maud recovered their bundle and examined the contents.

"They've brokken our eggs."

Despite their night start, by the time the old couple entered Wigton the town's streets were crowded. Such a clattering of hooves on cobbles; such whinnyings and cries! Horse dealers from across the North had arrived, tinkers, potters, gypsies with lucky raven's claws. And everywhere there were horses - broad chested fells, Clydesdales and Shires, old nags, snappy Shetlands, every colour, and every ploy used to show them off at their best. Men thronged Main Street examining, gossiping, bargaining. Into this shrewd crowd Fletcher and Maud moved, their charge in tow.

"Two pounds worth, then?" asked a man.

"Five bright sovereigns, and nowt less!" rejoined Fletcher.

The man laughed and pushed on. Another paused to examine the beast.

"Bit of age creeping' in theer. Where'd you get it, Noah's Ark?"

"Not thirteen years old," said Fletcher. "Good teeth, every one of 'em."

"Aye, a good knacker's buy."

"Knackers!" protested Fletcher, but the other had moved away. More folk prodded at the pony. Some examined its feet, others its teeth. No one seemed over-interested.

"And what do ya want for your old nag, then?" asked a voice.

Fletcher's hopes rose. He gave his hands a quick scuff of a clap, recognising a genuine customer.

"Eight," he said, eyeing the other's raincoat. "Sovereigns."

Slowly the man walked round the pony examining its fetlocks. Fletcher was relieved as the man's hands came away clean.

"It doesn't look too lively."

"Full of fire most of the time," assured Fletcher.

"Is that so?"

Fletcher struggled hard: "But quiet with it, good with the bairns."

The man's bloodshot eyes were upon him.

"You talk a load of bullshit." He stretched a tight dealer's smile. "But I like thee. Would three pund be a fairer do?"

Fletcher cuffed his hands again.

"Seven pund, or nowt," he said emphatically. "Bleeds me to be parting with it."

"I might come back," said the other. "I've a friend who would be interested in seeing this un. How would four pund suit ya?"

"All right, then," said Fletcher agreeing. "Six - but it would be robbery."

"Aye," said the dealer. "As I said, I might be back."

The man moved away.

"He'll be back," said Fletcher excitedly to Maud. "I reckon we've got a sale."

But an hour passed and the dealer did not reappear. The babble grew as the crowd increased. Shouts and curses mingled with the stamping of hooves. Farmers' wives in black skirts and straw hats poked experimentally at Fletcher's nag. No one stayed long enough to buy it.

"You should be sellin' in the ring, you should," bawled a crimson faced man.

"Mind your business and I'll mind mine!" rejoined Fletcher, who recognised one of the auctioneer's drovers.

Then only yards away up the street a fine bay mare was sold.

Fletcher's ears fairly burned at the price.

"Nine guineas," reported Maud. "It was a real good 'un."

Fletcher looked on in envy.

"You'll 'ave to be taking less," advised his wife.

The old man shivered inside his melton.

"It's a fact, I'd be better playing me old fiddle and begging than this carry on."

At noon they ate oatcakes and shared the broken eggs.

"We've not even got tuppence for a drop of ale," said Fletcher.

A lively snort made him turn sharply. The nag was perkier looking than it had been and with a pang of unease Fletcher realised that the laudanum might be wearing off. It might after all be better to get off home quick and have done with the whole thing.

"We could allus 'ave a bit of horse meat," he told Maud.

"Not after all this work," she said, shocked.

Business at the main sale ring was brisk. As fast as horses arrived buyers were ready with purses fat with sovereigns. In the less grand corners of the town, though, trade was at a low and Fletcher shared none of the profit making. By mid-afternoon he was desperate.

The sky had clouded badly and both felt perished. To make matters worse, the pony was growing distinctly militant. A hard glint was showing in its eyes.

"Whoa!" called Fletcher nervously. For the second time in minutes the creature dragged at its halter and tried to back away.

"Perhaps we'd best be getting home," said Maud. She cast a fearful glance at their charge.

"Come on, you ugly turnip!" Fletcher dragged at the nag's head.

As luck had it, down Main Street now appeared a trio of musicians. Their timing could not have been more unfortunate. Ragged and unwashed, they shuffled single file through the crowd playing a strident cacophony on trumpet, whistle and drum, recognisable as *The Bluebells of Scotland.* This discordant mixture, whatever it did for the crowd, proved too much for the nag.

"You blathering gowks!" yelled Fletcher.

Too late he grabbed at the tether. A trumpet blast completed the damage. Alarmed shouts broke out as the nag began backing up. This time, before anyone could stop it, it went too far.

A crash of breaking glass sounded as the pony hit a billboard and sent it crashing into the window of a baker's shop.

"Get hold of it!" bawled Fletcher. "Get hold!"

Glass and a dozen cobs of bread tumbled underfoot. Given a second more, the frightened pony would have bolted - except that this was Wigton and the crowd a knowing one. After the first moment of surprise, sure hands seized the creature firmly on both sides. Two thickset farm lads held it steady in the confusion and after a nasty moment, led it trembling to one side.

Through the noisy throng two men elbowed a passage. Maud saw them coming and shrank back dismayed. The first was the man with the bloodshot eyes, the dealer, and the other was the farmer, John Dykes of Keswick.

"Theer, John," cried the dealer. "Tell me if that isn't thee nag?"

Dykes stared hard at the trembling pony.

"By God," he exclaimed. "I do believe it is!"

He barged through to the front and arrived as an enraged baker rushed out from his shop. He was a big strong looking man.

"It damn well is!" roared Dykes. "Here, what the devil are you doing with my nag?"

The noisy demand cut through the babble. But it did not quite produce the expected result.

"Oh," cried the baker nastily. "Your nag, is it?"

"Aye, that it is!" snapped Dykes. "Don't think a bit of blacking fools me! I'd know this un a mile off!"

"In that case," said the baker weightily, "you're the very man I'm wanting!"

Dykes found himself grabbed by his jacket.

"Your nag's just broken my window . . . and you'll be the one to pay for it!"

Dykes squirmed in alarm. The baker, he realised, was a lot bigger than he was.

"Wait, you're making a mistake."

"Not as bad as the one your nag's just made," glowered the baker.

At the edge of the crowd Fletcher caught a dismayed look from Maud's long face.

"I tell you," bellowed Dykes indignantly. "My 'orse was pinched."
"And I tell you," retorted the baker, "you owe me a new window!"
"You don't understand!" bellowed Dykes.

Two tired figures trudged through the dark along the back ways into Cockermouth.

"It'll be turnips again termorrer," said Fletcher despondently.

The old woman trailing him sighed heavily: "Don't go on about it."

"And turnips again after that . . ."

"It's that poor old nag I keep thinking of," said Maud, her shawls clutched about her. "It's done nowt to deserve a load of bother."

"It'll end at the knacker's same as the rest," said Fletcher bitterly. "Us too at this rate."

Maud sighed: "It's hard on poor folk these days."

Fletcher wiped away a dewdrop: "We're all of us losers in this wretched world, that's a fact, but some of us loses a damn sight more than others."

They walked on, the old man and the old woman, Cockermouth hardly a couple of miles away now. Above them the sky was cloudless again and crackling with cold. For as far as Fletcher could see there were millions and millions of stars shining clear down to the horizon, and in a strange kind of way sight of them made him feel a little less miserable.

"Aaay," he said sadly, a shabby old man trying to come to terms with the glittering universe. "Aaay, but I could murder a bit of giblet pie."

The Dressmaker

Had there been no smoke from the chimney Miss Ivinson might at first have mistaken the huddle of stone buildings as being deserted, but there was just a trickle rising into the morning air, and as she pushed her bike up the track two black and white curs raced into the open, barking furiously. By the time she had reached the buildings a man stooped out of a doorway.

He was not quite what she had expected. A farmer, yes, though more academic looking than she might have supposed in this remote dale, almost a teacher.

"Good morning," she called, a little uncertain. "This can hardly be Scobold's yet, can it?"

She was hot and wishing now she had not worn her heavy cycling cape and bonnet. Three miles hauling the bike up the valley had been hard going.

He gave a half-shy stare: "No, you're just at Gillerthwaite - and you must be the dressmaker."

He spoke slowly, and his voice was appreciative for Miss Ivinson's firmly moulded figure and general air of well being were not lost on him.

"I heard you were coming."

She smiled primly, enjoying the knowledge that she too knew what was going on. She was after all born and bred in Cumberland and little stayed secret for long, even in a valley as lonely as this.

"That's right. I'm here for the week."

The man waved a hand.

"Scobold's spot is on a bit yet."

He eyed the bike and the sewing machine strapped to the pannier. "You've mebbe not met the Scobolds before?"

"Never. But we've corresponded."

He paused as if wondering whether to say more.

"You'll have known him a long time?" she said helpfully.

"Oh aye, many a year. He's . . . well mebbe he's not the kind a lady like yourself is used to."

She had heard already.

"Rude, is he?"

He seemed confused by her directness.

"As it happens," said the dressmaker, "I've got his character already from a friend."

A mean old Cumberland bugger was how it had been expressed to her.

He guessed she was a year or two younger than himself. Perhaps thirty seven or thirty eight.

"He can be awkward, but he means nowt by it."

"I'm sure we'll get along."

Really she was not sure at all but it seemed to satisfy him.

"He's about a mile on. Ower the second bridge."

Gripping her bike, she pushed out onto the track, the curs racing round her.

A bit awkward, was he.

"Bridge!" exclaimed Miss Ivinson. The path had turned into a rough scar, twisting up the valley floor. Never before had she been so encompassed by mountains, though they were not the cause of her dismay. She stared askance at the two tree trunks which lay across the rush of river. They were braced together with foot planks but had no handrail. Crude wasn't in it.

On the other side, half hidden, low slate roofs butted out among the grass slopes. Scobold's for sure.

Crossing was an ordeal. She edged her bike along, her button boots finding each step before she dared to trust the bridge with her full weight. A drop of hardly ten feet, but scaring enough.

The farm crouched defensively into the land, a rough stone house with a barn on one end. Relieved, she propped the bike and knocked at the door. The dressmaker had arrived.

A tiny woman in a black dress and a white apron looked out. Her hair was parted exactly in the middle and drawn down tightly at the back of her head.

Miss Ivinson smiled. "Mrs Scobold? I'm Hannah Ivinson, ma'am."

"Oh," said the older woman. She looked startled. Her fingers went uncertainly to her lips. "So you have come?"

"Well, yes."

Clogs clattered in the gloom of the passage.

"Who is it?" demanded a voice.

"It's the dressmaker," said Mrs Scobold anxiously. "She's gone and turned up."

"Oh, has she now!"

A shabby figure thrust forward and Miss Ivinson found herself being examined by William Scobold. He was small like his wife, but skinny and watchful, his face tightly stretched.

"And what brings you here?" he demanded sourly.

Miss Ivinson was surprised. This was hardly the welcome she had expected.

"You wrote . . . I've come to do repairs and make Coronation dresses for your children."

"Hah! Thoo hasn't," said Mr Scobold. He glared at her. "I wrote saying we'd changed our minds."

Miss Ivinson's smart cycling outfit seemed to grow a shade tight across her chest. Then, remembering, she felt in the pocket of her jacket and produced the letter. Already it was becoming crumpled.

"I'm afraid this is all I've had, asking me to attend all week."

She held it out.

"Aye. Aye. That was so . . ."

The little man took hold of the note reluctantly, his face dark.

"Willie, Miss Ivinson must step inside, now that she's here," said Mrs Scobold worriedly.

The farmer ignored her while he read the note.

"That damn Tyson's forgotten to send on the other!"

He stared at the dressmaker as if it were her fault.

"Willie . . ."

"Well, step in, then. Step in! As you've got this far there's no cause to stop on the step."

He waved her on inside.

The kitchen was spotless. A tall iron range shone with black lead. The slate floor gleamed like satin.

"There is plenty Miss Ivinson could do," said Mrs Scobold.

"Aye. Aye. You can say that. There's allus work." He looked peeved.

"There's two pairs of your breeches, and Emma's coat to lengthen."

Scobold swivelled round, his eyes searching. "Two shillings a day?" he demanded suddenly.

Momentarily Miss Ivinson was taken by surprise, then she recovered.

"Half a crown," she said firmly. "Two shillings and sixpence, that was the agreement."

"Never was no agreement. I sent a letter cancelling."

"A letter I have not received."

Her generous mouth set in a determined line.

"Well half a crown's too much. Farming's in a bad way."

"And dressmakers," countered Miss Ivinson severely, "have got to live too."

If he were surprised at her response he did not show it.

His wife glanced at the dressmaker and for the first time gave a weak smile of encouragement.

"Miss Ivinson's a hard worker, Willie. Everybody knows it."

The man stared at his wife and Miss Ivinson as if he were seeing them both for the first time. His shoulders sagged and he turned away.

"Aye. Aye. Well as you're here you'd best stay! But I'll not be paying any bills till Martinmas. There's not a penny in the house."

He gave a small malicious smile.

Miss Ivinson was not having that. "Our agreement was payment promptly, at the end of the week. The same as everybody else."

To her surprise the farmer gave a terse laugh. He stared into her face as if searching. "Nay, nay. Just testing! Just testing. Now, Maggie, show the woman where she'll be sleeping - and get her started, or we'll be paying her for doing nowt."

"At two and sixpence?"

"Yes, yes. But not today, only half a day today."

Uneasy at this brusque treatment, Miss Ivinson followed the farmer's wife up the staircase to a tiny bedroom. For the present she had little choice. The prospect of an immediate return down-valley was too daunting. But it was a queer spot and no mistake.

And then the children arrived home from school.

"This is Jenny, and this is Kate . . ."

Two small girls, two bright faces, two little Cumbrians, painfully thin, but tremendously lively . . . Miss Ivinson's heart warmed as the Scobold girls started to rush in with torn bodices, a patched skirt, a frayed pinafore.

"Goodness, you must have been fighting the Boers!"

"Take no notice of the bairns, Miss Ivinson," said Mrs Scobold. "These are all for turning into proddy rugs."

The two women laughed.

"But mother, I like this pinny! It's the pretty one."

"Kate, stop that face right now!"

Miss Ivinson examined the pinafore. It was worn out.

"No need to worry," she told Kate. "Once my machine's set up, I'll make another in no time; two in fact. One each. Dresses with them!"

The girls grinned excitedly at this offer but were quelled by a look from their mother. Mrs Scobold seemed strained.

"Have I said something wrong?" said the dressmaker.

"I'm afraid you don't understand. There can be no new clothes for the girls. Only repairs . . . I thought you realised."

Miss Ivinson paused, not sure of the other's meaning.

The farmer's wife looked uncomfortable, then she said in a rush: "The material we bought, it's had to go back to the shop. Willie wouldn't have it stay in the house."

She looked at the dressmaker apologetically.

Miss Ivinson was dumbfounded. "But you wrote saying it had already arrived."

"Aye, so it had. But it's gone again."

"Then why ever was I asked here?"

It seemed incredible to be engaged to make dresses and then be told there was no material for the task.

Mrs Scobold glanced uneasily at the girls.

"The dresses were my idea, and Robin's . . . at Gillerthwaite. You passed his spot . . . Robin said the girls would look nice in summat special, for the Coronation and I agreed. So did Willie at first, till the bill came."

Miss Ivinson did not speak. Slowly she took off her bonnet, releasing her ringlets. She was conscious of being watched by three blank faces.

Twenty minutes later she was hard at work putting a new seat into an old pair of cord trousers. Old? Ten years if they were a day. Miss Ivinson sat at a table in the kitchen window, her machine whirring, her mind still angry at the farmer's behaviour. She wore a pair of gold-rimmed spectacles and looked primmer than ever. Alongside on an upended box two dozen reels of cottons were set out in a bright splash of colour: Coates best six-cord. Well, she would need few of those, that seemed certain, not the finer ones anyway.

By six the family was preparing to eat. A tangy smell of tatie pot filled the kitchen as Mrs Scobold set the long board table. Despite the impending start of the meal, and a growing awareness of her hunger, Miss Ivinson worked up to the last moment.

A clatter of clogs signalled Mr Scobold. He hardly glanced at the dressmaker.

"What's this, then?" he demanded. "Five places?"

"Aye . . . she'll eat with us, won't she?"

"The woman will eat when she's done at eight o'clock."

"Nay, Willie . . ."

"That was the agreement. Eight till eight. And she didn't get started till gone one."

His wife bit on her lip.

"I'm the one who finds the money, woman, not you!"

Miss Ivinson's machine whirred, the needle flashed, every stab a spear of dislike. The meal clattered through, subdued and awkward while she worked.

The dressmaker finished the trousers as seven struck. They were a good strong job and would last a year or two more. She reached for a second pair. Later, she lay in bed seething with anger. The material, sent back to Whitehaven! It was past belief.

"Mean isn't the word!" she said again.

She tossed uncomfortably on the old horsehair mattress; it was lumpy and felt badly aired. She was unable to get to sleep. She had eaten her tatie pot alone at the big table, Scobold stretching his legs out before the range, the children playing in whispers in a corner, Mrs Scobold in a rocking chair knitting. Their sparse attempts at conversation had been stilted and embarrassing. What price a few yards of material? She doubted he was that penniless. She'd met poor farmers before.

Come ten o'clock, bed had been a welcome escape.

"Damn!" said the dressmaker. She pounded the mattress trying to flatten a lump. Outside, the dale was in darkness, silent and warm. In its own bed, the river rushed out of the valley as fast as it could go.

Early on Tuesday Miss Ivinson started to work on repairs. Porridge had been eaten with the family long before seven, then the children set off to walk down the valley to school, and at five minutes to eight Miss Ivinson began. The heap of clothes was enormous. For the most part they were plain farming wear - cord trousers and heavy Herdwick jackets badly torn, cotton dresses their seams split, and a long black skirt in need of a new brush braid where it swept at the ground. Miss Ivinson saw herself with plenty to do, but that was what she was paid for.

At mid-morning Mr Scobold brought back the first pair of trousers. She tensed, her shoulders stiffening imperceptibly.

"Nay, but that's an uncommon good job," he said gruffly, waving them at her.

"Why, thank you," said Miss Ivinson, surprised.

"But you've forgotten the binding along the ends. I allus has 'em with binding."

She tried not to snatch them off him.

Later, from outside came the distant double bangs of a shotgun. Each bang rumbled about the crags. Scobold, no doubt.

At noon Mrs Scobold set the end of the table. Scobold ate alone, his wife busying herself at the range. He soon went out. Mrs Scobold said: "Perhaps you'll have a bite with me?"

The dressmaker nodded gratefully. "I could do with something." In fact she felt famished.

The farmer's wife laid out bread and cheese.

"You shouldn't judge Willie too badly. Life can be hard up this dale at times."

She seemed to be inviting confidence.

"Well, it's just the children," confessed Miss Ivinson. "Their Coronation dresses."

"Aye. That was a pity. He's hard on his bairns at times. Doesn't want 'em spoiled."

The girls had been on the verge of tears, but had remained silent.

Mrs Scobold poured two mugs of tea and was careful not to make it froth. Miss Ivinson relaxed.

"He's my cousin, really, a distant one anyway. And he's got his good side when you know him. There was a year we lost half our sheep in the blizzard . . . Willie was out for days searching. Kept finding 'em dead in the drifts, their eyes pecked out."

She broke off as she remembered. Her face was lined, even a

little grey. Perhaps inside she felt unwell, but there was no possibility of giving in to it.

"We'd to manage on taties and little else for long enough. It makes a body careful when you've starved a bit."

Miss Ivinson felt a wave of sympathy for the little woman.

"And the sheep?"

"It's taken years to get the numbers back up again."

Outside a bird trilled and fluttered past the window. Winter was hard to imagine in this warm spring dale.

All afternoon Miss Ivinson worked, patching, strengthening seams, making good. She was short of repair material but was loathe to ask while there was a possibility Mr Scobold might overhear.

Good sighted though she was, she was glad when the afternoon was nearly over. She had wrestled with the skirt braid till her eyes ached and eventually she was obliged to work by the light of a small oil lamp on top of the machine. Outside something seemed to be happening to the weather for the dale was filling with a moody yellow light.

The girls arrived home, breathless with running. A storm was coming. They stood by her machine as she worked and eventually Miss Ivinson broke a rule and allowed them to finger the precious reels of cotton.

Mrs Scobold said unexpectedly: "Willie's away to market tomorrow. If you're agreeable, he wants you to eat with us tonight while he's got time."

Miss Ivinson was unsure whether to feel pleased at the invitation or not. Something of her uncertainty showed for Mrs Scobold added quickly: "It's nowt special to eat, but Willie says you're to join us"

"Thank you," said Miss Ivinson. "But I'll be wanting to work on after we've eaten. And I've been wondering if you can find any more bits I can use for patches."

It was a meal she was unlikely to forget. A crack of thunder filled the dale. The rumble rolled heavily until it seemed to be directly over the farm.

The oil lamps were already lit as Mrs Scobold set the pie on the table. The crust was golden brown and looked delicious but to Miss Ivinson's surprise the children seemed to be apprehensive.

Not so Mr Scobold who seized a knife and cut into it.

"A special treat for our guest. Meat pie." He gave a mirthless laugh, glancing at the dressmaker.

Emma said: "Father, can I just 'ave crust?"

"You'll eat the same as the rest of us," he snapped.

"But father . . ."

Mrs Scobold said quickly: "Willie, be sure Miss Ivinson has breast."

There seemed almost a warning note in the way she said it.

The farmer loaded each plate, steaming hot slices covered in gravy.

"Reach up," he ordered. "Don't let it get cold."

An unpleasant aroma assailed Miss Ivinson. It was like nothing she had previously encountered, strong and pungent. The taste proved to be equally unpleasant. A first piece of dark meat choked in her throat.

Scobold ate noisily, mopping at the gravy with slices of bread, but the others only pecked half-heartedly at the strange dish, leaving most of it on the sides of their plates. For her part, Miss Ivinson ate only the crust.

"Not hungry, then?" Scobold glowered down the table.

"I . . . it's rather strong," said Miss Ivinson.

"Crow usually is," said the farmer.

Using a lump of bread, he wiped up the last of the gravy.

"Crow?" said the dressmaker. She remembered the shots. So that was it. Never in her life had she tasted anything so unpleasant. The gall rose sharply within her.

"Waste not, want not," said Scobold. "It's meat like owt else."

Miss Ivinson felt her face turning white. She saw that Scobold was simply enjoying her discomfort.

Mrs Scobold quickly began to remove plates.

"Usually the breast's not too bad," she said apologetically. "But there's rice pudding for afters."

Miss Ivinson could eat nothing more. Deep inside her the conviction was growing that the meal with the family was not the charitable gesture it had first seemed. Scobold had planned the whole thing to upset her.

Outside in the privy she retched and it was some time before she felt well enough to concentrate on sewing.

Holding a candle steady, Miss Ivinson watched as Mrs Scobold raised the lid of a bedding chest. The two women were on the landing and the children in bed.

"There's this bit," said the farmer's wife lifting out a piece of linen. A waft of lavender came with it.

"It's good, but too stiff I think for lining. Cotton would be more like."

"Aye. Well mebbe there's better lower down."

She began taking out bits and pieces.

"I'm sorry about the pie," said Mrs Scobold.

Miss Ivinson smiled grimly. She was over it now.

"We only 'ave crow once in a blue moon . . . I don't know what got into him, but he said it was no good letting 'em waste once they were shot."

Miss Ivinson felt she knew well enough how Scobold had been thinking.

Not until the chest was nearly empty did she lean forward more intently.

"Why, what are these?"

Mrs Scobold lifted out two folded lengths.

"Curtains, but they're too grand for us. They're some Willie's aunt left him years back when she was in service at Workington Hall."

"But they are beautiful," said Miss Ivinson enthusiastically. "I do believe they are silk."

Pale blue folds gleamed in the candlelight, soft and lustrous.

Opened out, the curtains proved to be in perfect condition.

"They are silk, and I'm sure they are Chinese!"

"Aye, well mebbe they are. His Aunt Ella - our aunt really, but she always preferred him to me - anyway she worked for the Curwens and they were often abroad, always bringing stuff back. Lovely, a lot of it."

Miss Ivinson grew enthusiastic. "You know, these could just be what we need for the children's Coronation dresses."

Mrs Scobold's face clouded with anxiety. "We can't be using 'em. Willie would go mad."

Miss Ivinson smoothed a hand over the material. "It's such wonderful quality. Perfect for dresses."

"Well, I don't really know. Though it does seem a shame for 'em to be hidden away in this box all these years."

"I'd have to measure to be sure, but I do believe there would be about enough."

"Do you think so?"

Mrs Scobold seemed to be wavering.

It was sufficient for Miss Ivinson. She suddenly had no doubts. "Somehow I'll find the time. If you are agreeable, before I leave on Saturday I'll make your girls two of the prettiest dresses they could wish for!"

Mrs Scobold looked frightened, but at the same time glanced at the material. It was truly beautiful.

"He'll never agree to it . . ."

"Mr Scobold," said Miss Ivinson, refolding the silk, "need not know anything till they're done. We can just say we found the material and thought we would save him money. He'll understand that well enough."

The little woman was at a loss. She had never heard of such a thing. Miss Ivinson, however, was excited. The girls' disappointment was firmly in her mind, and at the same time she saw a neat way of getting back at the farmer for his meanness.

"You won't really have enough time," said Mrs Scobold hopefully. But yes, said Miss Ivinson, there was enough, and suddenly it was all settled. Perhaps it was the look of confidence that imbued the younger woman; somehow she was reassuring, and in the end Mrs Scobold seemed to accept it too. After all the girls had been close to tears.

From first thing on Wednesday morning the sewing machine whirred. It was going to be a race, for one thing the pile of clothes in need of repair seemed as high as ever and partly this was because Mrs Scobold had arrived with another load, which she put under the others. The dressmaker gave her a surprised look, but the farmer's wife only smiled and went out again.

Then Scobold clattered in.

"Getting on, then?"

"There's plenty to do," acknowledged Miss Ivinson.

He eyed the heap of clothing.

"Enough to keep thee busy till I'm back by the look of things."

She did not stop working, but to her discomfort he went on watching and eventually the cotton snapped. She was struggling with the thread when unexpectedly he said: "You think I'm a hard man, don't you?"

Inwardly she despaired. She could have done without this. She strove to get the thread through the eye of the needle, but for once it wouldn't have it.

"I don't know what you mean."

"Admit it. You think I'm being hard."

"Well, the girls are disappointed."

"The girls are spoilt!"

Miss Ivinson bent closer to her machine.

"If you really want to know what I think, Mr Scobold . . ."

Her voice was low; she seemed intent only on the wayward thread.

"Aye! Aye, I do. Just what does a dressmaker think!"

Dare she say it? She knew that sometimes she was too outspoken; she'd been told so before.

"I'm waitin'," he said.

"I think you are being a bit cruel."

The farmer's face hardened. At this moment he could have dismissed her on the spot. A tiny vein pulsed on the side of his nose, then without speaking he turned and went out.

Later, as she sat working at the window, she saw him setting off down the valley, round shouldered, a cow in tow on a rope. It was a long walk to the train and then on to the market.

From an upstairs window, Mrs Scobold was also watching. There would be just the four of them in the house for the next two nights. She knew he would stop over in town at his cousin's and not be back till Friday.

She went downstairs.

"He's away."

Miss Ivinson gave the little woman a smile of reassurance.

"I'm afraid I may not be able to finish all these . . . the dresses will take all my time for now."

"Bless you!" Mrs Scobold bustled and began pulling bits and pieces out of the pile. "These is just for proddy rugs and the like! I pushed 'em in to make him think there was plenty to keep thee busy!"

"Oh. How very clever of you!"

The two women laughed. They were in it together now.

"And you really can do it?"

"Of course! Never doubt it!"

To keep the Coronation dresses a surprise, Miss Ivinson decided to base them on the girls' Sunday best. The women spread them out on the big table.

Soon the patterns were ready.

And the beautiful silk curtains chalked out.

Then the long scissors.

"Nay," said Mrs Scobold.

"Don't worry," said the dressmaker, cutting quickly.

"If only he'd not gone and sent the other lot back, not that it was as lovely as this."

No pausing now.

At noon they ate bread and cheese. Later Mrs Scobold brewed a pot of tea.

"What about when the lasses get home from school? What shall we do? To keep it all secret?"

"Can't they do anything outside?"

"Aye, they can be off back to Robin's with me a while."

"Even an hour will help," said the dressmaker, busily pinning. "It'll take me all of tomorrow."

The girls arrived, wanting to play with the cottons. The silk had been concealed in a cupboard. They protested about going out again but their mother had her way and towed them back down towards Gillerthwaite. Alone once more, Miss Ivinson bent over her machine, working carefully, expertly.

Supper - steaming broth, bread and butter pudding - and later the girls, still protesting, at last in bed. The task was resumed.

"I must get on."

"You look terrible tired."

She was, but she persisted, an oil lamp on either side of the machine. Her back ached, her fingers were sore, but the first dress was shaping up.

"Perhaps I can sew a bit by hand?"

"That would be a help," agreed Miss Ivinson gratefully

For another two hours the women worked away. "There's to be pleats in here and here."

"Aye, that'll be pretty."

"And I wonder if you can find anything we can use for sashes, perhaps light blue?"

Eleven was striking before they stopped. The first dress was still a way off completion.

"I've never seen such a pretty thing, it's going to be just beautiful," said Mrs Scobold admiringly. "And out of curtains at that."

"We're not done yet," warned Miss Ivinson. Nonetheless she was pleased. She'd show the skinflint.

Thursday dawned brightly. Another fresh May day. Warmth and light filled the dale. In distant villages and towns, though, doubts were beginning to emerge. Would the king be well enough; would the Coronation take place as planned? Despite the uncertainly, bonfires were being built on prominent heights,

flags were being made and parties planned; if it were to go ahead then all must be ready.

At the Scobold farm, remote from the great run of the outside world, Miss Ivinson finished the first dress just before mid-morning, and as Mrs Scobold took over and began the delicate job of pressing it, the dressmaker started on the next. With the experience of the first fresh in mind, the second proved somewhat easier.

The girls were packed off to bed early for a second night. There were howls but it made no difference, their mother insisted.

"The little devils! They know summat's up," laughed Mrs Scobold putting on the kettle. "Worse than Christmas Eve, it is!"

Miss Ivinson smiled. She was weary but they were doing well. She worked until half ten, then had to give in. Tomorrow morning would be their last chance before Scobold arrived home.

And that was how it worked out.

Friday . . . the clock on the kitchen dresser was striking eleven as she set down the iron on the hob for the last time. "There!" she exclaimed.

Both dresses lay on the long table, shining in the light.

"But they're as grand as owt!" said Mrs Scobold full of admiration.

"Let's hope they like them!"

"Like 'em? No question on it. They've never had owt as pretty."

Miss Ivinson thought carefully.

"It might be best if they were wrapped. It'll be more of a surprise."

"Could his Aunty Ella only see her curtains now."

Far down the dale the girls came into sight. And later, as the sun wheeled still further westward above the craggy heights, a third figure followed. As Miss Ivinson picked him out she felt a touch of unease and wondered if she had gone too far.

Yet from the moment Scobold arrived home it was clear that he was feeling pleased. Miss Ivinson saw it as a good sign and waited for the right moment. It seemed to come soon after the family had finished tea.

"You'll be away in the morning, then?" said Scobold, settling into his fireside chair.

"The work's all done," acknowledged the dressmaker.

"Aye. Well, you must have a decent breakfast before you set off down the dale."

"Thank you," she said and glancing at Mrs Scobold added: "There is a small matter . . ."

"Aye. Aye. Not just now. I've summat to be on with."

He spoke impatiently: "Come here, my lasses."

Miss Ivinson had to wait while the girls were called over. Scobold seemed oddly animated.

"Now then, have you been working hard at school?"

"Of course I have," said Kate.

"Both of you?"

"Yes," said her sister.

"Do the pair of you know what I've been doing these past two days?"

"You took a cow to market."

"Aye, and got precious little for it. But do you know why I was selling yan?"

The girls looked blank. Even Mrs Scobold looked up from her knitting.

"It was so I could be getting these for thee."

The farmer bent down. He felt around for a moment then he pulled a parcel from under his chair.

"Go on," he ordered. "Open it."

Her mouth open in horror, Miss Ivinson watched as Kate and Jenny tore open the wrapping and took out two dresses.

"Father! For the Coronation . . . "

"Mother, look! Father's brought us some new dresses!"

Their delight was unbounded. As they fell to hugging their father, Scobold shot a look of triumph at the dressmaker.

Mrs Scobold, her face a picture of dismay, said: "Willie, what have you gone and done?"

"Done! I've fitted the girls out with new dresses, haven't I? That's what you wanted, wasn't it?"

The farmer's wife looked ashen faced at Miss Ivinson.

Desperately the dressmaker spoke first: "Why they are just beautiful! Are you going to try them on?"

"No they're not," snapped the farmer. "They're for the Coronation and not before."

"But father . . ."

"Not another word. Now get 'em put away!"

Miss Ivinson, conscious of the second parcel by the machine, glanced desperately at Mrs Scobold. For an instant their eyes met. Whatever happened, no one must know.

"It's a really nice present," she told him lamely.

"Well, do you think," said Scobold scathingly, "that I'd let me own lasses down!"

His voice held a note of triumph. The little man had scored and he knew it.

"I feel so ashamed," confessed Miss Ivinson.

"You've no cause to be."

The two women stood outside the farm looking towards the river. It was just seven in the morning and the dale still patchy with mist. The excitement of the evening was over. The girls would go to the school Coronation party in new dresses after all, though not in the way Miss Ivinson had planned.

"I'll see he pays you before Martinmas," promised Mrs Scobold. "He's got no right to hold back your money this way."

Miss Ivinson checked the pannier straps.

"I only want pay for three days," she said.

"Aye, well, if you insist . . ."

"I do. I couldn't charge for dressmaking time - in view of last night."

A hard gleam lit Mrs Scobold's face.

"I shouldn't be saying so, but I reckon he bought them dresses out of spite. That would be like him! He wasn't thinking just of the girls."

She spoke bitterly.

"But what about the silk ones?"

Mrs Scobold shook her head.

"I've hidden 'em where they come from, back at the bottom of the chest."

Up on the fell a dark figure moved among the sheep.

"I'd best be away."

The dressmaker smiled at the little woman and Mrs Scobold looked suddenly blank. The days had sped rapidly.

"Perhaps you'll be up again sometime?"

"Perhaps I will."

"Robin will allus be glad to see you . . ."

Miss Ivinson smiled.

High above a skylark trilled. It was going to be another scorching day.

"But I'll have a tale to tell the lasses one day, won't I!" said the little woman. "I mean, about yon curtains."

She was still thinking this long after Miss Ivinson had safely crossed the bridge and had set off to push her bicycle down the dale.

Winter Wake

It was the middle of November and the woman sitting on the bedside chair was putting matters straight.

"So the mare," said Martha Herdman, "the mare goes to Isaac?"

Bob Herdman nodded. "Aye, that'll be right." Their fell pony would need a good home.

"And your clothes . . . to Peter?"

"Not me best," he wheezed. "Me best I'll be wearing."

His head shifted on the pillow, his one pale eye staring at her to make sure that she understood.

"I'll see it's all done properly," she promised.

Outside, the rain drifted along the crags of St John's in the Vale and came seeping in through gaps in the slates of their farmhouse. A patch of damp ran down the wall in a long stain behind Martha.

She pulled the chair closer to the bed. She was a small bowed old thing in a brown dress and a shawl that was too comfortable to throw away. Her man began scrabbling at the bedclothes with his fingers, his head a stubbly patch on the pillow. All his life he had worked in a quarry but his hammers and chisels now lay rusting in the outshed.

"You've done it, then," said Martha, nodding. "You've outdone the old Queen as you always said."

Queen Victoria had scarcely made the new century herself,

dying a year ago in 1901. For long enough it had been a joke that Bob would last out longer.

He coughed in the chilliness of the room, his mind on other things.

"There's one matter we've not settled," he said weightily.

Martha had anticipated what was coming. She clicked her tongue in a show of disapproval. "Now you'll not be starting that again . . ."

"I've said it before, I'll say it again, I don't want burying here at St John's," said Bob firmly. The light glinted in his eye. "Not while any of me brothers is living. I'll go to Stoneside whether the buggers like it or not."

"Shush, shush," she protested.

He tried to shift himself around but the bedclothes tangled, holding him fast.

"I'll see 'em damned."

Martha fussed and freed the blankets.

"After all this time you belong here, more than ower that mountain. Use your common sense."

"Missis," said Bob, "I won't let 'em get away with it."

Beyond the valley head against the great wall of Blencathra the blackness flared in a sudden glare of sheet lightning, blanking sight. The thunder sounded long afterwards in a drawn out roll. A man on a horse came down the vale. Soon steps sounded on the stone staircase.

"There's someone to see you," said Martha pushing open the door. "It's the doctor."

Her announcement brought a snort of protest.

"Keep that grasper out of here!" grumbled the old man.

"It's not Dr Hargreaves," whispered Martha. "It's the new one." And in a louder voice: "Come on up, won't you?" She lit his way up the narrow stairs with a candle.

"Oh," said Bob, turning to look. "So it's the new one, is it?"

Dr Durham, young and broad shouldered, had been in the dale just a few months. A gust of cold air assailed him as the layer of hessian that did for a ceiling billowed gently. He sat himself down on the chair and eyed the figure in the bed.

"And how is the patient?" he inquired cheerfully.

"I'm failing," announced Bob.

The doctor was embarking on the difficult apprenticeship of understanding dale folk.

"Is that so?" he said, opening his bag briskly. "Now, that'll hardly be the right spirit, Mr Herdman, will it?"

A disagreeable weathered face glared at him from the blankets. "And just how," said the patient, "must a dying man talk, then?"

"Bob!" cautioned Martha.

The doctor realised that the patient might not be far from the truth.

"I'll ask just the once," said Bob, wheezing back into the blankets. "You don't have to wrap it up. Can you do owt for me?"

The doctor glanced at Martha.

"Go on," said Bob. "I'm busy waiting."

"Well, I'll do my best."

Bob was having none of that.

"To hell with thee best, lad. Can yer cure me?"

The grizzled old man eyed him fiercely out of the covers. The doctor folded away his stethoscope.

"I think you might beat me there in the end," he said gently.

"Hah!" The old man grunted. "Well, you're honest, I'll give thee that. But that's no good to me. If you can't cure me you had best be about thee business, 'cos there's no sense me paying bills for nowt!"

When Martha came back up the stairs she said: "Too sharp you were, Bob. I thought he was an agreeable lad."

"Lass, we can all be agreeable, as you say, if we're being paid handsome. Now remember on what I said: Stoneside, or nowhere."

"Aye, I'll remember," she promised.

"Then I'll be content with that."

Martha sighed. He had been stubborn the day they had met, and he was no different now.

The old man lasted two more days. About the same time that he died the weather worsened. The starkness of winter had settled on the vale.

Without any bidding, a sturdy middle-aged woman arrived at the kitchen door, wrapped in a thick shawl.

"You'll be needing company, Martha," announced Anne Towler.

The two women clasped hands briefly.

"He was a grand man," said Martha simply.

"Aye," said her neighbour, "but he does look peaceful now."

Martha did not ask Anne how she had known. Carefully, the women straightened out the body, washing it from head to toe, and slowly Martha dressed her man in his best clothes. As signs of respect, they closed the blinds at the windows, covered the mirror, draped the furniture in white sheets and shut all the doors, then turn and turn about they sat beside the corpse watching.

For the first day Bob lay waiting for his coffin, and when it was carried into the parlour by two subdued farmers he was lifted into the box where he lay dressed in his Sunday suit, illuminated by an oil lamp on the dresser.

Then there was the bidding. But Martha preferred not to call it that, to her she was seeing old friends.

She knocked at Isaac's farmhouse door. As it opened she said in a strained voice: "One from this house is invited to the funeral of Robert Herdman." And then, knowing this was too formal, she added: "You'll be coming, Isaac?"

The tall man had a stoop and a long Norse face. No one knew how many generations his forebears had lived among the mountains.

He nodded slowly.

"But not here in the vale?" he said, having heard.

"He'll be buried over at Stoneside," said Martha.

Isaac looked troubled.

"Across the fell road? What's he want being buried away over theer?" He spoke without rancour.

"It's an old score," said Martha, but she offered no explanation.

At each cottage and farm she gave her invitation.

"There'll be no funeral tea after," she explained, "because of the journey, but all are welcome the day before."

Isaac called later, drenched, and sat by the hearth till his clothes began to steam. "It's not a fit road this time of year," he told her.

She busied herself at the kitchen table, mixing the arvel bread, traditionally given to mourners at funerals. In the parlour Anne Towler and Margaret from Howgate were keeping a whispered vigil.

Martha said: "I've walked to Keswick market and back for fifty years, a few miles ower the fell road won't hurt."

"The first is true," the man conceded, "but there's a black sky and a fresh storm brewing. The going will be bad every bit of the way."

"It'll make no difference. I promised him I'd go, and go I will."

The wind rushed in the wide old chimney, drawing the peat to a bright glow.

Isaac eased his back where it ached from the cold.

"An old score, you say . . . that'll be his brothers?"

"Aye," said Martha. "Fifty four years gone! It should have been done with and forgotten, but it isn't. Not yet."

"I'll be on time," he promised.

The day before the funeral a stream of dale folk called to offer condolences to the widow and to take final leave of the old man. His body had been covered with an ironed linen sheet leaving only his head showing at one end of the coffin and his brightly polished boots sticking up at the other. In the gloom of the parlour each caller touched Bob's face briefly, and each time this happened Anne Towler watched to see if the body bled.

When Isaac followed suit, Anne confessed: "There's been a few scared faces here this day, I'll tell you!"

"You and your superstitions. We're in the new century now and no one murdered the old devil; he died like the rest of us will - wanting breath."

But Anne shook her head. Let each man or woman show they had no part in Bob's death. The touch was the test. Martha wanted it this way, just as it had been in her mother's day.

Isaac and Anne's husband Richard cleared the barn and set out a long plank table.

Twelve folk arrived for the first sitting, keeping their coats on to combat the cold, then it went on into the afternoon, callers arriving in ones and twos - roadmen, farmers, quarry workers, Jackson the miller, the men and women of the dale, though noticeably among them were no kindred, neither from Bob's side, nor from Martha's. The valley observed and those closest to the Herdmans said little, for they knew something of the matter already.

The vicar, a little uncertain, said: "Bob belongs here at St John's more than anywhere, Martha."

She nodded that she knew, but it would make no difference. In the morning Bob was going back over the tops to Stoneside.

"It's all been arranged, thank you," she explained. It was embarrassing to her, too. The vicar was a good friend.

At the end of the day Martha went to sit with her dead man and tried not to think of the morning.

Eight muted men and women arrived at the farmhouse door battened in coats against the rain. Each mourner was given a black scarf. Martha, dressed in her heaviest long coat and bonnet, knew the scarves should have been silk but expense precluded it, so she gave cotton instead. She welcomed the mourners into the warmth of the kitchen and as they passed the parlour door they glanced in and saw that the lid was on the coffin.

It was only eight in the morning but she asked: "You'll have a tot?"

The kitchen filled with talk. Isaac carried in a bundle of empty sacks for use as capes, and waved at the wet outside. Martha saw to their glasses a second time - the Walker brothers, Jacob and Aaron; Peter Redshaw from the quarry; John Bateman, Richard and Anne Towler, Jim Chapman and Isaac. Eight would set off with her up onto the heights.

Peter slipped away to the barn while the rum set them talking.

Martha said: "I thank you all for coming."

Anne said: "It's a fearful day to be taking the fell road."

"We'll manage fine," said Isaac. He was anxious to make a start and was relieved when Peter announced that the cart was ready.

The coffin was carried out to the yard where the Herdmans' pony Bessok was already in the shafts. To Martha's surprise and gratification the yard was full of people.

A woman touched Martha on the arm. It was John Bateman's wife, Margaret.

"We wish we were all able to go over with you today."

Martha nodded, suddenly unable to speak.

The cart was the simplest of its kind, two wheeled, open at the back. The men slid the coffin in over the tail end and it was just a fit. A wreath was tied on top.

The vicar intoned: "Let us remember our maker . . ."

In the grey November morning the dale folk sang *Abide with Me* and only after the last voice had died away did Isaac lead the cart across the cobbles. As Bob Herdman's last journey began, those remaining followed into the lane after them, the men doffing their caps while they watched him go. It was fifty-four years since he had come to Threlkeld and now he was going back to his old home. Past and present were soon to meet.

The axe glinted as it swept down and sank into the barn door.

"He's a maniac!" wept Martha Jackson bitterly. "He'll kill us both before he lets us be."

Blows smashed at the wood until a plank began to splinter.

Robert raced to roll the cart against the inside.

"Martha! Set down the lantern and help me push!"

Both were young. They had fled the house the moment his brother Simon had appeared. One glance at the blotched angry face showed that yet another fit was upon him. In the terrible minutes that followed, Simon hacked their bed to pieces with the axe, stopping only when his frenzy had run to a state of near exhaustion. During the lull they escaped down the back staircase and got across the yard into the barn.

Simon pounded at the planking as Martha, barely nineteen, dragged at the cart, matching Robert. She was strong and buxom, but afraid.

"He'll get in!" she said. "He's possessed again."

"He'll not!" said Robert.

Outside in the night an angry voice sounded: "No Jackson bitch will get a wedding bed in this farm! D'ya hear? I'll see you both dead first!"

"Go to hell!" shouted Robert.

They rammed the cart hard against the door where the wavering light from the lantern threw their shadows in fearful patterns. A dance of death, thought Martha.

"I curse thee Simon Herdman!" she shouted. "And all your vileness!" And then quietly: "Oh, Robert, there's no sense in this fighting. I don't want to go on staying here. It was bad enough when your father was alive, but Simon is never going to stop now."

"I'll not be outdone," said Robert grimly. "The farm is to be shared."

The pounding stopped. Martha listened for a time then sank beside him, holding his hands. "He's still there, waiting."

"Be patient," said Robert. "His fit will end. I know him; he'll be like a baby once it's passed. He's allus the same. He blubbers."

"But what are we going to do?" Her face filled with dismay.

"We all inherit: Dadge, Simon, me, even Spencer, equal shares. I want no more than what's mine."

"We must go. Simon is never going to change!"

"So what's to be done? Run away? Leave 'em to it? A man can't farm without land."

"We can do summat else, 'stead of farming."

"Aye. Beg likely, and starve."

"We'd not starve," said Martha. She shivered. Dismally she picked up a sack and wrapped it across her shoulders. "Better get out now while we can."

Robert knew she was right but he did not like losing what was his.

"Just be patient. Simon's fit will pass."

Outside Simon huddled in the gloom. He strove to conjure Martha's face but the harder he tried the harder it became. He remembered the day he cornered her on the stone staircase in the downhouse. But Robert had arrived and pulled her clear. His long-standing dislike for his brother had welled within him. Robert had set her against him. Always had. A second chance came by the stile and Martha had heard nothing until he had hold of her and dragged her to the ground. She had fought like a vixen and then the looming figure of his father had seized him. Pinned down to a sandstone wheel, Simon had wept in rage as the whip turned his back into red blood wields. Simon's hatred grew into an unforgiving bitterness. His day of revenge would come.

And now it had. He had caught them in bed. He would teach whore and brother a lesson of his own.

Dimly he was aware that he was drooling. One foot was twisted where he had slipped on the staircase and had caught his ankle.

"I'll kill you, you devils!" he cursed.

Yet already he was too late, there was a noise of shifting wood and the barn door was swinging. Simon was still struggling to stand up as Robert and Martha escaped up the track to the fell. They had decided their future. They had left everything.

The mourners struggled through a slough of mud.

"Push harder!"

The mare, Bessok, bred for mountain toughness, was floundering. They were scarcely half a mile along the vale and constantly one or the other was forced to grab and steady the coffin.

"Peter, Richard, give us a hand!" called Isaac. He was gaunt faced, strong looking, his hair wild in the wind. The others pushed. The mud was deadly.

Twenty minutes later the track divided. They turned up from the valley floor and got some relief as they found better going on a stone track. It was the start of the old fell way and ran past a farm.

"We'll rest," said Isaac.

But Jacob Walker protested: "No, this is not a fit resting place for the dead! This place is not blessed."

"We'll rest," insisted Isaac, mindful of the women. "He's dry enough in his box."

"You'll have the devil on us!"

Isaac ignored him.

They paused and regained their breath, Jacob muttering angrily. Above them loomed the misty fell side. They would need all their strength to get over it in this weather.

Noisy barking broke out at the farm and in the gloom a man came towards them.

"Shelter yourselves in the yard!"

Martha recognised Ben Tomlinson. He waved at them to move on in but she shook her head.

Isaac said: "We must get on."

Tomlinson stared at the women: "I fear the road'll be washed out in this lot!"

"I thank you, Ben Tomlinson," said Martha. "But we cannot afford to linger."

She looked out from under her umbrella.

"There can be no turning back."

They began to climb up the side of the fell, a cluster of shrouded figures and the cart. As they gained height gaps came in the rain, affording glimpses of the slopes above where the track twisted towards a sprawl of quarries.

Jacob spoke in an undertone to Anne: "I am thinking we should never have stopped his body back there. I am thinking it was a wrong place."

"You are a believer in the old ways?"

"And are you not?"

Anne panted along slowly.

"There's places it is unholy to stop, that's true."

"It should never have happened," said Jacob fearfully. Something bad would come of it. He felt it in his bones.

Isaac passed the halter to Peter Redshaw and waited for Martha to catch up. She climbed slowly, her umbrella a hindrance now that they were more exposed to the wind.

"How are you managing?" he asked.

"Better now we've left the mud."

"There'll be more yet," said Isaac.

Unexpectedly a harsh rattle sounded in the mist.

Jim Chapman turned quickly, his face drawn. "For God's sake, whativver's that?"

Isaac laughed: "It's nobbut a ewe. I'd have thought you'd know that, Jim."

But no one else laughed. Several glanced sharply at the coffin. No one liked being on the fell with a corpse.

Then the track seemed to vanish altogether under water.

"I know this place," said Anne. "It's the well."

"Nay," said Jacob. "The last thing we want is more watter!"

The well had overflowed, gushing across the track. They splashed through, no longer attempting to keep their feet dry.

Anne said to Martha: "Why don't you ride?"

Martha shook her head. "It's enough that one of us is in the cart."

She waded on after the others to a stone bridge. A peaty cascade roared in its rocky bed and thrashed on down the fell.

"But that's a sight," said Anne.

"We rest here," said Martha. "The first of the blessed places."

The mourners clustered in the lea of the wall while Martha fumbled with cold hands at the wreath, sliding it to one side.

"Can I help," said Isaac.

"Yes, I want the lid off."

Several heard despite the roar of the beck.

Jacob came close. He looked angry. "You'll have us cursed again!"

Martha ignored him. She wrested the top off the coffin and felt inside.

"Here," she said, and while the white face of her dead man was lit again by the stormy world, she passed out cheese and loaves and a bottle.

Road to Paradise

"You don't think," she told the astonished mourners, "that Bob and me would let you do all this without being properly cared for, do you!"

"This is cursed for sure," vowed Jacob, eyeing the rum. "But it's a blessing on you both."

Huddled below the wall, they ate and drank till the bread and cheese had gone and the bottle was empty.

The three young hunters had their prey trapped. Slowly the brothers closed in, widely spaced, covering the gaps between the buildings. Rain had left the farmyard cobbles glistening and slippery. There was no easy escape.

"You bastards," cried Robert. "He made a will, and you know it."

Each of his brothers had a fencing stake. Simon, the oldest, held his like a club, his muscles taut.

"I've the same right to be here the same as any of you," shouted Robert.

Simon spat at the ground. "You lost that right the day you left with the whore. Dadge! Cover the gate!"

Dadge moved across, his clogs clattering. The third brother, Spencer, licked his lips unsure of what he was about.

"We don't need hurt him, much, do we . . . just scare him, eh?"

He laughed nervously.

Simon glowered, his eyes on Robert who was backing against the barn side.

"He's going to learn his lesson. If it means we beat him for shaming us, then we'll beat him."

Robert edged back still further. The yard was out of sight of the house. It was early morning and no one alive now but his three brothers, who ran everything - Simon the money, Dadge and Spencer the beasts and the land. He should never have come back, never have let himself be cornered, but his resentment burned fiercely. He was entitled to a share of the farm. They were out to rob him.

His nailed boots and hardened quarry hands were his only weapons.

Ducks splashed by the gate where Dadge waited. Dadge, minion to Simon, small, solid, a surly face. Spencer was across at the other side, by the long barn door. Spencer, dirty, unshaven, twenty-six years old, still wetting his bed. And in the middle, Simon the bully, heavy, given to fits of rage, determined to own everything. Simon was the vicious one.

Robert knew he must act swiftly or not at all. They were too close. Lunging, he grabbed up a fallen piece of fencing.

"Stand back!" he shouted. He clutched the stave, poised to strike, alert, tense.

"Get him!" snarled Simon.

Robert swung at the oncoming man, smacking him on the side of his head, spinning him about in a lash of crimson. Simon, blinded in his own blood, reeled away screaming.

Dadge had Robert locked with thick arms, pinioned against a wall, pounding him in the groin with a knee. Spencer was shouting and punching blindly at his face. Robert, creased with pain, twisted his head, and bit hard at Dadge. A bellow filled the yard as his teeth tore at one of his brother's ears. Blood splashed their clothes, then he was free and stumbling towards the gate.

"Blast you!" screamed Dadge. "I'll murder you!"

A piece of flesh tumbled down inside his shirt.

Robert, panting, ran a few more steps then slipped on the stones. The last thing he remembered was Simon's clog smashing into his face.

Cartwheels bucked and turned in frenzied rings. Alarm and confusion! The mourners were careering down a steep slope knowing they were going too fast. The women had decided to ride in the cart after all, but already they were regretting it.

Isaac shouted angrily at Jacob. "Easy man with that whip!"

They had lingered too long and were still several miles from the graveyard.

"You must stop the cart!" shouted Anne, clutching at the coffin. "Stop it, will you!"

Martha, robbed of breath, clung white faced as the wheels scattered showers of stones.

Where the track snaked below a black line of crags the cart hit a boulder. As a wheel spun off, the women and the coffin were pitched into the bracken.

They abandoned the cart. There was no immediate way to repair it. Limping and dejected, the mourners moved on through the mist, scarcely aware of direction, and now little caring. Belts and bracers had been sacrificed. They had hoisted the coffin on to Bessok's broad back and tied it on as best they could. Now the men walked alongside to make sure it did not tumble again.

"I tell you it was the cursed drink that brought this on," snarled Jacob.

"You supped your share like the rest," scowled Anne. The more she listened to the man the less she liked him.

"This is no place to quarrel," said Isaac. "We're badly late."

Soon the track would turn down off the tops, with the church a mile or so further.

Peter said: "I don't know how anyone can tell where the road is in this lot."

"I can tell," said Isaac.

Then Martha had to pause.

"I'm sorry," she said suddenly, "I need to stop."

Her face looked whiter than ever.

"This is no place!" snapped Jacob.

Isaac said: "It won't do to sit overlong in this mist, Martha."

She sank onto a rock.

"I'm feeling a bit strange . . ."

Dismayed, they clustered round.

The old woman needed to make sure.

"Isaac, if I don't see it through, you'll do the right thing won't you?"

"Don't be talking that way! You'll see it through."

"But if I don't?"

"You will. There's not far now. But get your breath and then we'll go on slowly."

Unattended, Bessok stirred uneasily. Several times the crudely fashioned thongs had slipped and the coffin had been retied. But the forward bindings were giving again and slowly the long heavy box began to tilt down the mare's back. Startled by the sudden shift of weight, Bessok edged forward, and then went on again. Before anyone noticed properly she had moved off into the mist.

Isaac was the first to realise.

"The pony! Where's the pony?"

They turned, scarcely understanding.

"Who left her unattended?"

No one answered.

"For God's sake," he shouted. "Get after her! The coffin won't stay on by itself!"

The men swore. This was all they needed! Hurriedly they set off into the mist along the bleak edge of the fell.

Alone, the two women huddled together on a boulder.

"They'll never find Bob in all this," said Martha.

"Of course they will!" said Anne. She spoke more confidently than she felt. "Bessok can't be far off."

"We are cursed like Jacob says!"

"Never! That's his foolish talk."

"Aye, but it's a wrong thing we're doing today . . . coming back here. I shouldn't say so, but it is."

Robert had been twenty-two, Martha nineteen. Martha's tired face filled at the memory of the day they fled from Stoneside. "Mother and father died when I was a baby, and the Herdmans had allus looked after me. When Bob and me ran away we committed the unpardonable sin."

"But surely," said Anne sympathetically. "Running off, that wasn't so terrible?"

"Mebbe not. But Bob and me we never were wed, not ever. And you know what some in the valley think of things like that."

Anne stared. Yes, that was a surprise.

"We're not the first to manage without a preacher, and like as not we'll not be the last."

"And you never come back here to Stoneside?"

"Aye, the once, Bob did, but it was a cruel meeting. He came back after his father died. I begged him not to. That's when he lost an eye fighting."

The old woman sounded bitter. "He should never have returned."

"Then why now," said Anne, surprised.

Martha's face hardened. "Bob's getting his revenge! He made me promise. He'll be back among 'em now whether they like it or not. They'll have a hard job to be rid of a dead man. The farm was as much his as ever it was theirs!"

Muttering angrily, Simon dragged a glistening stone out of the ground and lodged it in the wall. He seized a cobble and threw it aside, preferring sharper brutal rock. He could not remember how it began, the first few pieces, the dull idea that had grown into a battlement, and now was a harsh line of hatred edging yard by yard along the fell above the farm. As time had passed, the weeks, the months, a year and longer, the blackness of the wall had grown until all in the valley were conscious of it ranging along the heights where the intake ended and the bracken began.

Sullen moods began to cloud Simon. His hair had grown wild, his face unshaven. When Dadge or Spencer came near he chose neither to see nor to speak, but muttered darkly and sought shapes in the stones, finding the harsher lines, keeping his back towards his brothers.

Dadge, at a loss to combat Simon's behaviour, struggled to maintain the farm.

"He's no good to us or hissel."

Within the house disorder grew. Paper littered windowsills; dirty dishes filled the stone sink; floors were unswept.

Spencer tapped a finger at his head and leered. "Gone soft as shite," he chanted. "Soft as shite . . ."

Dadge scowled at his younger brother.

"That's all you're good for isn't it! Cussing and pissing your pants! And him mazed as a thwarted bull."

Winters and summers came and went. A crack in the gable-end stonework widened; the sag in the barn roof became deeper. Dadge knew they had to do something, but Simon did not help and Dadge floundered. Only the daily round of minding the sheep and cattle kept them steady.

Then for two days Simon disappeared.

At first they did not look.

"He's buggered off!" said Dadge desperately. "Left us to look after every bloody thing! That damn wall's got him bewitched."

A mile beyond the farm, where the fell began to steepen, the wall-end gaped unfinished. They found Simon lying behind it in the bracken, rigid.

"He's here!" said Spencer, frightened. "He's dead!"

Not dead, you damned idiot! Simon screamed.

Dadge, still registering a first glimpse of the twisted body, closed his mouth slowly and bent over his brother. Simon's eyes were open wide and unmoving. Dadge touched the flesh. The body was cold and stiff.

"The lord have mercy on us," whispered Dadge.

Help me up! screamed Simon. *Don't just stand there staring!*

"He's as dead as a stuck pig."

Spencer's eyes were clouded with fear. He twisted grubby hands. "I ain't picking him up. I ain't touching him! Not for no one, see!"

"You'll help me carry him down, or I'll make you stop all night with him by yourself!"

"I don't like dead bodies, Dadge, you know that."

God in heaven, I ain't dead! bellowed Simon. *What's the matter with them! Christ!*

Rough hands seized the body, towing it to the farm. Mud splattered Simon's cord breeks where they dragged him through the mire.

And all the way from the wall to the cobbled yard and up to the door Simon shouted and told them to put him down.

I ain't dead! he screamed. *Listen, will you!*

But it seemed as if his brothers were not listening, or didn't want to. They went inside leaving him propped against the door jamb while they decided what to do next.

The two men, clad in unaccustomed suits, crossed the farmyard stiffly. "He's bloody well gone and left us to run this damn place all by ourselves," cursed Dadge.

Spencer shuddered as they entered the house, remembering the deaths of their parents years before. His clothes still smelt of mothballs and old sweat. He had refused to touch Simon's body a second time. Even the undertaker had been uneasy. No one had been able to close the corpse's eyes, even when the lid had gone on the coffin. They had just stuck wide open stiffly and no one could remember anything like it.

Dadge went into the dampness of the little-used parlour and took two glasses from a cupboard. He poured two whiskies. Spencer gulped his down and Dadge refilled the glass.

"I just couldn't touch him," said Spencer again, his eyes still seeing the body.

"No," said Dadge. He drained his own glass and poured more. For one terrible moment as the coffin lid had been lifted into place he had imagined that one of Simon's eyelids had flickered.

"No," he said again.

Greatly relieved, Isaac came up with Bessok in the mist. The pony was covered in moisture.

"God protect us," said the farmer.

The coffin lay on the ground spilled open. A length of white satin lay twisted on the grass, but Bob's body was not there.

For an age Isaac quartered the peat hags desperately searching for the corpse. The land was too soft to step on and he was obliged to tread warily. Twice he returned to Bessok to check she was all right.

"Whoa, whoa," he said softly each time, but the pony made no further attempt to move. Wearily, Isaac set off to search the hags again.

Time passed until far away in the greyness came the faint sound of a man calling.

"Listen!" said Martha.

They shouted, guiding him until a bulky figure came looming.

"It's Isaac," said Jacob.

"Thank the lord," said Anne.

The farmer led Bessok up to them, the coffin tied across the pony's broad back.

Peter Redshaw said: "We'd all but given you up!"

"She'd gone near on a mile," Isaac told them.

Martha got to her feet. The rest had done her good and she was feeling stronger. "Thank you. We'd best try and make up some lost time."

They descended a hillside and moved in among the shelter of trees. Mud-stained, they passed a dilapidated farm. At the gate before the huddled greyness of the church a robed figure hurried out to meet them.

"Thanks be to God you are safe," he said. And then, not pausing: "I am the resurrection and the life . . ."

In a slow shuffle they carried the coffin into the church. They were thirteen in number, the mourners, the vicar, a verger and, at the back, in the gloom of a smouldering oil lamp, two old men on a bench. Only their eyes seemed to move as the coffin was set down in front of the altar. No one acknowledged their presence and their voices made no more than a mumble in the service that followed. When the service was over the pew where they had been sitting was empty. No one had seen them leave.

The grave had been dug in a grassy bank below a rhododendron. The coffin was lowered quickly and earth scattered. Martha looked hard at a second grave alongside the pit. The headstone had weathered and the name was not easy to read, but she knew well enough who was buried there.

Turning back to the pit, she threw in a sprig of green and said softly: “Be at peace, Bob.” Past and present lay side by side.

When all was over the mourners trailed along to the inn. Jacob walked with Isaac and for a while did not speak. The little man seemed subdued.

“There’s no need to say owt to Martha,” he said finally, “but I reckon there was summat wrong about Bob’s coffin.”

Isaac listened, suddenly watchful.

Jacob cleared his throat uneasily. “I mean, we left the rum bottle inside with him.”

“Yes,” said Isaac. “That’s so.”

And then he added, as a reassurance: “Bob wasn’t one to mind an empty bottle.”

“Mebbe not . . . but it’d be best to say nowt to his missis. She might think it improper.”

“You’re right. Not a word.”

At the door of the inn Isaac said to Martha: “You must be fair tired.”

“It’s a strange thing,” said the old woman, her face breaking into a smile. “Now it’s ower I’m feeling better.”

Anne said: “Come along, we must get summat to eat or we’ll all find ourselves lying along there with Bob.”

“He’d not have wanted us miserable,” agreed Martha.

She moved inside. “Did you see, in the church . . .”

“Aye,” said Anne.

“His brothers, ” said the old woman. “Dadge and Spencer.”

“I guessed it was them. What happened to the other?”

“Simon died years back of a stroke,” said Martha. “Allus a lot of trouble he was. Well they’re lying side by side now.”

She sighed heavily. “Aye, but it’s a terrible thing when families fall out.”

The Wooden Folly

John Gilchrist took his time on the uneven floor and carried two tankards of ale across to the bench well aware of the other man's gaze. He realised that the next few minutes were likely to be important, perhaps for both of them.

"A proposition, you say? A good paying one I hope?" He laughed, though he guessed he was being a bit clumsy. A bit too direct. "I've always room for more work."

"I'm glad to hear it," said Aaron Dixon. He eased the bench beneath him and had another good look at the shipbuilder. Cautious by nature, he was still undecided whether the man was the right person for the job.

They were in a pub at Penny Bridge, uphill from the river. Outside, the land was encased in snow and bitterly cold, but inside alongside the fire it was warm enough.

"Up here, at the Bridge," said Dixon. "You have nothing pending?"

"Oh aye, there's repairs and such."

"But not another vessel?"

The shipbuilder acknowledged reluctantly that there wasn't. He did not elaborate, but an ill-timed bout of 'flu had set him back just as he was preparing to put in a bid to build a sloop. Disastrously, the commission had gone to a shipyard down at Ulverston.

The two men were an unalike pair. Gilchrist, stocky, rough faced, his balding head crossed by a few gingery strands of hair, concerned about the future; and Dixon, master mariner of Ulverston, painfully thin, his skinniness not improved by an overtight frock coat and britches, keen to own a new vessel, keen to get one built.

The mariner took a long slow sup. Gilchrist looked reliable enough, practical, he'd give him that. But was the man's work good? Dixon knew he needed to speak his mind.

"I don't want you to be taking this personally, it's just there are folk saying how ships built here at the Bridge have been having a bit of bad luck these days . . ."

Gilchrist almost laughed, except that it was a damned serious matter. He had heard some of the talk himself.

"So it's bad luck now, is it? And who spun you that one?"

"I own that it is simply gossip," said Dixon.

"Someone down river? Greenodd way likely?"

The two villages had been shipbuilding rivals for long enough.

Dixon changed tack. He spoke quietly: "The sloop, the *Laura* . . . was there never a trace?"

That was the hurt of it.

"None." Gilchrist looked bleak. He had a right to be for he and his workmen had built the vessel. "She sailed from the Bridge one Monday bound for the high seas and that was it. We've not heard of her since."

It was a bitter memory.

"We reckon the damned privateers got her."

Dixon eyed the shipwright with some sympathy, but a lost ship did not make for a good omen. He risked a more dangerous line. "Some have suggested the *Laura's* timbers might have been unsound."

Gilchrist glared angrily. "And who says that? Some idle devil I've sacked, I'll warrant!"

"It's just gossip."

"Then why repeat it! Solid oak went into the *Laura.* Given the same job today, I'd build exactly the same! She was a good ship. First rate."

Dixon's face remained impassive but he gave a slight nod of acknowledgement. He was impressed by Gilchrist's manner. In any case, gossip mongers aside, there were others who had recommended the man.

The merchant's eyes flitted to the landlord. Suddenly decided, he lowered his voice.

"As you've gathered, I am thinking about commissioning a vessel. But it's fatter game than a sloop."

Gilchrist's hands opened and closed in a clench, his anger still evident, though his attention was sharp enough.

Dixon said: "What would you say if I asked about building something special . . . something bigger?"

That was a surprise.

"Bigger? How much bigger?"

"How about a fast schooner?"

Gilchrist pursed his lips.

"A hundred and sixty tons," said Dixon.

"Nay . . . that sounds more like an Ulverston job."

"Ulverston," said Dixon, his voice still low, "has one vessel building already. Leven likewise, so it needs be down river at Greenodd. Or else up here at Penny Bridge."

Gilchrist frowned. A schooner . . . it would be a Godsend and provide plenty of work. But a hundred-and-sixty tonner would not launch at the Bridge. So why was Dixon looking to his yard? It did not make sense. He grew wary.

"Down river it would work better. Deeper water."

"Perhaps," said Dixon. "But up here at the Bridge there's likely to be more folk interested in buying shares. And have the ready money! There's little spare these days at Greenodd."

That was true. Gilchrist knew it.

Dixon leaned forward eagerly. "What I want is a two-master that can sail fast and get in among the Home Trade. But could the Bridge raise money soon enough to make a quick start?"

Gilchrist gave a wry smile.

"Money is not the problem. The problem is the river, whether the Crake would carry enough water to launch her."

"You have serious doubts?"

"Aye! A hundred and sixty tons is almighty big. The biggest vessel built here was the *William and Fanny*, in my father's day. She would be about a hundred and fifty tons. But that's years ago, and she almost didn't make it. My father said she got down river only by the grace of God."

"But she did get clear!"

"Aye! She's still afloat."

"A good sign! So it is not impossible!" Dixon's face lit enthusiastically. "Let us suppose it would launch . . . what then?"

"It depends on the terms."

"The terms are simple! Thirty-six shares to be funded by myself and by my old Aunt Nancy - she's grossly rich and has finally decided to do something useful with her money! Twenty eight more you would place as you thought fit . . ."

"Twenty-eight!"

"Never fear!" said the merchant reassuringly. "There must be plenty of widow's money in the valley. I'll warrant few will resist a slice of a new merchant schooner!"

On the strength of my goodwill, thought Gilchrist. But perhaps Dixon was right. There was money in the valley, though getting purses to open wide enough would take some effort.

The real problem was the river. If the tides were not right, all the money in Furness would not make a launch possible.

The shipbuilder stared into his tankard. "I need to study the tides."

"Then you are interested?"

"I might be," said Gilchrist cautiously. "First the tides. We must be certain it is possible."

Dixon nodded. He appreciated a cautious approach.

"A good two-master!"

"As long as you don't want anything built in iron!"

"Iron! Let them build in iron as wants," said the merchant. "They'll be trying to make granite float next!"

There was not much to Penny Bridge itself, a cluster of rough houses stretching down towards the bridge, with another inn on the far side. Yet it was an important crossing place for the mail coaches. Half a mile down-river lay Greenodd where the Crake joined the bigger channel of the Leven and ran south into the bay and the sea. Ships sailed in from distant parts to both villages, unloading all manner of goods for carting on through High Furness. And out of one place or another poured a reverse stream of iron and copper ores, slate, flax and such surprising varied products as ovens, anvils, hatter's irons and weighty cannon shot, used in past times for blazing away at Napoleon.

Gilchrist moved quietly, approaching the empty slipway where he paused, still unable to resolve the argument within him. It was hardly dawn and the mist moved with the current, trailing ghostly wraiths in its wake. Patches of snow and ice encrusted the heavy timbers. Here his father and his grandfather before him had worked on many fine vessels. Here he had learned his own trade and in turn had built three sloops, the *Jessie,* far away now trading in the New World, the *Helen,* away up to Shetland, and the third lost without trace and a grievous memory.

But now came this merchant's proposal. A schooner! And a hundred and sixty tons. In the village opinion was fiercely divided about the likely outcome, and that was the root of his concern, for he was not totally convinced that the doubters were wrong.

Given the tonnage, he calculated the vessel's probable length at about a hundred foot and a beam of twenty-two. She would certainly be hard to get away down the Crake, but would it be impossible? It was a tremendous challenge. He had never built anything so large before.

Long into the night he calculated tidal figures and was making little of them when he had an unexpected stroke of luck, one that certainly seemed to change everything. Next March's spring tides were going to be extraordinarily high. He checked again to make sure he was not mistaken. Excitedly he saw that the tides would be among the highest for a decade. It was a significant discovery.

Midnight was striking as he went to bed, his mind still racing. If he could build the ship and have it ready a year from now, then surely even a hundred-and-sixty-tonner might get down to the sea? The water would never be deeper, nor conditions better. For the first time he began to feel optimistic.

His chief carpenter was appalled.

"A hundred and sixty tons!" protested George Bewsher incredulously. "It can't be done! We'll never launch owt that big in the Crake!"

Gilchrist sighed. Doubts, doubts, doubts!

"Don't tell me, George, you're another without faith."

Bewsher sat uneasily in Gilchrist's parlour, a short nervous man, quick to show his fears. The whole idea filled him with dismay. "Faith, Mr Gilchrist, aye, when it's sensible! But this 'un, she'll grind the mud first go."

Gilchrist reached into a cupboard and brought out a bottle and glasses. He had convinced himself it was possible. The high tides for next March were clear enough.

"She'll not stick, George. Given next year's good spring tide she'll float out without bother, I'm sure of it."

"Then I'm glad you are," said the carpenter, "because I'm not! For a start, I can't see us getting rid of the shares. No one's going to risk their money."

He did not add 'after the *Laura* disaster' though he could easily have done so.

The shipwright poured two generous measures of rum and handed the carpenter his glass before answering: "I've placed eleven already."

Surprised, Bewsher swivelled on his chair.

"And who's been foolish enough to put in this quick?"

"Two to the vicar . . ."

"Holy Moses! And how long has the vicar been sea-legged?"

"You do him an injustice. He loves the sea. Three to the major. One to Widow Rennison."

"That's six, you said eleven."

"Four to me."

"You'll be a ruined man."

"One to your good self . . ."

"But I haven't agreed!" howled the carpenter.

Gilchrist was not put off.

"A schooner! It's just what the yard needs."

"Hah! Your years are getting you."

Gilchrist smiled. "The difference between you and me, George, is that I'm still an optimist, years or not. There'll be no shortage of shareholders. And you know as well as I do, we need the work."

"She'll not have the pleasure of being sunk," predicted Bewsher, "because she'll never survive the launch."

"Your health!" said Gilchrist. Their glasses clinked and they knocked it back. For a moment Bewsher allowed himself a fleeting smile of acknowledgement. "You'll not be winning me round with alcohol."

"Of course not," said Gilchrist topping up the other's glass.

Mid-January already. They had until March next year, just about fourteen months. It was precious little time. The shipwright stood in the parlour window enjoying the weak sun. A thin covering of snow lay everywhere, though more could yet come. At the quay a sloop was waiting for the next tide down to the sea.

Gilchrist said: "Tomorrow, we'll need a new sawpit, Big Tom on the sawing . . . we'll build a schooner the like of which has never been seen 'afore at Penny Bridge."

Bewsher sighed heavily. "If she ever floats!"

"Aye? Well I can let your share go, George, since you're so bothered."

"No, I didn't say that."

Gilchrist laughed. "When the time comes she'll float out like a swan."

He held up the bottle. Just a drop left. He shared it between them, his face alight.

"I must finish the model. We'll show Greenodd a thing or two about ship building!"

Word spread rapidly. In ones and twos villagers, the doctor, and local members of the gentry took up the shares. It proved easier than Gilchrist had expected. Thus Jack Rigg, sail maker: "One will do - providing, of course, I get the order for the sails."

"Of course," agreed Gilchrist.

At the start of February a group of men met in the shipwright's kitchen, some wanting hiring, some already in his employ. Gilchrist's wife Alice, after a shy "Good morning," flitted into another part of the house and left them to it.

The shipwright knew them well enough - joiners Edward and Thomas Askew; carpenters John Tomlinson and Bert Casson; handyman Isaac Ellwood from up-river at Spark Bridge; labourer Billy Parke along with lean faced Marly Shepherd, the father of five other young Shepherds. These men would help form the core, though others would be needed. A schooner this size would need more than his usual men.

"And what's happened to Big Tom?" said Gilchrist.

A deep voice sounded in the doorway. "Here I am, Mr Gilchrist."

A large framed man stooped in, six foot or more and broad with it. He was followed by George Bewsher.

The shipwright's face brightened.

"Now then, Tom, a good man as top sawyer!"

Big Tom beamed. He and Gilchrist had worked together for many years. His presence was reassuring. Skilled sawyers were essential, doing all the cutting and yet, despite their bulk (it often being a characteristic of their occupation) they were men of considerable delicacy, working with long bladed saws to fine limits. Big Tom was such a man.

The sawyer said: "A schooner, eh! We'll build us a good un, Mr Gilchrist."

"Well said Tom! That we will! Now lads, take a good look at this."

Gilchrist turned to a long table where a sheet covered a lumpy object. All in the room knew well enough what lay hidden underneath. He lifted the cover clear and the men crowded round to get a good look.

It was not the conventional wooden model of a two-masted schooner, it was only a half-model, for it was sliced exactly down the middle. On one side it presented a finished vessel, but on the other it was a careful cutaway from stem to sternpost, from deck to keel, showing the inside in great detail. The whole thing was three foot long.

"Now that's a beauty!" said Big Tom enthusiastically. "A real beauty."

Gilchrist smiled, pleased.

"Perfect to scale!"

It had taken him a long time to make and now it was ready. From this model the men would build the real thing.

The shipwright produced a bottle. "A toast before we start . . ."

"Nay, Mr Gilchrist, sir." Shepherd interrupted him. The man glanced nervously towards the door. "There's one more yet wanting hiring."

"Oh, is there? And who might that be?"

Shepherd shuffled uneasily, his undernourished face leaner than usual. "Come on, step in now."

A boy was pushed forward. The shipwright recognised him as one of Shepherd's sons.

"Aye, now, it's Master Peter, isn't it? How you've grown! And what do you know about ship building, young sir?"

The boy glanced anxiously at his father but received no encouragement. The boy was on his own.

"Nowt much sir." And added quickly. "But it leaves me head terrible empty for putting in learning."

Laughter filled the kitchen.

Gilchrist observed the boy's build, and turned to the sawyer.

"You could do with a pit boy, Tom?"

"Aye," boomed the big man. "Given the right one! All right . . . we'll put the lad to the test. Let him try the saw, but I'll not be having him if he's no good."

"Of course not. Then that's settled. A glass for the boy."

A small measure of rum was poured, watched by a passive faced father.

Gilchrist held up his glass. "Here's to the ship, me lads."

"The Ship!"

They downed the rum in one go and Gilchrist filled up their glasses again.

Next morning Parke and Shepherd set to and began to dig a new sawpit in the back of the river slope. Down at the Bridge hardly three feet of water was running.

Bewsher peered into the hole.

"You're too near the river. It'll flood."

"Not before March next year, it won't," said Parke.

The carpenter's worried face grew tighter. "All right, all right, I was only saying."

A cool wind ruffled the water.

The pit was finished the following afternoon. Long and narrow, it gaped near the slipway, close on eight foot deep and lined with packed logs.

At Big Tom's signal, young Peter set a ladder down into the hole. Across the top a hefty length of larch lay on wedges, stripped of its bark. The sawyer drew a thick yellow thumb nail along the wood and surprised the boy by scoring it deeply.

"Now, me lad, you mark this saw? Well you does the down pulling, and I does the guiding, up and down. Has your head got that?"

Peter's head had got it.

Tom stood on top of the log and set a six-foot blade against the timber as the boy went down into the hole.

"Take a proper hold on that end and we'll see how you go. Now off you go, and keep your strokes steady or I'll be sawing off your ears by mistake!"

A cluster of men watched as top sawyer and pit boy began their trial partnership. The first few strokes wavered falsely, then the blade settled and soon each cut developed a healthy harsh bite.

A dozen strokes and the boy was being showered in sweet-smelling sawdust.

"Steady, theer, lad. Take it steady or you'll not last."

Peter was finding it hard to maintain a proper rhythm.

By fifty strokes the boy was panting badly.

At eighty he was gasping as if he were going to die.

". . . eighty-seven, eighty-eight, eighty-nine . . ."

As the saw bit deeper into the wood the watchers had increased in number, chanting encouragement.

". . .Ninety! Ninety-one . . . ninety-two . . ."

"Don't stop now!"

Peter scarcely heard. Sawdust rained around him, blurring the world. He was wanting to die.

". . .ninety-nine . . . a hundred!"

A cheer rose from the men.

Eight feet down from the world Peter let go of the handle and fell to his knees.

"Well done, lad! Well done!"

Shipwright and sawyer stood at the top of the pit and looked down at the boy.

"Well, Tom?"

The giant-framed man smiled grimly.

"He's a sight short of a few mutton chops, but given time he'll manage fine well."

Peter struggled to the ladder and Big Tom reached a hefty hand down to haul up the new pit boy.

"A shilling a week," said Gilchrist.

Marly Shepherd heard and nodded appreciatively.

"We'll want your mark, lad. And while we're at it, we'll find you clogs. No sawyer of ours needs go bare footed."

An hour later, Peter, the colour back in his cheeks, made his mark, and pledged himself to live under a shower of sawdust. Time would show that this was not the worst that lay ahead.

Once the news about the schooner got out Greenodd folk greeted it with scorn and disbelief. In the bustling Ship Inn Gilchrist's foolishness was a frequent talking point. Mariners in from the sea walked the half-mile up-river to stare at the slipway. Some predicted disaster and a few were looking forward to it with a sharp pleasure. A failure at the Bridge would put useful business elsewhere.

February sped by and the slope between river and road was transformed. A team of horses began hauling in timber from Gilchrist's wood yard at the top of the village, building it into stacks at the sawpit. Sheds were erected and an iron stove was fitted in one of them to feed the long steam chest, which would bend the planking. The chest was a major construction in itself, forty feet long and two-foot square. For Big Tom and his young apprentice there was now continuous sawing. If others around them were cold, those at the sawpit were not.

On Gilchrist's directions, the labourers had dug out the overgrown slipway.

"We've got to be longer yet," said Bewsher measuring up again.

"Still more?" said Gilchrist. "Then it'll have to be up at the topside."

"Another six feet should do it."

The carpenter was beginning to wear a look of deepening interest. Only occasionally did underlying doubts trouble him.

The weather held good as the sawyers cut the keel blocks. These were laid on the slope, each one four foot apart and three foot deep, leaving space for a man to work in between. The venture was young. It went well.

As March came a distant cry across the river of "Hold back theer!"

announced the arrival of a slow moving load from Abbots Reading. The men turned to look as a team of six horses struggled down the road beyond the inn. Pressing in behind on heavy wheels lay a great elm bound in chains.

"Whoa, there! Steady, boy!"

The wagoners' warning shouts rang out as the horses struggled to hold back the trunk. Hooves sparked on stones and the noise brought folk hurrying out of the inn in time to see the tree go past the door and rumble on across the bridge towards the waiting ship-builders.

The great trunk was scrutinised carefully and Peter listened as Gilchrist, Big Tom and Bewsher examined and argued about the grain before working out the cuts.

The elm was eased on a derrick over the pit.

"But what's it for, Mr Tom, sir?" asked Peter.

"The keel, me lad. The keel. You and me's going to be sweating before we've finished with this 'un."

Chalk marks made, the two prepared to start on their long task.

"We're going to need another sawyer," said Big Tom.

Gilchrist nodded. Time was still on their side, but Big Tom was right. It was vital they kept it that way.

Hard days of toil followed before the keel - cut in three pieces - was scarfed together and set firmly on the blocks. It was a significant stage. Everyone felt better now that they could see the first timbers were in place.

Elsewhere another urgent search began. Consultations started at the timber stacks to find the right lengths for the stem and sternposts. The labourers rammed in cant hooks, turning over the piles. Bewsher and Gilchrist rejected piece after piece before two were chosen with something like the required shape in them.

And now as spring came the weeks began to go swiftly. To speed the cutting Gilchrist took on another top sawyer, a Myrus Atkinson, along with a lad out of Spark Bridge, Bobby Turner. A second sawpit was dug out and lined.

The sawyers began the tricky work of cutting moulds from

soft wood. Set against pieces of oak, chalk marks were drawn round each mould and the sawyers once more cut the shapes demanded by the shipwright.

"Now you know why we're good spitters," Big Tom told his apprentice during a break for a mug of tea. "Get a gob or two of sawdust and you learn to spit like a trooper!"

"But Mr Tom, sir, my mother doesn't like us spitting."

"Mebbe not, but you'll learn. I mind a dandy woman sawyer once with muscles like fat cods and she could spit so you'd think a cannon had blasted. Five foot in a straight line she could!"

At this stage Peter tended to believe most things the sawyer said.

Another coal ship arrived at the Bridge. For the shipbuilders there was scarcely time even to glance. At last the stem and sternposts were hoisted onto the keel and methodically the carpenters began to build in the apron piece.

The weather, astonishingly good until now, finally sagged. In blustery showers the men rigged up canvas shelters and began to drill long augur holes through the apron. For hours on end they took turns, twisting a crossbar at the augur head, cutting little by little until there were holes eight foot long. Fat copper bolts were cut and Parke, Ellwood and Shepherd started work as a team, hammering them through the augured holes. Peter, attracted by the noise, watched awestruck as each man swung his sledgehammer in a fast mesmeric rhythm, pounding the metal through. One misdirected blow would buckle a rod. Never once did he see anyone miss.

Gilchrist was anxious to start cutting out the first of the frames, the ribs of the vessel. Using moulds, the shipwright and Bewsher matched each one against the hard wood, marked the cuts they wanted, and set the sawyers to work. Numerous reshapings were demanded before both men were satisfied, and then at a signal each frame was hoisted up, carefully aligned and bolted to the keel.

It was suddenly much warmer. Summer had crept up the valley. Shirts came off and as the heat grew one of Marly Shepherd's youngest boys, Tim-lad, was engaged at a ha'penny a day to supply the men with drinking water from a spring. In all this activity, the boys working down in the sawpits had the coolest jobs.

Bit by bit the schooner began to take shape until a day came when the last frame was bolted to the keel and the sides were truly framed up. The ribs were in place and it meant that planking could race ahead.

Vivid swearing from Billy Parke and a long struggle with a reluctant iron stove finally resulted in clouds of steam gushing from the planking shed. Soon a comical race began. As the steam chest softened the planks for the ship's sides, gangs of men hurried down-slope bearing scalding lengths of wood, and then the plankers sweated and swore and heaved as they worked at high speed, fitting each hot plank and nailing them in place before they cooled and became unworkable.

Passers-by stopped to watch in growing numbers. Not all were welcome.

"Bas-tard ship! Bas-tard ship!"

The dishevelled figure of a swineherd scuttered round the staging, stopped, shook an angry fist, and hurried on to the road again.

"She'll never float!" yelled Old Greety. "Never!"

"Bugger off!" called Ellwood.

A jagged stone whipped past the handyman's head.

"You old adder!" bellowed the enraged Ellwood.

No one at the yard trusted Old Greety. He had been caught once before stealing tools and beaten for his troubles.

The swineherd fled.

Pedlars and farmers stopped; and children on their way to and from school. A distant trumpeting of a post horn signalled the Kendal-Ulverston coach. Four horses clattered past, the coach swaying heavily on the dusty road, the passengers striving to glimpse the vessel as they crossed the river. September came and Gilchrist at last began to feel happier for the job was going well. There was a lot to do yet, but the deadline was still a long way off.

As the days shortened a change took place at the sawpits. Naphtha flares were suspended overhead and the sawyers began to work on late into the night. The idea spread and prompted Gilchrist to light the up whole yard so that shift work became possible. A score of lanterns shone, ghost like and eerie.

The leaves of a new autumn flared into brilliant reds and yellows. And all seemed well. Then one morning a gang of men stood in a sullen group on the slope above the sheds.

The boat builders paused.

"It's the Greenodd lot," said Bert Casson nervously.

Gilchrist walked out into the open, brushing down a whisp of hair.

"Whisht! Trouble," hissed Ellwood. He closed a hand on a stave.

Gilchrist said firmly: "And what's it with you lads?"

One he recognised as Giles Random. He was a shipyard worker from Greenodd, solid set, good at his job but a man with a reputation for dark humours.

"Just admiring, Mr Gilchrist. Just admiring."

Gilchrist said: "Good of you to say so, Random, but I can manage without admiration, thank you."

Several around Random sniggered. Mostly they were in their early twenties, one or two out of Ulverston, a bit rough looking.

"Just thought we'd make sure," said Random. "Make sure you aren't having bad luck with any rotten timbers, Mr Gilchrist."

The shipwright tensed, patches of red coming to his face.

"Are you here just to insult me?" he began, but a bellow of anger sounded from the road. Big Tom appeared behind the Greenodd men. He was armed with a hefty stick.

Random missed being brained by a fraction. The strangers scattered, floundering on the slippery ground, then quite suddenly they fled, cursing as they went.

"Rotten timbers," bellowed Big Tom. "Come back, you scum and try this 'un for strength!"

The shipbuilders stood about in the road, their routine disrupted.

"They just might," said Bewsher. "Come back, I mean."

"Aye," said Gilchrist, his face etched in thought. "He's an odd man is Random. Works for Marsden, the new man at Greenodd. I allus got on well with Random's father, but never the son. His old man helped me fit out the *Jessie*."

Bewsher said: "We'd best take turns and sleep here nights from now on."

Gilchrist shook his head. "I don't think it'll come to anything."

"I'll split Random's spleen if I catch him fiddling around," said Big Tom.

The others drifted back to work but there was an air of unease and from time to time men could be seen glancing up at the road when strangers passed.

It was now that they realised tools were going missing. First an adze, and then a bevel gauge.

Edward Askew, dismayed, searched everywhere for the bevel. "I've had that 'un twenty years. It was real ebony."

Others helped to look. They failed to find it.

Gilchrist said: "Well, that settles it. We'll take turns and keep a night watch. But we could have done without this."

Young Peter's turn to stand guard did not come until the start of December. Wrapped in a layer of sacking, he huddled by the stove in the planking hut and struggled to stay awake. He was sorely afraid of ghosts but he kept his fear to himself and told no one. One dusk on the old Coniston road he and his father had stumbled on a body of a man lying in the track, sodden with rain. The cart had gone on in front and no one was missing the driver. Horrifically a crow had been standing on the man's face pecking. Peter, limp with fear, hated crows from that moment.

He crowded wood into the stove and set it roaring. He knew he must keep a good lookout, though the night could not pass quickly enough and he longed for dawn. Despite his good intentions he fell asleep.

At one o'clock he stirred and raked the embers back to life;

then he dozed again until a loud noise jerked him awake.

The boy crouched in the dark, the hair on his neck stiff with fright. What had wakened him? The ashes were near enough out, hardly a glow. It must be three o'clock. When nothing more happened he got to his feet and moved to the entrance. Flakes of snow blustered in at the door but he could see nothing of the hull, though it was hardly fifteen feet down-slope. Full of uncertainty, he stood listening.

Hammering filled the night. It was so sudden it turned Peter rigid with fear. Someone was down at the ship pounding! Peter's senses raced. It sounded as if the supports propping the vessel were being knocked away.

Grasping a caulking mallet he edged forward, feeling his way. Each step was a nightmare. He touched the side of the hull. In falling snow he listened, then began a slow circuit of the vessel. Four steps, five, six . . .

Abruptly the hammering stopped. The silence was as bad as the noise had been. Scared, Peter yelled: "Who's there?"

As he spoke a figure rose up among the keel blocks and aimed a blow at his shoulder, and then struck again, hitting him between the eyes.

The news spread rapidly. Doors opened at cottages. In the cold of the winter morning dismayed faces watched as Edward Askew and Billy Parke carried the inert figure up through the village on a ladder. Marly limped alongside, his face ashen.

All that day Peter remained unconscious. A stream of people called at the Shepherds' crowded home with small gifts of food and expressions of sympathy, but not until dusk did the boy's eyes open and a slow recovery begin.

"I'll murder 'em!" vowed Marly bitterly. He clenched his fists and scowled. He was certain he knew who was responsible.

Some of the scaffolding at the slipway had been knocked aside. The discovery brought forth more anger.

Bewsher groaned: "It's a cursed ship, for sure."

"Nonsense," said Gilchrist, though he too looked grim.

"Random will get the edge of my whip if I gets hold of him," vowed Big Tom.

Gilchrist said: "No one knows it was him for sure."

"Who else then?"

The sawyer and Marly exchanged a swift glance.

Bewsher said: "There's a third badness to come. Mark my words, bad luck runs in threes."

Gilchrist was anxious to change the subject.

"We must get back to work. We can thank God the snow has eased."

The following morning Big Tom did not appear.

"I told you," said Bewsher. "Always in threes."

"Well, where is he!" demanded Gilchrist. He stood impatiently by a sawpit where Atkinson and young Turner were shovelling away the snow.

"We don't rightly know, Mr Gilchrist."

Gilchrist fumed: "Half-eight and not a stroke done. Someone get up to his croft fast and find him!"

Edward Askew stumbled off through the drifts but was soon back looking worried.

"He's not at home." He shifted about on one foot, and then the other. "He's in Ulverston."

"Ulverston?" The carpenter looked ill at ease. "Edward, tell me straight - what's happening?"

"Aye, well, he's after yon feller Random."

"God save us!" exclaimed Gilchrist. "Get me my horse. There'll be bloody murder in Ulverston."

It was a Thursday morning. Market day, almost Christmas. A roar came from the crowd. Big Tom and Random rolled over on the cobbles, punching and biting.

"Beat a lad, would you, who can't help himself!" bellowed the giant sawyer.

"Stop it, you damn fool! I never touched him!" shouted Random.

Either Big Tom did not hear him, or he pretended not to.

"Try this for size!"

A massive fist slammed into Random's stomach. Both men were bleeding. A gash on Big Tom's face spattering blood on the stones. One of Random's hands was bleeding.

The crowd was excited, locked in a dense circle round the two men. A market day fight was a lucky bonus to the morning's trading.

Random butted his head into the sawyer's face, and followed it with a kick to a shin. Big Tom's bellow of pain filled the square. The crowd yelled its delight, then another hefty blow sent Random reeling away into a line of tethered ponies.

"Come back you sea scum!" shouted Big Tom.

"Scum yourself!" yelled Random. He struggled out of the jostling animals. The sawyer hoisted a basket from the pavement edge and hurled it bodily. Catcalls swelled as Random was showered in potatoes.

The men circled, striving to regain their breath, then they tumbled again in among the stalls punching furiously. The crowd loved it. Trading in the tiny square was at a standstill.

The fight lasted several more minutes until suddenly it was as if both men had had enough. Random, weak at the knees, swung a fist and pitched over onto a stall where he vanished in a cascade of flying vegetables.

Big Tom, one eye half closed, his smock crimson with blood, swayed while Ransom was dragged from the wreckage.

"I'll murder yer!" panted the sawyer, but the promise was never fulfilled.

Police whistles sounded. Two hefty constables pushed through the crowd accompanied by the town watchman. Jeers and boos filled the market place. It was the best fight the town had seen for years.

Big Tom was hustled down a narrow alley.

"This'll cost you a fortune," snapped a constable.

The sawyer spat a tooth onto the cobbles.

"Every penny will have been wuth it!"

He was bundled into the town lock-up where he nursed his aches behind a barred window and there he stayed until Gilchrist arrived on a sweating horse and bought him out.

The fight in the town had one good result; it greatly raised the spirits of the shipbuilders. In good heart they returned to their task determined to make up lost time. It also increased the number of visitors. Instead of the casual passersby, suddenly whole groups of people appeared on the road above the slipway. Members of the gentry paused in their carriages to stare, some of them dismounting and walking round the caged-in vessel. Many keen eyes examined Gilchrist's ambitious project.

The decking had been fitted, and the two masts, for months chained together in the seasoning pool above the bridge, had been cut to shape and stepped. These were simply the lower masts, the topmasts would wait till the proper fittings after the launch, but they made a further big difference to the appearance of the vessel. Likewise great trouble was taken in fitting the bowsprit.

From morning till night now the riverside resounded to the hammering of the caulkers as they worked the oakum in between the planks, making the hull watertight.

Aaron Dixon reined in his old nag on the heights above the village and looked down. He had ridden out from Ulverston. The water was low and the vessel stood out against the tidal mud, a growing thing. She looked good, her sides fully planked and yet, as he stared, his misgivings increased. The craft simply looked too massive for the river.

At the slip he found Gilchrist measuring timber. The smell of hot pitch was everywhere.

"Good progress," said the shipwright. "We 're doing well."

Dixon nodded uncomfortably.

"Does she not please you?" asked Gilchrist.

"Aye, that is, I don't want to be morbid, but I have just had fresh doubts about the river."

The shipwright laughed: "Never fear! She'll sail out beautifully my friend."

Dixon, his coat shabbier than ever, bit on his lip. A lot of money was at risk.

"Mid-March, the highest spring tide for years!"

"If she fails I'm a ruined man."

"You'll not be ruined. But have you decided on a name?"

"Aye. She will be called the *Nancy.*"

Gilchrist looked surprised, and then pleased.

"It's my old aunt's name," said Dixon. "The least I can do. This has taken a great deal of her money. And she keeps offering more!"

Gilchrist thought about the name and marvelled at the way coincidence worked, but he said nothing.

"A good name. I like it a lot." The *Nancy*, eh!

In a sudden lunge, the man grabbed at the boy and got him by an arm. Peter let out a cry of surprise.

"Ah, now, you sprat! Just the one I've been wanting to see."

The man loomed above him.

"What's these lies you've been telling about me? What's this about me beating you?"

They were in Lipp wood above the valley, following a snowy path. By chance alone Random had come on the boy taking a short cut.

He looked into Peter's face.

"Nowt to be feared of if you've nowt to hide! Do you hear me?"

"Aye, Mr Random . . ."

"That's it, *Mister* Random. So you telt 'em I went and cobbled you did you?"

"N-no," blurted Peter. "It wasn't me alone. We all guessed it was you!"

"Oh, guessing was it!" Random's face, still scarred, filled with understanding. "And what if I tell you you guessed wrong! And I was nowhere near that ship? Never! What of that? And what if I tell you I didn't raise a finger at you, me lad! Now you'd believe that wouldn't you?"

Peter bit his lip. Could he have escaped he would have done so.
"Well, me lad?"
"Aye, Mr Random, sir."
And then Peter spoke out rapidly: "It wasn't me that said owt - but with you and Mr Gilchrist daggering we were sure it was you hitting at the ship."
"Ah, you were sure. Well there's summat you need to know!"
The man's voice dropped.
"Giles Random builds ships, not knacker's 'em. Do you understand? And me father the same. He built 'em, too. Good ships! Remember that and you and me will get along fine. But if I catch you lying there's going to be bad trouble. D'you hear?"
Peter nodded vigorously and Random seemed satisfied.
"As to who did it, that's a mystery to me, and to everyone. My boss and Gilchrist included!"
He loomed over the boy.
"Now get off with you!"
Peter waited no longer. He raced away through the trees.
"You remember what I telt you!" shouted Random. With a soft laugh he set off down the hill, startling a wood pigeon as he went.

A carriage drew up on the road above the slip, a very fine carriage. Gilchrist had a visitor, a well dressed one.
"Who the devil is that?" exclaimed Parke.
Bert Casson stared.
"That's Marsden! The new boss at Greenodd. The bloke who's taken over the shipyard."
"What the devil does he want?"
No one knew. They watched as Gilchrist and Dixon ushered the visitor into the hut. He was dressed in a blue velvet suit and looked very grand. Minutes later the shipbuilder appeared at the door and asked Parke to organise a brew of tea. Then back inside he went and no one down the yard knew what was taking place.
Nor did Gilchrist say anything when his visitor left an hour later.

The yard was rife with speculation but no one could read his expression, except he was looking grim.

"Summat nasty's brewing, for sure," said Bewsher.

The shipwright did not tell them the bad news until the next morning. It had come from an agitated Marsden. A new turnpike was planned. It was going to be built across part of Marsden's own shipyard at Greenodd, hence his concern, but the worst aspect was that a bridge was going to be built over the lower reaches of the Crake, cutting Penny Bridge off from the sea.

"Cut us off! They can't do that!" said Bewsher incredulously. "How are we going to build ships!"

Gilchrist shook his head wearily. He had hardly slept all night. "We won't be able to. The *Nancy* may yet be the last vessel anyone will build up here."

Dismayed faces filled the yard. No more ships from the Bridge, after all these years! It did not seem conceivable.

"Then what of the *Nancy?*" demanded Big Tom. "How are we going to fit her out? If we can't fit her out on shore we must find another way."

"That is the one bit of good news," said Gilchrist. "It was why I saw Marsden. He's agreed to rent us his dry dock down at Greenodd so we can finish the job. Ironically, though, for us, he's gone and made Random the dock foreman!"

"Random!" howled Bewsher.

Gilchrist shook his head resignedly.

"He's an odd man, I'll grant you. But whatever else, he is good at his job. And Greenodd is going to solve a lot of our problems!"

He said no more. Marsden's offer had not come cheaply, but Dixon - via his old aunt's fortune - had agreed to pay for the hiring and this meant the ship would get finished.

Snow engulfed the shipyard slope. Christmas had passed mildly enough, but as January arrived the weather turned severe.

Gilchrist despaired. Work halted as drifts buried everything. His men dug out the slip making pathways until fresh soft storms swept in over the hills and drowned the valley. It was a bitter start to the New Year. Not until January 27th did work begin to get back to normal and the race to catch up started afresh.

The final few weeks passed rapidly. As February moved into March an evening came when Gilchrist had a final look round. The schooner stood on the slip, still needing the final fitting once launched, but she was as near ready for launching as ever she would be. A good craft. As good as any he had built.

"Tomorrow," he said. "The big day."

"We nearly didn't make it," said Bewsher.

"No." Gilchrist sighed. "Come on, let's have a tot. The Lord knows we've earned it."

No one at Penny Bridge had anticipated the size of the crowds. Soon after eight in the morning the rutted tracks leading to the huddled village became alive with people. Horsemen and carriages churned the dusty road out of Ulverston, at first in ones and twos and then in a steady stream, bringing cottagers to their doors amazed at the numbers. From Torver and Coniston, from hovels and farms people set out to walk to the normally placid river valley, and the reasons were plain: not only did people imagine that it was likely to be the last ship to be built at the Bridge, but few people believed it would ever get away.

Exasperated, Gilchrist struggled to hold back sightseers from the slipway.

"Another rope! Get it across, sharp now!"

Two farmers had joined them and hammered in a line of fence posts between the vessel and the road. Big Tom, dressed in a new cap and a clean smock, was constantly ordering youths back up onto the road. Launch day, and everyone seemed as if they wanted to touch the vessel.

"They've come from all ower!" said young Peter marvelling.

"Aye," said Bewsher. "Come to see the disaster."

"It'll not be that, will it Mr B, sir?"

The note of dismay caught at the carpenter. He looked towards the ship looming on the muddy slope. It was big, bigger than anything that had been built there before. Whatever the tide, she would need both luck as well as skill to get away smoothly.

"To be honest with you lad, I don't rightly know . . ."

The sun strengthened and the carnival atmosphere grew. Spectators crowded both banks as newly arrived carriages struggled to find open spaces. People stood five deep on the Bridge and soon nothing on wheels was able to pass in either direction. The inn on the far side had been expecting more trade but the huge crowd took the landlord by surprise. Folk swamped the premises. Benches were dragged into the open and soon the first two barrels of ale had been drunk dry.

Gilchrist went down to the river's edge and looked at the marker on the side of the bridge. "It's started! The river's started to rise."

"Let's pray," said Dixon, "for God's help and a good launching."

"Amen," said Gilchrist solemnly. "At twelve-forty we'll know."

Both men waited apprehensively, watching the water creep up the stonework.

At last the moment came. They climbed on board.

"Twelve-thirty nine! It's now!"

"Bert! Quick man! The depth! "

Bert Casson sank the marker over the stern until it touched bottom.

"Ten foot, five inches!"

Gilchrist reckoned up swiftly. If she floated clear of the mud it could give ten inches of water under her, perhaps a foot.

"It will do! We'll risk it."

"Stand by!"

"Ready Mr Gilchrist!"

"Madam . . ."

On a temporary wooden platform Mrs Abigail Dixon clutched a bottle. She stood poised momentarily, a big bosomed woman in a large hat, with flowing curls and a long scarlet coat, an overwhelming figure whose style of dress contrasted sharply with her shabbily attired husband. Their guest, Mr Marsden, easily matched her in his own velvet attire.

"Now!" urged Gilchrist from the ship's rail. "Now!"

The river was full up to the bridge. The tops of the arches had disappeared. The crowd swayed, tense with expectation.

"In the name of God and all here at Penny Bridge," began Mrs Dixon. "I do name this fine ship the *Nancy*. Long may she voyage over all the seas, far and wide . . . and long may . . . the men who built her . . . and all those . . ."

"Abigail!" cried her husband waving. "The bottle!"

"I have not yet finished," said Mrs Dixon.

"The bottle!" cried the crowd.

Glaring, Mrs Dixon stared round her, caught sight of several severe looking faces, then brought the bottle a hefty crash on the vessel, splintering glass.

". . . and all who sail in her."

Down on the slipway the labourers let swing with sledgehammers. A barrage of blows sent the chocks flying. A second ticked by in which nothing seemed to happen, then the looming hulk of the *Nancy* started to glide down the slip into the swollen Crake.

A roar rose from the crowd as the vessel met the water; a second excited shout followed as a bow wave began to roll towards the opposite bank. the *Nancy* surged forward weightily, full of promise and momentum.

"The hawser!" yelled Gilchrist. "Keep that hawser taut! Don't let the ship get too far!"

The call was wasted. The men on the stern hawser knew what they had to do but they failed to do it. Over eager, a helper on the rope slipped and lost his balance. Amid shouts and confusion, men began to stumble over his body and at this crucial moment they failed to take up the slack fast enough.

Gilchrist was still calling as the deck lurched. A dull grinding came from deep down in the timbers as the keel churned the river bottom. The noise lasted for seconds then the vessel went stern first into the mud of the far bank.

Men tumbled and shouted. On shore arose a disbelieving gasp of dismay. Gilchrist was the first to recover and ran frantically to the bows.

"Pull!" he yelled at the men on the riverbank. "Pull!"

The vessel began to list as the flow of water bore against her.

"Pull, damn you!" bellowed Big Tom.

Men rushed to haul on the trailing hawser rope.

Gilchrist swung round and snapped: "Spread your weight! Don't just be standing at the rail!"

"We'll never do it," groaned Dixon helplessly.

"No." Gilchrist stared at the bridge. Slack water. Twenty of the longest minutes he had ever known followed but the vessel did not stir. Then a gap showed under the top of the arch.

"The water's falling! We're too late!"

Angry shareholders met the shipwright as he landed.

"You and your tides!" stormed Widow Rennison. She shook with rage, her face patched in red. "You've tricked us John Gilchrist."

"No, no," protested the shipwright.

"Mrs Rennison is right," chimed in the schoolmaster. "Everyone knows the river could never take a vessel this big."

"Please be calm," urged Gilchrist. "We're not finished. There's still tonight."

"Calm!" snapped the schoolmaster scornfully. "Our savings are sinking in mud and you tell us to be calm!"

More angry protests sounded.

On the road Giles Random stood watching. At the rush to the ropes he had almost pushed in with the rest, but he held back. In any case the ship was badly stuck; it was obvious they would not shift her easily now. The immediate need was to prevent damage. The flood was ebbing fast, exposing wide banks of mud. In this messy expanse the *Nancy* would need a good deal more than a couple of rope gangs to move her. Begrudgingly he had to admit that she was a fine looking vessel.

Angry voices came up the slope.

"Get her off in the dark?" exclaimed the irate widow scornfully.

"Just a moment," stormed the schoolmaster. "Did you say tonight's tide will be higher?"

Gilchrist said: "About another foot we reckon."

"Then why was the launching not tonight!"

People engulfed Gilchrist. He looked about him, momentarily helpless, his few whisps of hair blown awry unheeded. Pride was the short answer. The satisfaction of watching a ship go down into the water, of seeing the work of his yard riding the river where all could admire her, that was why he had chosen a daylight launch. In any case, ten foot five inches deep should have been enough. But that was only part of it.

"Night launchings are much harder. I wasn't prepared to risk it."

"No," cried a voice in the crowd, "but you'd let the ship go aground."

Gilchrist felt the blood rush to his face. "Arguing won't help . . . twelve hours and it will be high water again. If we are to free her we must start working at it now."

He broke away. A ragged figure dragged at his sleeve.

"Bastard ship! Bastard ship!"

Gilchrist's scowl quelled Greety and the old man shrank back.

At the top of the bank Dixon met him. It was the moment Gilchrist had dreaded.

"Over-proud I am," said Gilchrist. "And pig headed."

"No," said the merchant. "All of us can make mistakes . . . a higher tide tonight! We must work fast."

Their eyes met. Dixon of course was right. Gilchrist gave a smile of gratitude and turned to look at the stranded vessel.

"It couldn't have been worse could it?"

The schooner made a forlorn sight.

They pushed through knots of spectators, walking round and examining her from both banks.

Finally Dixon said cautiously: "An extra foot of water might not be enough."

"Can't tell, but no it might not." Gilchrist cracked his knuckles. "We just might manage it with block and tackle . . . and no one on deck who needn't be there. Eleven! That was far too many. I should have known better."

"Once the water's rising, she'll have to be dragged off the mud first."

"Aye. And then another cable to turn her into deeper water afterwards."

"Let's get on with it."

The afternoon raced by. As the water level sank labourers stripped to their waists and waded alongside the vessel, shovelling the mud and gravel to try to free up the hull. It was a filthy task and soon they were unrecognisable. On shore, carpenters were realigning the winch. Gilchrist was everywhere, supervising, urging, conscious of the race of time. Unexpectedly, on a short cut between two sheds, he chanced on a weeping figure.

"Now then, lad. What's all this?"

Peter made no answer, turning away shamed faced.

"If only the winch was stronger," said Dixon. "But what's the matter?"

"It's young Peter, taking on . . ."

Beside the slipway the labourers built a heavy timber platform and bolted down the winch. Early evening saw a cable lacing across from it to the vessel's bows. At the same time, a second rope was run out ready for a gang to haul by hand. The men's wives were busy too. Up in the village they were turning out cupboards, so that a collection of oil lamps began to grow on the slipway. With all this going on no one noticed Marly Shepherd set off alone.

Along the hurrying Crake, beyond the forges of Spark and the lush river lands where Norse settlers long ago had cleared the scrub, a cart track turned steeply up through the coppice to the ridge. In these woods lived the old woman called Bessy. She had lived there for so long now that folk called the track Bessy's Bank.

"Tell me what you heard," demanded Marly yet again. The hovel was unlit, built against the hillside.

"I know nowt," said Bessy. The old woman huddled in a corner by the heaped ash. She was grimy like smoke, her voice a rough rattle.

Marly's face showed his disbelief.

"You know for sure," he insisted darkly. "I've been told you know."

She did not answer. Her eyes flickered, taking in the leaf-wrapped object in his hand. She was sorry about the boy and his injuries.

"The first moment I clapped sight on him I thought he was dead," confessed Marly. "All the blood."

He sucked in air. The den was airless. A black womb, a part of the hill.

"Revenge is a wicked bitterness," said the old woman. But he ignored her.

"Some are blaming Random, but I don't think so. Another devil's done it, I'm certain, and I'm going to find him."

The old woman scraped her clay pipe with a twig. Her ulcerated lip was sore.

"There's just ale-house gossip, that's all."

Marly strained forward trying to hear her. Was she about to tell him?

"What ale house?"

"I take no heed," she said.

That was no help. She put the pipe in her mouth and sucked softly. Like the ash heap on the floor it was unlit.

They sat in silence five more minutes, then Marly sighed, disappointed. It had been a waste of time after all. The old woman knew nothing, or if she did she was keeping quiet. He pushed the packet across a barrel towards her, for she still must be paid.

"It has a bad smell the whole thing," she told him.

"Aye," said Marly, no wiser. Then he added: "But I'll get the devil in the end, with or without help."

One of Bessy's hands closed on the tobacco.
"It has the smell of pig," she said.

Almost midnight. Chains of lanterns flickered in the dark on both sides of the river. Other lanterns hung along the ship, turning it into a ghostly mass of pools of light. High water was fast approaching.

The minutes ticked by.

Young Peter was shouting excitedly: "Mr Gilchrist, sir! Top of the arch!" His lantern swung from the bridge parapet.

Big Tom's voice boomed out. "Stand by to haul, lads!"

It was one o'clock. It was now.

Gilchrist, on board, drew his breath sharply. He waved his own lantern shoreward. "Take her up!"

A light signalled back. Nothing more happened for a moment, then a wavering chant began and the slow clicking of a ratchet started.

"*Haul a-way my John-ny, O . . .*"

The winch cable tightened, and after it the second lighter rope began to lift out of the water as the men got a better grip.

Savage creaks came from the winch. Eight of the strongest men were turning the handles.

"Heave, me lads! Heave!"

Peter leaned dangerously out over the parapet watching the water. Another inch higher - and another, but how much more would the river rise?

Gilchrist gripped the ship's rail. Full tide. It must be full tide by now. This time there were only three on board, two carpenters and himself. Eight people lighter. Damn it! Why didn't she move? He held a lantern aloft, lighting the cable where it stretched in a taut glistening line shoreward. He paused, listening, and it was now that he detected a first faint tremor.

"Heeeeave, me lads!"

Had he been mistaken?

But it was not the vessel. On shore alarmed shouts filled the darkness. Around the winch came a flurry of movement, then as if they were flecks of flotsam, the men manning the handles were flung aside as the winch wrenched out of its mounting. A scream punctured the night as iron spiked down through flesh and bone.

In the blackness high water came, held, and sank away leaving behind the stricken vessel and a dream that was fading fast.

Haggard and cold, Gilchrist crouched before a stove, a sack around his shoulders. Others were in the shed but for once he did not care. The warmth of the fire barely seeped into his chilled frame. Two o'clock in the black of the night. Most of the men had gone home. It was too late now, but he should have thought the launching through far more carefully than this: he should have fixed chocking to the slipway; he should have kept down the speed of the launching. It was a dismal prospect, yet depressed though he felt he knew that he could not give up.

"We've got to have another try," he told Dixon.

"But the best tide has been lost," said the mariner, surprised. "What chance have we now? The tide will be inches lower - it simply won't be possible!"

Gilchrist felt sour and angry. It was not just the ship; there had been young Peter attacked and left unconscious; and tonight Isaac Ellwood, a leg spiked and three mouths to feed. Bastard ship, aye, it was a bastard all right!

Bewsher said: "We could take out the mast footings . . . "

"We're not touching the masts!" snapped Gilchrist. That would simply undo good work, though he knew he was wrong in this.

"It would usefully lighten her," said Dixon.

"They stay. Now leave me."

Dixon went white.

"Now see, Gilchrist, I've as much right to decide on this as you."

"I'm the one who's building this ship," said the shipwright. "And I'll get her down to the sea. She's not yours till she's afloat and you take command. Until then I'll be obliged if you and all here allow me time to think."

He glared round the hut. Billy Parke looked at the door and after a moment they all left.

The fire in the stove died away. Alone, Gilchrist stared into the gloom, and as the embers settled lower a sapping weariness overcame him. He half listened to the sound of distant hooves on the road and reflected dismally that it had been the worst day of his life. So many mistakes. He had judged badly, there was no denying it. The team on the rope should have been hand picked. Despite his moment of optimism, he knew that freeing the stranded vessel grew more and more difficult.

A murmur of voices sounded outside. Who the devil was coming at this time! He was only half listening as a short solid-framed man stepped into the light.

"Aye, now, Mr Gilchrist," said the newcomer.

The shipwright, surprised, rose to his feet.

"Whatever's this? It's still the middle of the night!"

It was Giles Random.

Random said straight out. "The boss, Mr Marsden sent me. About yon ship."

Of course, Random, the new foreman . . . Gilchrist stared at the newcomer and became aware that this was not quite the man of their previous meeting. Random stood his ground and slight though it was he seemed to have an air of confidence that had not existed previously.

"The ship," said Gilchrist, "is practically a disaster, as everyone knows well enough."

"Aye, Mr Marsden says the same! Unless you get it away quick!"

"Oh, yes?"

Random was not put off.

"Aye, he reckons that you need a good winch. And I tell him how you need a big un! The biggest there is." He waved a hand at the door. "He tells me to bring you ours."

Gilchrist had never been sure about Random, had not altogether trusted him. Still uncertain, he looked into the night and was greatly surprised. Standing on the road were four horses with a cart, and behind just visible in the lantern light loomed a giant winch. Gilchrist recognised it at once. It was Mighty Jack, off the quay at Greenodd.

"Well, I'll go to the devil," he said softly.

"It'll do the job," said Random. "Built at Rutherglen! It was one of T. B Seath's."

"There's none bigger," acknowledged Gilchrist.

Every shipbuilder round the Cumbrian coast had heard of Mighty Jack.

A figure pushed forward.

"Aye? " growled Big Tom suspiciously. "And why are you being so busy doing all this, then?"

Random glowered: "The straight answer is me father and me hates to see a bad waste of a ship. And if you're wanting to make summat of it . . ."

"No, no," butted in Gilchrist quickly. "Your father? He's still alive?"

"Aye, but he's a bit badly now he's getting on."

Gilchrist listened more carefully.

"We used to be friends, him and me."

"That's so."

"But the winch," said Big Tom, "Marsden?"

"Call it a loan!" A note of triumph sounded in Random's voice.

Gilchrist hardly took it in. He stared at the road as if for the first time and the flicker of excitement began to grow. The lanterns were wavering and it was at this instant that the shipwright realised the answer to his problem was standing there in front of him.

"God help us Random! I think you've just shown me how I can save the *Nancy.*"

His voice was dry with excitement. He hurried up the slope.

"Dixon, here's our answer!"

But he was not looking at the winch.

"Horses, Dixon. Horses! By God, we'll pull the *Nancy* out!"
Dixon and Random stared at Gilchrist strangely.

"Not just four of 'em," exclaimed the shipwright, seeing it all clearly. "But twenty - and more! Thirty, forty if we can get 'em! If we can chain up enough we'll drag the *Nancy* into deep water!"

"Surely it's not possible!" said the mariner. But his eyes lit with excitement. "It would take a whole army . . ."

"As many as we can find! And carts. As many carts as we can muster."

"Carts?"

"Then the winch?" said Random.

"Yes, Mr Random, we'll use Mighty Jack, and right gladly and I'll tell Marsden so myself . . . but it's horses we need. We must act! Right away! If it's to work we must get 'em here by morning, and there's precious little time. The midday tide."

He swung round. "Tom! Get the men out of their beds! Billy, get to Benson's. Wake him! Tell him we want all the quarry waste he's got, tell him . . ."

He spoke rapidly, galvanised, naming farmers, friends, anyone likely to lend a horse. And soon his tired labourers and carpenters, called from their beds, were stumbling off into the night, and for miles around doors were being hammered and lanterns lit as the shipbuilders roused surprised householders and begged for help.

By the first light of morning thirty-seven horses arrived at the river. It was an astonishing response. Nor was it over. Even as Gilchrist was counting them more were being led in. They were exactly what he had hoped for, Clydesdales and Shires, the giants of the land, the slow moving descendants of the Great War horses of the Middle Ages, bred for strength, harnessed to farm and forest. Whatever happened at sea, on land horse was king, and now was their chance to prove it.

Big Tom shook his head and marvelled.

"We'll never see the likes of this again! "

The creatures were being marshalled into teams on both sides of the river, trampling mud as they were chained up. Still more were arriving down behind the inn until more than sixty were there.

Every man knew the plan. First drag the schooner off the mud, then turn her down river into deeper water. It was a formidable task. Gilchrist left the wagoners to organise the hitching. His attention was urgently needed elsewhere.

Two hundred yards below the bridge the shipwright and Dixon stood in the reeds and examined the river's width.

"This has got to be the spot," said Gilchrist emphatically. "There's nowhere better. We've got to dam it as high as we can."

Dixon stared at the riverbanks.

"I can't believe it'll work. It'll be swept away before it gets a chance."

"We must try! We need to hold back enough water to get her afloat, that's all. Once down river a bit she'll do all right. You must time it properly. That's critical."

"It's going to be a near thing."

"Five hours to high water," said Dixon.

"I'll leave it to you," said the shipwright.

Big Tom looked after the near bank, Dixon the far. A heavy-jowelled farmer led in the first load of quarry waste. It was one of the Parkes of Nibthwaite.

"And where's it to be then, Tom?"

"Right here, Jim, thank you."

The farmer backed up the cart and tipped the load into the water. It disappeared immediately.

"You'll need two or three more," he observed.

Forty more, sixty, eighty . . .

Dixon had the harder task. The carts had to come farther to get to his side. Even so three hours later the riverbanks on both sides were unrecognisable. Low walls of earth and rubble were advancing towards one another. Every few minutes strings of carts arrived from the quarry where a gang of shovellers had loaded them.

"We could win," panted Dixon to Ellwood.

"Do you think so?"

The gap had narrowed to some fifteen feet, but the water seemed to eat each load away as fast as it went in.

"The tide's begun turning!" shouted Big Tom.

"This won't be enough," shouted Dixon. "We need more!"

Would it really be possible to dam a river at full tide?

Gilchrist stood on the deck of the schooner, his eyes cast down.

"Oh God, my maker," he said softly. "Let this thy ship yet sail to the open sea."

The Crake was rising fast. A mass of waiting horses was whinnying impatiently on both banks as they sensed the excitement. Everywhere people were getting in the way.

At the dam Big Tom shouted: "It's nigh on full water!"

Eight feet, seven feet, six . . .the gap was narrowing. As fast as a load sank in another cart was already backing up. The wall was massive. It must work!

"Hie! Hie! Hie!" Excited cries sounded down-river. The milling crowd at the Bridge strove to get a better view. Why were they shouting?

"They've done it!" It was young Peter. "Mr Gilchrist, sir, they've blocked the river!"

Then it must be now, thought Gilchrist.

"Now!" he cried. He yelled it. "Now!"

Not only was the ship at stake, so were the savings of many valley folk.

Cries of "Giddy-up theer!" and "Forrard, you devils! Forrard!" rose from the waggoners. Long lines of horses began a tremendous jostle. Shouts and curses filled the day as hooves sought to get a purchase, and the watching crowd saw the two bow cables lift slowly from the river, streaming curtains of water. Alongside a third cable began to rise as a team of men began to turn the giant Greenodd winch.

"This time it must work," said Gilchrist.

The noise of floundering men and horses filled the valley.

The water was at the top of the arch, but only just - it would surely rise no higher.

A single huzza sounded on shore. The shipwright realised he was clenching his teeth. It must work. It had to!

And the huzzas grew and swelled.

Gilchrist hurried to the side and stared at the struggled mass on the slipway.

And suddenly there was continuous cheering. Chaos had gone, horses were no longer sliding on the churned earth, they were beginning to move in one mass so that all at once it happened . . . the *Nancy* was beginning to drag free.

"She's shifting!"

And shift she did, a moment more and the schooner was wrenched out of the river's grip, sucking mud and gravel as she came.

Gilchrist stood poised, waiting for the exact moment. And it came.

"Cut her free!" he cried.

As the vessel's stern dragged clear of the mud, Tomlinson and Casson hacked furiously with axes at the bow cables. Both lines parted with gun-crack reports.

Chaos erupted on the slipway. Horses and men were pitched into an unwieldy confusion as the lines snapped back towards them. But Gilchrist was not watching. He was already at the stern.

"Pull!" he yelled shorewards. "Pull!"

Men and horses were waiting down river for just this moment. A jangling mass of chains chimed as the lines began to tighten.

"Heave, me beauties. Heave!"

The fresh horse teams took up the struggle. The schooner, fully righted, began to swing, her keel grating as the animals strove to bring their weight to bear. For moments more nothing seemed to happen then the vessel began to turn and almost imperceptibly she started to move down-river. Huzzas rang out along the flooded shores. Excited men splashed through the shallows calling and whistling. Three yards, four, six, eight and suddenly the *Nancy* was moving easily in deeper water.

"She's clear," said Gilchrist softly. He stared at the vessel scarcely believing it. "Oh Lord, our maker, she is clear."

The cheers increased. They had won.

The horses were eased off. Stern anchors sank away and the vessel was safe and riding on a full head of water. She was barely in time. Down river the dam was caving in.

Big Tom was turning a cart away as the barrier noisily sagged in two places. A crash of water boiled through and in minutes the efforts of hours of toil was pouring seawards. But the schooner was afloat.

Through the gloom of the winter dusk a lantern flickered across the marsh. It bobbed along among walls of frozen reeds, advancing slowly, now visible, now abruptly gone. Old Greety was on his way home.

He came, unsuspecting, muttering in an incoherent grumble, his ill-shod feet squelching through mud, his lantern drawing the world close in around him. Concealed in the heart of the marsh, where the land formed a low buttress, stood a thatched hovel. Extending at one end was a crudely fenced plot of ground with two pigs belly-deep in mire.

The swineherd did not sense anything was amiss until he untied the string that secured the hut door. The knot came apart awkwardly and at this he paused knowing it was different. He was still wondering why as an arm locked round his throat.

"Well now," grated a voice. "It's Greety, Old Greety the pig man."

The swineherd's lantern crashed to the ground.

"Help!" he yelled. "Help!"

"Aye," said the voice heavily. "I'll help - but not yet!"

In a rush, the man rammed the swineherd against the door, forcing it inward with a crash. Greety screamed as he pitched into the room and tumbled to the earth floor. Panting with fright, the swineherd lashed out with his clogs, catching the man on the leg, then he struggled towards the only other opening, a hole to the sty and plunged forward. It was as far as he got. He collided with the barrel, carefully placed to fill the gap.

It seemed an age before the swineherd came to his senses. It took a while to realise that his face was bleeding and he became aware of the candle burning on the floor. Facing him sitting cross-legged in the pool of light was Marly Shepherd.

"Aye," said the labourer grimly. "It's me, young Peter's father."

Greety was terrified.

"What do you want?" he whispered, and then in a whine: "What do you want, scaring an old man . . ."

The labourer reached into the dark beside him and placed an ebony bevel on the ground between them.

"Revenge," said Shepherd softly.

Old Greety's denials filled the hovel and flew away with the marsh wind.

"Beat him, didn't you?" raged Marly. "Beat my lad . . . Aye! Well Marly Shepherd's been thinking what he'd do with a pig minder who spills a boy's blood . . . what attacks him in the black of the night."

Greety wept and pleaded, and then for a time he only blubbered as Marly sat, sharp and watchful. Finally, exhausted, the swineherd stopped his noise.

Alongside Marly lay a stick. The labourer might even now have picked it up and thrashed the man as he had planned, but in all this he held back.

Gradually he saw that the swineherd was scarcely more than a wretch, thinner even than himself, nothing but an old man, pathetic and mean, but mostly just old.

"Aye," he said softly. "You can stare. You're not even fit to be beaten."

But the anger in him had not subsided enough to leave it at that. There had to be a quittance of sorts and swiftly he grabbed hold of the old man and pulled him to his feet.

"Don't kill me! Don't kill me! I didn't mean to hurt him!"

"No, I'm not going to kill you," said Marly solemnly. "I've another little treat for you, you thieving wretch."

Hoisting him up, the labourer carried the swineherd bodily out into the night. The filthy tatters of the man's smock seemed little more than a sack full of skin and bones. Marly almost dumped him on the ground and walked off but his sense of justice demanded just a little more.

In the gloom of the partly risen moon he carried him round the edge of the hovel to the pen, and there he lifted him up above the sty and gaffed his smock onto a gable stick.

"Let me catch you hurting any of my childer again, you old viper, and I'll murder you!" said Marly menacingly. "Do you hear?"

The old man blubbered incoherently.

Marly turned away and set off to pick a path back through the marsh.

Greety's cries still sounded on the wind long after the labourer had arrived home at Penny Bridge. Not until the best part of the night had passed and the moon was well overhead did the swineherd's smock split apart and drop him into the sty.

This same night a second person also had a visitor. He lived three miles outside Greenodd.

"Joseph?" Gilchrist stood in the half-open door at the cottage, undecided whether to push in or not. The place seemed to be unlit.

"Joseph, it's me, John Gilchrist, do you remember?"

Coughing broke out in the kitchen at the back of the living room. A moment or two passed then an old man hobbled through carrying a lantern. He was in his shirt and trousers, and unshaven. Gilchrist was shocked as he recognised Joseph Random, his old friend of past times. The man had aged terribly.

"Oh, so it's you, is it?" said Joseph blinking against the daylight. "Well, come in, and don't leave the door open and let all the heat out."

Gilchrist sat down alongside the remains of the fire.

"So what are you doing coming here, then?" said Joseph, his eyes looking first into the boat builder's face, and then at the bottle in his hands.

Gilchrist smiled: "I owe you a drink, Joseph, you old devil - if you'll take one with me, that is."

Joseph did not answer. Instead he reached for two tumblers off the dresser.

"So you got her launched."

"Aye, we did! Just."

Gilchrist poured generously.

"It's been a long time since we had a drop of rum together. And if you will take it how it's meant, here's to you and to Giles. We owe it to both of you."

Joseph's pale eyes had lit up.

"The *Nancy*, eh?"

"That's right."

"My old lady, she was called Nancy. Do you remember?"

Gilchrist smiled. He leaned forward and poked the fire back to life.

"Of course I do. You don't mind do you?"

Joseph nodded as if to himself, remembering how she used to look after him. He smiled and it seemed to knock the years off him just like that, for a smile always was a way of looking younger.

"She'd have been pleased."

Gilchrist nodded, satisfied.

They talked on, Joseph in his day a shipbuilder Greenodd style, John Gilchrist, still toiling, Penny Bridge style. Both were stubborn. Both had a lot in common.

"Our Giles," said Joseph. "Did he help?"

"That he did! Especially at Marsden's. We managed well enough thanks to him."

It had been a surprise to Gilchrist as well as to his men.

Joseph emptied his glass and held it out for more. "He's a funny cuss, is our Giles. But you can be sure he always puts ships first. I told him as much."

On a bright summer's morning the *Nancy* set sail for the Bay and the open sea under her Master Aaron Dixon. The schooner would be back at Greenodd from time to time, though she would never again berth up at Penny Bridge, for in the years ahead the bridge was built just like many had said.

But on this golden morning, the vessel broke out her sails to the sound of cheering from the onlookers on Greenodd quay.

The news of the departure had been known for days and as the ship stood down channel knots of people stared from the heights as far as the rounded Hoad Hill at Ulverston. The schooner made a fine sight and in Furness would be remembered as the ship that only just got away.

Gilchrist and his workmen stood in the crowd, subdued but pleased. They watched until they could see her no longer and then they turned away.

Big Tom's pale eyes looked into those of the shipwright.

"Well, Mr Gilchrist, sir, I'm thinking we're in for a bit of a rest - back to our old jobs, like. Repairs and such."

"Seems so, Tom."

"And the yard?"

"Something will turn up, Tom, never fear."

The shipwright glanced out towards the sea.

It was the moment he disliked, when men were about to be paid off. Tom, Bewsher, his carpenters, Tomlinson and Ellwood - the skilled team - they and a couple of lads would stay for now, but the rest would have to go.

"We did a good job."

Bewsher said: "We did, but I'm thinking we should have dug the river bottom out first!"

Gilchrist laughed. Already the heartache of the launch had passed.

"True enough! Now what say you we surprise the Greenodd men and sup in their own inn? By God, I might even risk buying Random a pint, I've grown a terrible thirst."

They crowded inside, a garrulous gang of working men,

the uncertainty of the future set aside for another day. Another vessel had passed down channel, leaving an empty feeling, almost of loss in the men who had built her, and often it was like that, though they told themselves that next time somehow it would be different.